Natalie removed her blouse and Derrick wiped his hands—all over her body, trailing his fingers around her breasts, down her stomach, and finally to her core. Sliding his finger inside made Natalie let out a soft sigh of pure delight.

Tracing the trail he left behind with his tongue, he nibbled on each breast, leaving no remnants of the sticky treat. Going lower, he licked and tasted her stomach before moving even lower. With his tongue, he reached up to caress her breast and moaned at the sugary taste of her.

Unspoken Love

Doreen Rainey

BET Publications, LLC
http://www.bet.com
http://www.arabesquebooks.com

ARABESQUE BOOKS are published by

BET Publications, LLC
c/o BET BOOKS
One BET Plaza
1900 W Place NE
Washington, DC 20018-1211

All Kensington Titles, Imprints, and Distributed Lines are available at special quantity discounts for bulk purchases for sales promotions, premiums, fund-raising, and educational or institutional use. Special book excerpts or customized printings can also be created to fit specific needs. For details, write or phone the office of the Kensington special sales manager: Kensington Publishing Corp., 850 Third Avenue, New York, NY 10022, attn: Special Sales Department, Phone: 1-800-221-2647.

First Printing: January 2006

10 9 8 7 6 5 4 3 2 1

Printed in the United States of America

This book is dedicated to all the readers that continue to give me their unconditional support. Thank you!

Chapter 1

"Marry me."

Natalie Donovan sat directly across from him at a small table in the back of the café when the heartfelt words left his mouth. Not missing a beat, she slid her cup toward the waitress. Pouring two cups of steaming, freshly brewed coffee, the waitress, who had overheard the request, barely acknowledged them. Leaving flavored cream and natural sugar on the table, the waitress walked away without so much as a backward glance.

Eyeing the small, black box he placed on the table just a few inches in front of her with casual indifference, she added a touch of cream and a pinch of sugar. Taking a few seconds to stir, she raised the cup to her lips, blew softly, and took a sip. The rich mocha flavor felt smooth going down her throat.

"Perfect," she said, opening the morning newspaper she always brought with her. Pulling out the business section, she passed the front page and sports to him.

Expecting a quick response, he hid his impatience, taking the paper but setting it to the side without glancing at its contents. Whatever was happening in the world or with his favorite sports team was irrelevant to what was taking place right now.

His eyebrows rose inquiringly and he leaned forward. She had never had a hearing problem, but he decided to check anyway. "Did you hear me?"

Setting the cup on the saucer, Natalie reached past the small jewelry box and picked up a warm, gooey cinnamon roll that had been placed in the middle of the table. She usually went the healthy route for breakfast, choosing fruit or whole wheat toast, but when she had stepped inside the revolving doors this morning, a fresh batch of the rolls was just coming out of the oven and she found it impossible to resist.

With icing sliding down the side of her hand, she took a big bite and immediately relaxed her shoulders, sitting back in her chair. Closing her eyes with the roll practically melting in her mouth, she lost sight of everything around her and entered a place of sheer delight. Without opening her eyes, she took another bite. "Umm . . . this is soooo good. You have got to try one of these."

Dr. Derrick Carrington watched her body go limp and listened to the moans and sighs coming out of her mouth. His eyes were magnetically drawn to a small piece of creamy white icing making its way down the side of her lips toward her chin. Fighting the urge to lean over and kiss the cream off her chin, he watched her tongue dart in and out, licking up every drop.

What with the sensuous sounds coming from deep in her throat and the erotic motion of her tongue and lips, every male part of him came fully alive. Adjusting his body to accommodate his sudden discomfort, he let out a frustrated breath. No amount of changes he made in his seat would compensate for his body's reaction to her. Hoping to regain her attention—and focus on his question—he cleared his throat loudly. When that didn't garner a response, he decided his only option was to sit back and be patient. She had to finish her breakfast sooner or later.

As it turned out, it was going to be later. With each bite she took, she determined to savor the flavor, concerning herself with nothing of the things around her—including him. Derrick, on the other hand, hadn't touched his coffee and couldn't have cared less about a pastry. Not only because he waited anxiously for a response to his question, but because, after watching what she did with her tongue and mouth, he could barely keep his lower body in control. Checking the clock on the wall, he pondered how much longer it would be before Natalie would come back to earth.

Natalie enjoyed every morsel of her food, refusing to rush. Carla's Café had the best homemade pastries in the entire Washington, D.C., area and she wasn't about to ruin this moment just to answer his one little question. Neither the coffee nor the roll would taste the same if she let either of them cool off. She liked her food fresh and hot.

Located in the hustle and bustle of the business district, Carla's Café was a popular morning spot, having a constant flow of traffic from the minute they unlocked their doors every morning. With its coffees from around the world, pastries baked fresh every day, and its bright colors that gave a little island flavor, it was clear to see why so many people made this their first stop before starting their workday.

When the last bit of her roll was gone, she licked her fingers one by one, before using her napkin to wipe her mouth. Taking another sip of her coffee, she finally turned her attention to the man sitting in front of her. "What I just ate will probably cost me an extra forty-five minutes on the treadmill tomorrow. But I just couldn't help myself. I swear whatever is in that icing is addictive. I wonder if she would be willing to share her recipe. I've eaten quite a few of these in my lifetime at other places, but none quite like this."

"Natalie," Derrick said, refusing to fall into her trap of changing the subject.

Noticing his plate was still full, she reached across the table and ran her finger across his plate, scooping up some of the icing that had melted off. Putting it in her mouth, she sucked her finger for a few seconds before removing it.

Derrick watched the motion of her hand and wondered how he was going to make it through the rest of this breakfast when all he wanted to do was satisfy the burning desire that she created by just eating her food.

Seemingly unaware of the sexual charge she was giving off, she eyed his plate. "You're not going to eat yours?"

"I'm not that hungry," he said.

Hearing the rising tone of irritation in his voice, Natalie decided to ignore it. "Really?" she asked innocently. "I was practically starving."

Derrick moved the plates to the side and pushed the box closer to her. "Now that you've had your fill, I'm waiting for you to answer my question."

Casting her eyes downward, Natalie stared at the box for several seconds before raising them back to him. "Aren't you forgetting something?"

Derrick's attempt at a blank expression failed and he ignored the accusation in her voice.

"Let's see," he said thoughtfully, checking things off his imaginary list. "I'm here . . . you're here . . . I asked the question . . . I have the ring . . . what could I possibly be forgetting?"

Natalie skipped his stab at humor and scolded him with her eyes. "How about the fact that you already have a wife?"

"Minor detail," Derrick countered calmly, seemingly unfazed by her reasoning.

"Ha!" Natalie said, looking around for the waitress. If she was going to be on time for her first meeting of the day, she'd have to leave in the next few minutes. "Maybe it's just me, but having a wife when you're asking another woman to marry you is not what most people would classify as a 'minor detail.'"

His lips curved into an irresistibly devilish grin. "Well, maybe it's just me, but when I ask a question, I expect to get an answer.

Folding her newspaper and putting it back in her briefcase, she prepared to leave. "Let's have a little review . . . shall we?"

Crossing his arms at his chest, he nodded for her to continue. "I'm listening."

"You and I have an understanding . . . remember?"

"I'm clear on our understanding," Derrick said, watching her gather her sunshades and purse, but not the ring. Reaching across the table, he stopped her flurry of activity by taking her hands in his. Rising out of his chair, he leaned forward and sweetly kissed both of them. Lowering his voice, his eyes brimming with tenderness and passion, he said, "I understand that you love me and I love you."

Natalie rolled her eyes heavenward and removed her hands from his, continuing her preparations to leave. It could be so easy to be taken in by his sexy voice and charming smile, but Natalie held her ground. "I will give you partial credit for that answer. What you just said is, in fact, an understanding, but it's not *the* understanding."

"Then please," he said, giving her the floor. "Refresh my memory."

"With pleasure," Natalie said, knowing full well he knew the next words to come out of her mouth. "There will be no discussion of you taking another wife until you get rid of the one you have."

Snapping his fingers, Derrick appeared to have been given a revelation. "Oh, *that* understanding. Such high demands you have of me," he said, pretending to be insulted, as if she were being unreasonable.

"Not demand*s*," she said sweetly, "just one demand. Take care of that one tiny, little thing and then . . ."

"You'll marry me?" Derrick asked. The question was asked with more hope than confidence.

The waitress placed the bill on the table and cut her eyes from Natalie to Derrick. As she shook her head in amusement, her mouth split into a wide grin. Her light laughter resonated in the air as she moved to the next table to take an order.

Natalie stood and slid her shades on her eyes, completely ignoring his question—again. Picking up her coat from the back of the chair, she slid her arms through the sleeves, covering the smoky gray pantsuit she wore. "I suggest you pick up that small box and put it in a safe place before you leave it—or worse—someone takes it."

"My intention *is* to have someone take it," Derrick reminded her, leaving the ring exactly where it was. "You."

"Good-bye, Derrick," Natalie said, refusing to carry this conversation any further. Picking up the bill, she focused on the total. "I'll see you at dinner tonight. It's a special occasion, so don't be late."

When Derrick arrived this morning, he had every intention of getting Natalie to give him an answer, but as he watched her prepare to leave, it became painfully clear that that was not going to be the case. Standing, Derrick reached for the check. "You're not paying for breakfast."

Moving the bill just out of his reach, Natalie opened her purse and flashed a confident smile. "I let you pay for the movie last night."

"Correction," he said, grabbing for it again. This time he was successful. "You didn't *let* me do anything. I wanted to."

"Well," she said, removing her wallet and taking out some cash, "you paid for the ice cream last week, so it's my turn."

Carla Powers stood by silently, unable to surpress her laughter any longer. Overhearing the ridiculous conversation of two of her favorite customers was like watching *Comedy Central.* Dr. Derrick Carrington and Natalie Donovan came in for breakfast at least three times a week—and argued at least three times a week. On days she wasn't working the dining area, she made a point to take their table whenever they came in—mainly because she wanted to see what subject would have them going at it.

The topics might change, but it was fair to say that whatever they were discussing, they would somehow end up on opposite sides. If they weren't having passionate debates, as they liked to call them, over who would pay the bill, they were quarrelling over the latest political issue, a movie they saw, or where they should eat dinner. Last month, they spent thirty minutes in a heated discussion over who had the best football team. Natalie couldn't believe Derrick would choose the Dallas Cowboys over the Washington Redskins. Carla often asked herself how they had managed to stop arguing long enough to develop a relationship.

Derrick took a deep breath. He'd said it before, but judging by her behavior, it was worth repeating. "We don't need a scorecard to track who pays for what."

Natalie raised her brow at his tone. He may have been trying to hide his frustration, but he wasn't doing a good job. His words were clipped and spoken through a tight jaw and closed mouth. A twinge of guilt hit her and she considered what he was trying to do.

She wasn't trying to give him a hard time, but Natalie had been raised to be independent, never to depend on anyone for anything, especially a man. Her mother had been left by a married man and ended up raising Natalie on her own. The hard lessons Margaret learned early in life had been passed on to her daughter. The last thing Margaret wanted for Natalie was for her to go down the same path.

Graduating from college, buying her own home, and starting her own nonprofit organization demonstrated that the lessons taught by her mother had been learned well. She was able to take care of herself and this way of living had never posed a problem for her . . . until now . . . until Derrick.

Early in their courtship, it was a constant battle for power and control. Who would decide where they would go? Who would pay? It started to wear both of them out.

Challenging her way of thinking, Derrick showed her that it was OK to let someone else take care of her every now and then. Letting him do for her wasn't letting her guard down, it was allowing him to demonstrate just how much he cared. Natalie had been learning the art of compromise. *Let the man pay for breakfast.* "Fine, but next time I'll—"

"Next time you'll do nothing," he interjected, waving Carla over. Natalie was, by far, the most stubborn person he'd ever met. Rarely wanting anyone to do anything for her, she found it hard to accept anything from him. If Natalie had her way, everything about their relationship wouldn't be fifty-fifty—it would be 100 percent to zero.

"I'll leave the tip," she volunteered, taking money out and putting it on the table.

Picking her cash up, he held it out to her. "Natalie, take this money. Breakfast is on me."

Taking a step toward him, she grabbed his shirt and pulled him close, giving him a quick peck on the cheek before taking the money out of his hand. Turning to leave, she gave a quick wave. "I'll see you later."

After taking several steps, she paused. Slowly turning back around, she relaxed her stance and tipped the corners of her mouth into a sexy, seductive smile designed to entice. Walking slowly toward him, she swayed her hips from side to side. Stopping a few inches from his body, she clasped her hands behind his neck and stood on her tiptoes to reach her destination. She placed her mouth on his, and this time there was nothing quick about the kiss.

Feeling the softness of his lips, she coaxed them apart and slipped her tongue inside. His short intake of breath told her she'd captured his full attention and the tension that had existed between them just moments ago suddenly disappeared.

Just as they were about to cross the line of making a public spectacle of themselves, she released her hands from his neck and placed them at her side. With a final kiss she took two steps back, winked, and headed for the door. "Don't be late tonight."

Sitting back down, Derrick touched his lips and let out a soft sigh. Watching her cross the street to her car, he waited until she was safely inside before turning away. He shook his head at what just transpired between them, partly in amusement, partly in frustration. The things that drove him crazy about her were the very things that he loved about her. Strong. Independent. Self-sufficient. Able to take care of herself. Sexy. Smart. Alluring. Fascinating. Captivating. Charming. Natalie Lynette Donovan was all those things—and more.

She called her own shots, made her own way, created her own destiny. She would find a way or create a way. If that wasn't possible, that still didn't mean that she would ask for help. It was a well-known fact to anyone who spent more than five minutes in her presence—she didn't need anything from anybody. Sometimes, Derrick felt that included him.

"How many times are you going to pull that box out before you realize she's just not interested?"

The hilarity in Carla's voice didn't make Derrick feel any better. When did his proposals become common knowledge? He picked up the box and stared at it. "I don't think *interest* is the problem."

Carla took the cash from his hand, smiling gratefully as he indicated that she could keep the change. "Doesn't much matter what you call it—it all adds up to the same thing."

Derrick eyed Carla with weary eyes. Older than his thirty-eight years by at least a decade, she paraded around the café, dishing out unsolicited advice as if she were the next Dear Abby. Her petite frame was quite misleading. Just barely topping five feet, she had no qualms about butting into other people's conversations. He'd heard her say, on more than one occasion, that if people didn't want her in their business, then they shouldn't have come to her café.

Her warm spirit and easygoing manner could make anyone open up—and rumor had it that they usually did. And while Derrick didn't take to sharing information about his personal life with strangers, he pushed aside the feeling that he might regret his next words and gave her the expected response. "What does it add up to?"

Carla took the seat Natalie had vacated and Derrick smiled. Give her an inch, she'd take ten miles.

"Your question, plus that box, equals her saying no. What is this—the second time this week? And it's just Tuesday," she said, astonished at realizing how many times she'd watched the proposal play out. "I'm not even going to mention last week and the week before that."

Setting her order pad and pen down, she continued with her assessment of his current situation. "You must truly love her or you're a glutton for punishment. Pride alone should keep you from asking her over and over and over—"

"Don't you have other customers to attend to?" Derrick interrupted. The last thing he needed was a reminder of how many times he'd professed his love and offered the ultimate commitment, only to be given the brush-off. He especially didn't need it from someone who seemed to be enjoying his state of discontent.

Derrick turned the box around in his fingers, and Carla watched his expression move from agitation to disappointment. As her compassion kicked in, her face became serious. "Has she even opened it?"

"Oh yeah," Derrick said, thinking back to that romantic dinner almost three weeks ago. He'd made arrangements for a limo filled with all of her favorite things, including fresh orchids, a bottle of champagne, and Hershey's Kisses with almonds, to pick her up. Bringing her to her favorite restaurant for a private dinner, complete with five-star service from the chef, a violinist, and a harpist, Derrick had taken care of every romantic detail. "I waited until dessert had been served. After telling her she was everything to me and that I wanted her to be a permanent part of my life, she popped open the lid, gave a slight nod of approval, slammed it shut, and put it back on the table."

"Ouch!" Carla said, covering her heart for extra emphasis.

"My thoughts exactly," Derrick said, snapping out of the memories from that night.

"So what are you going to do about it?" Carla asked.

Derrick stood, put the ring in his pocket, and picked up his keys. "That, my good friend, is the million-dollar question."

Natalie put the Jamison Enterprise files to the side just as her assistant stepped into her office. Her morning had been jam-packed with client meetings and this was the first time she'd had all day to catch her breath. It was almost one o'clock, and she would have to grab lunch on the go again if she was going to make her two o'clock meeting on the other side of town. She hadn't had anything to eat since breakfast. Thinking of breakfast caused a secretive smile to crease her lips. She loved starting her day sharing breakfast with Derrick. It was hard to think back to a time when he wasn't in her life.

Carla's Café had become routine for them. They'd started the ritual soon after they met and it continued to this day. With her office located less than ten minutes away and his practice less than that, they had made it their own personal hangout.

"Umm . . . excuse me, Natalie?" Jea asked. "Are you OK?"

Realizing she must have ventured into la-la land with her thoughts, Natalie cleared her throat and tried to get her mind back to business. "Sorry about that, Jea. What's up? I've only got a few minutes."

Her boss's rushed tone was not new to Jea. Rarely a day went by when Natalie's schedule wasn't booked solid from morning until evening. There were client meetings, grant proposals, employee issues, and fund-raisers. Jea marveled that in the midst of a hurricane, Natalie managed to maintain her sanity. Always polite, patient, and attentive, she rarely lost her cool.

Always in a tailored designer suit, she wore neat and simple hairstyles that consisted of ponytails and buns. With minimal makeup, she appeared to be timid and meek. But that couldn't be further from the truth. This was one case where looks were deceiving. Jea could not recall a time when Natalie's accessories weren't perfect, her suit wasn't just right, or one strand of hair was out of place—the consummate professional. "I have a couple of things."

Graduating from American University two years ago, Jea had learned quite a bit working at Business Strategies, Inc., and from Natalie. Professionally, Jea admired Natalie for building a solid career as a CPA at one of the most prestigious public accounting firms in the country. After earning her MBA, Natalie shocked her colleagues by leaving the corporate world behind and starting a successful nonprofit organization, Business Strategies, Inc., or BSI as it was known. Her vision to design a company that would help ailing small businesses get their finances back on track had become a reality.

On the financial front, Natalie had it going on and Jea was impressed at what she had accomplished, including buying a large ranch-style home situated on several acres. On the few times that Jea had visited, she had fallen in love with the meticulous decorating that was cozy and inviting, yet sophisticated and stylish.

Then there was Dr. Carrington. At twenty-four, Jea was typically attracted to men her own age, but Derrick Carrington was superfine. Those eyes. Those lips. And he had money. What was there not to like? She had been working the day they met a year ago and perceived that Natalie had been walking around on cloud nine ever since. From the sidelines, Jea often wondered if Natalie's life could get any better. "Your phone has been on 'do not disturb' for the past two hours. I haven't bothered you, but there's a call holding for you and it sounds important."

Sticking papers and notes in her briefcase, Natalie didn't look up. "If I don't leave now, I'll never make it on time."

"I wouldn't even bring it up," Jea said hesitantly. "But it's your mother."

That little bit of information did nothing to change Natalie's disposition. Phone calls from her mother rarely constituted anything important, urgent, or requiring immediate action. Natalie could count on her cell phone ringing at least twice a day and her home and office phone at least once. Margaret Donovan could hardly let a day go by without reaching out to her only daughter.

Natalie had warned Jea about her mother over the years that they worked together, but the young assistant had trouble resisting Natalie's mother's persuasiveness. But time was ticking and Natalie's making her next appointment was crucial. The Executive Women's Network meeting had been on her calendar for months. There were over two hundred women waiting for her to share her strategies on successfully financing a start-up business. She couldn't take the call even if she wanted to. "Take a message."

"It's the third time she's called today," Jea said, hoping to sway her boss's decision. "I could have her call you on your cell phone and you could talk on the way."

Pausing, Natalie stared at her assistant in disbelief. "How many times did she call last Thursday?"

Jea hesitated before she spoke. "Four."

Slipping her arms through the sleeves of her light beige trench coat, Natalie said, "When I finally agreed to take her call, what was the pressing issue that needed my immediate attention?"

There was no use acting as if she didn't remember. They both knew the answer to this question. "To know which brand of chocolate chips would make the best cookies."

Without missing a beat, Natalie picked up her Blackberry. "How many times did she call a week ago Monday?"

"Three—but—" Jea started, feeling she needed to defend Natalie's mother.

Cutting her off, Natalie said "What did she want that day?"

Jea searched her vocabulary to find the words or phrase that could be used to strengthen her case. It was no use—there was no way to spin her answer to her advantage. "To ask what you wanted for Christmas."

In a gesture that only served to prove her point, Natalie pushed the calendar button on her Blackberry and turned it to face Jea. "What month are we in?"

Without looking or answering, Jea pleaded the case for Natalie's mother. "She said it was critical that she speak with you. It sounds like . . ."

Putting the electronic device in her purse, Natalie grabbed her briefcase and headed for the door. "It's March, Jea. She's asking about Christmas and it's March."

Watching Jea search for another angle, Natalie lowered her voice and reassured Jea with an understanding smile, "Believe me, Jea. I know my mother has a way of making it seem as if the world is coming to an end, but ten times out of ten, it's not that important."

Relenting, Jea followed her out into the reception area. "I'll take a message."

"Thank you."

Natalie walked out the front door just as Jea broke the news to her mother.

Heading to her car, Natalie made a mental list outlining the rest of her day. After her meeting with the Executive Women's Network at one o'clock, she was speaking at a late afternoon workshop to assist entrepreneurs with understanding some new tax laws that had recently gone into effect. It was just one more avenue that BSI used to reach those business owners to get them the knowledge they needed to keep their businesses thriving.

BSI had been her baby from the start and she couldn't have been more pleased with its growth. Passing the CPA before graduating from college, Natalie happily, and without regret, gave up her corporate job with a large firm and opted to help small business owners with limited financial access to professional services. Since starting the nonprofit agency several years ago, she'd helped almost a hundred companies recover from tax mistakes, mismanagement, and undercapitalization by providing them a plan for a profitable future.

Pulling out of the parking lot, she glanced at the number that popped up on her cell phone as it rang.

After two rings, she still hadn't decided whether she wanted to answer it. The Florida number flashed again. Needing to get in the right frame of mind for her upcoming meeting and presentation, she didn't want to get caught up in a conversation with her mother on what she should wear to go shopping with her neighbor or whether Natalie thought Florida would be affected by the hurricane season—which was more than five months away. Making her choice, she clicked the button and the ringing stopped. She sent her mother to voice mail.

When Margaret Donovan moved to St. Augustine almost two years ago, they both agreed it was the best decision for everyone. As a single mother, Margaret had endured a life filled with bitterness, animosity, and resentment caused by the abandonment by her married lover, Natalie's father. Having worked through some of that pain, Margaret decided to move to Florida for a fresh start. But living eight hundred miles away didn't stop Margaret from touching base with her daughter on almost a daily basis. Natalie loved her mother dearly, but she could be a little overbearing at times, testing Natalie's patience. If she talked to Margaret as often as she called, she would never get anything done during the day.

Her phone beeped three times, indicating a new voicemail message. Eyeing the small envelope icon in the right corner of her phone that blinked accusingly, Natalie felt a sliver of guilt seeping in. This wasn't the first time today—or this week—that she'd put her mother off. During the day she'd been too busy, and her evenings ended late if she had meetings or was spending time with Derrick.

Checking the time, she had at least ten minutes before she would arrive at her location. Just as she was about to call her mom back, her phone rang again. It was Christine Ware, her half sister who was hosting tonight's festivities. Thinking she might need her to take care of some last-minute details, Natalie answered, putting off her mother again.

Chapter 2

Dr. Derrick Carrington turned his Lexus SUV into the reserved parking space in front of the redbrick building that housed his medical practice. Taking note of the other cars, he could tell that most of the administrative and nursing staffs had arrived, as well as a couple of patients.

Located in the northwest part of the city, the four-story building housed several medical offices, including a dental office, a dermatologist, and three internal medicine offices. Located in an area with major employers and some residents, their practice was thriving and busy.

After leaving his practice in California, Derrick had reconnected with an old friend from his medical school days and begun to contemplate joining his practice. Dr. Will Proctor had been in several of Derrick's classes at Stanford, and while the two of them had quite a bit in common, they had their share of differences. They were both from the East Coast, enjoyed golf, and had plans to work in a practice that serviced families and corporations. With a high concentration of successful companies in the area, the executives of these organizations paid a premium for exceptional care to give their stockholders confidence that their leaders were healthy and strong.

However, when it came to social activities, they were miles apart. Will changed girlfriends as often as he changed his underwear. With the rigors of medical school, Will had found very little time to bond emotionally with women. Instead, he enjoyed the casual dating and physical connections. Derrick had never been into casual dating and often stood on the sidelines in amazement as Will juggled studying and several women.

When Will realized that Derrick was searching for a place to build his practice, they found out that another thing they had in common was their vision and philosophy regarding the type of medical care they wanted to provide. After several meetings and getting to know the other two doctors in the practice, Dr. Sherisse Copeland and Dr. Jeff Cain, Derrick came on board. No one since had regretted the decision.

The digital clock on the dash reminded Derrick that he had his first appointment in ten minutes. Thankful for the extra time, he turned the ignition off and leaned back in the plush leather seats. After dealing with Natalie ignoring his question this morning and debating who would pay the breakfast tab, he felt his frustration rising. It only increased when he spent the rest of his morning on a conference call with his attorney.

Talking to Philip Cox had turned his mood from slight irritation to downright exasperation. When the call ended, the scowl on Derrick's face served as a strong indicator of how unproductive that meeting had been. He and Philip had been in constant contact over the past months attempting to work out the details of his divorce settlement. He had hoped to finalize most of the outstanding points of contention, but the only thing today's conversation yielded was more negotiations and the makings of a major headache. Taking two extra-strength pain pills and a tall glass of water couldn't possibly offer any relief to the pain that was pounding in his temples. That's because this type of headache had a special source, and that source had a name—Mrs. Charlene Carrington.

How could a woman who claimed to want to move on from their marriage drag this process out? How could she create such drama in what should have been a very simple process? The lawyer fees alone should make her want to end this as quickly as possible. But Charlene didn't seem to care what it would cost to get what she believed should rightfully be given to her.

With his medical practice just getting off the ground when they got married, his potential for earnings was on the rise. Still, Derrick didn't believe in prenuptial agreements. Marriage was not a business deal to be hammered out and negotiated by two suits sitting across from each other at a conference table. Marriage was a decision and a commitment made from the heart and the soul.

His parents had been married for over forty years and he expected the same to be true of his union. Derrick wasn't naïve enough to think that everything would be perfect. He anticipated ups and downs, highs and lows—they were a part of any relationship. Not only did he expect to have them, he had every intention of working through them whenever they arose.

When he placed the diamond ring on Charlene's finger, his entire self was committed to the woman and their relationship. With everything in him, he believed that the union they were forming would be the cornerstone of the life they would build together. Unfortunately, the other person in this relationship didn't hold those same values. While Derrick looked forward to a future filled with making a home, building a career, and starting a family, Charlene looked to build her social standing.

Who would have imagined that he would be betrayed by someone who swore before God and three hundred people that she would love and honor him until death did them part? What a farce! The love lasted about as long as it took for her to get bored with their life—and him. And the honor? Well, that disappeared the moment she decided to sleep with his friend in his house and in his bed.

Replaying their life together, Derrick should have realized much sooner that things weren't right. But hindsight is twenty-twenty and you can't change anything in the rearview mirror. The only option he had now was to try to put this part of his life behind him.

The sound of his cell phone brought him out of his thoughts. Caller ID had been a godsend, giving him the option of dealing with someone or not. He debated for a few seconds before making the choice. Understanding that he would probably regret it, he said a quick prayer for patience and a contained tongue before pressing the green button.

"Why are you dragging this out?"

Her voice caused his head to pound harder and faster. That sound, at one time, had been music to his ears, offering encouragement, support, and love. Now it had become the equivalent of nails scraping down a chalkboard.

Derrick was not the least bit surprised by the call—it probably took all of five minutes for his lawyer to talk to hers. Derrick would bet his new truck that that's what this call was about. There was no doubt that she didn't like the information her lawyer delivered. "Hello to you, too, Charlene."

"Cut the pleasantries, Derrick," Charlene said, no doubt hearing the sarcasm laced in his tone. "There's no use in pretending that we actually want to be nice to each other."

"Fine," Derrick said, finally having something to agree with her on. "Then make this quick because I have a life."

Charlene shut her office door and lowered her voice. No need having the entire office witness her conversation. Having started her job as a public relations assistant just a few short months ago, she didn't want to start any rumors about her or her situation. "I just got off the phone with my lawyer."

Derrick didn't respond. After all, she hadn't asked a question.

"Did you hear me?" she asked through gritted teeth.

"Shouldn't you be talking through our lawyers?" Derrick asked. "I thought that was our agreement."

"To hell with what we agreed," she said, ready to do verbal battle with him.

"You should be good at that, Charlene," Derrick said. "We agreed to love each other. We agreed to spend the rest of our lives together. We agreed to raise a family together . . . and once again, you said 'to hell with what we agreed.'"

The calmness in his tone infuriated Charlene. The words were spoken without a hint of any emotion. "I didn't call you to rehash the past."

"Then please, Charlene, tell me why you've chosen to call me."

"Is this your idea of some type of sick revenge?" Charlene picked up the notes from her conversation with her lawyer. "Why are you fighting me on the china? The paintings? And the home in Vale?"

When he didn't answer, she continued.

"You never cared about any of these things. I don't think you've eaten one thing off those plates. You laughed when I brought the artwork home and you hate to ski."

This time, Derrick did respond—with a laugh. He could tell that pure, unhindered anger hovered just below the surface for her. She was about two seconds away from cursing him.

"What is so funny?" Charlene practically screamed.

"You," he said as if he'd just had an epiphany. "It just hit me how important *things* have always been to you. Even now, with a paid-for house, a paid-for car, and money in the bank, you still want more things."

"Well, Mr. High and Mighty, if things are so unimportant to you, why are you fighting me to hang on to them?" she asked smugly.

"I'm not fighting you," he clarified confidently. "Every one of those items was bought with my money."

He heard her take a breath to speak, but he cut her off. "If my memory serves me correctly, you bought three picture frames, eight CDs, and a set of place mats. I told my lawyer you were more than welcome to have all of those things."

The sarcasm in his voice made Charlene cringe, but she quickly recovered and found solace in reminding him of the facts. "Correction, dear. Those things were bought with *our* money. It's community property, Derrick. We have to split our assets."

Not moved by her words, Derrick was quickly tiring of this conversation. "At least I'm letting you keep the bed. You know, the one I found you in with my good friend, Scott."

The phone went silent for several seconds. Finally, Charlene said, "Why are you still hanging on . . . being so revengeful? Do you think we'll get back together? Are you still in love with me? Is that what this is about?"

From the outside looking in, one might think she had spoken the truth. But Derrick wasn't on the outside. He was dead smack in the middle of it and he knew the truth. Could she really think that he had any feelings left for her after what she had done to him—to them? "The simple fact is this, Charlene. You hooked your claws into me, but my money and my love just weren't enough for you.

"This is not about getting back together. This is not about still being in love with you. This is about me not being your meal ticket anymore. The reality is that this divorce could have been final months ago, but you're the one who can't seem to come to an agreement about some of our assets. So let me offer you a little advice. If you have questions about the settlement discussions, I highly suggest you contact my lawyer because I won't answer any more calls from this phone number."

As he disconnected the call, Derrick's smile quickly broke into a hearty laugh. Hanging up on her didn't change anything, but it sure made him feel better. Maybe the bed comment was laced with revenge, but he wanted to remind her of why they were in this situation to begin with. His laughter came to an abrupt stop when he remembered one of the most painful times in his life.

As Derrick's career began to take off, Charlene became more of a socialite than a wife—always wanting to entertain, attend grand affairs, and shop for the newest, the latest, the biggest, or the greatest. Initially, Derrick didn't see the harm. They could afford it and Charlene was happy. But gradually, Derrick began to feel that her feeding frenzy on material things and social activities had taken over their relationship. When he started to pull back from attending events, restaurant openings, and being a willing participant in her shopping sprees, things started to change for them.

Charlene began to spend more and more time away from home, and when she was home she was distant. Derrick tried talking to her, but it didn't seem to make the situation any better. Concerned about what was happening and wanting to work things out, he tried over and over again to get her to open up to him. When he suggested counseling, she waved off his anxiety, claiming every couple goes through a rough patch. Asking what was making their patch so rough would just cause her to shut down.

At the end of his rope, Derrick had finagled some schedule changes with other doctors in his practice to take two weeks off. Thrilled at the idea that came to his mind, he found the perfect way to spend some quality time with his wife to concentrate on what was going wrong and to work out their challenges. Stopping at a travel agency on the way home from work, he purchased a two-week stay in Maui. In a private bungalow on a secluded beach, he was sure that whatever wedge had formed between them could be removed and their relationship would be repaired.

After picking up the tickets, he had headed home early that day. Making reservations at her favorite Indian restaurant, he planned to surprise her with dinner and the second honeymoon. Noticing her car in the driveway, he entered the house and searched the entire first level for her. Getting no results, he climbed the back stairs two at a time to the second floor. Yelling her name as he made his way down the hall, he opened the double doors that led to the master suite.

A punch from Mike Tyson in his prime fighting days would have paled in comparison to the force that coursed through his entire body. Shocked. Astonished. Flabbergasted. Completely overwhelmed. His stomach twisted into a tight knot, his heart slammed against his chest, and the air was sucked completely out of his lungs. He blinked several times to confirm what had registered to his brain. Feeling his knees buckle, he leaned against the door for support.

As he focused on her for a brief moment, their eyes locked and he looked for anything in hers that would explain away the scene that was playing out before him. When she gave him nothing, his eyes then made their way to *him*. The man who had roomed with him his freshman year in college. The man who had celebrated with him the day he passed his medical board exam. The man who toasted him the night of his bachelor party. The man who stood at his side as he recited his sacred wedding vows. That same man who had been such a big part of his life was now tangled up in his sheets, in his bed, with his wife.

Scrambling to his feet, Scott Livingston rushed into an explanation that crossed between justification, rationalization, and apologies. In his haste, the covers fell to the floor. Horrified, Scott frantically searched around for his clothes. Reaching for his pants, his shirt, and bending over to pick up his shoes, he opened his mouth several times, but nothing came out.

Charlene, on the other hand, hadn't made a move or a sound. Without so much as an acknowledgment as to what was happening, she watched Scott dress in less than three minutes.

With Derrick standing in the doorway, blocking his exit, Scott had no escape. The room became eerily silent.

Finally, Scott took a few tentative steps toward Derrick. "Look, man . . . I . . . we . . ." He ventured a quick, desperate glance at Charlene for help, but none was forthcoming. Amazed at her look of indifference, Scott turned his attention back to Derrick.

Before he could say anything further, Derrick stepped toward him. "Get the hell out of my house!"

Not sure how to make this right but wanting to offer something, Scott searched his mind for any words that would somehow diffuse the situation. The attraction between him and Charlene had been growing for months, and Lord knows he had tried to resist. But her advances became more obvious and more frequent. Believing that it was just a matter of time before Derrick and Charlene separated, he crossed the line and began having an affair. "Derrick, man, I know what this looks like, but . . ."

Derrick's hand clenched into a fist. "But what, Scott?"

With the change in Derrick's demeanor, it appeared that this altercation was on its way to becoming a physical battle. "It's just that . . ."

"Are you kidding me?" Derrick challenged, with a sinister laugh. "Are you seriously trying to have a conversation with me about why I just walked into *my* house and found *my* wife having sex with *my* friend . . . in *my* bed?"

"Let me explain," he said.

"No," Derrick said. In a few seconds he might do something that would probably send him to jail for a very long time. "Let *me* explain. If I have to tell you to get out of my house one more time, you'll be leaving on a stretcher or in a body bag."

Seeing pure hatred in Derrick's eyes, Scott decided the best thing he could do was take his advice. Fearing for his physical well-being, Scott rushed past Derrick, never looking back at Charlene. A few seconds later, they heard the front door open and shut.

In the quietness of the house, Derrick waited for Charlene to say something. If anyone had any explaining to do, it was she. She should be the one telling him why she was having an affair, why she turned her back on their marriage, why she looked as if she couldn't have cared less that he just found out that his wife was being unfaithful with his friend.

Finally, Charlene stepped out of the bed, unashamedly naked, and walked into the adjoining bathroom. The slam of the door was unapologetic and final.

Unable to move from the spot he was standing on, he tried to make sense of what his eyes had just witnessed. His friend. His wife. In bed. Together. Focusing on the jumbled sheets that had fallen to the floor in Scott's haste to get out, he shook his head in disgust. They were the same sheets that he had slept on last night.

Scanning the room, he took note of the half-empty bottle of wine, the two glasses, and the ripped condom packages.

What had been shock a few minutes ago turned to rage. Was this what his marriage had become? After all he and Charlene had been through together? College sweethearts. The rigors of medical school. The challenges of his residency. His supporting her as she moved from one career to another, not quite finding herself in any of them. After a decade of loving each other, this was how it would end?

The bathroom door opened and Derrick turned his attention to her. Having put on a robe, she leaned against the jamb and stared at him. Her jet-black hair that reached below her shoulders settled into a sea of uncontrolled ringlets. Devoid of makeup, her skin, the color of nutmeg, appeared flawless. It was amazing that at thirty-eight, she still had the beauty of the young woman he had met in college.

He'd been captivated by her spirit and had fallen in love with her ambition and drive when she walked into his history class during his freshman year. She understood the rigors of being premed and stood by him as he pursued his dream of becoming a doctor. Wanting to support him through medical school, she was right there with him when the pressure consumed him and he didn't think he was going to make it. The day he passed the boards was the day he proposed. And since that time, he'd thought they were on their way to living a good life together. But somewhere along the line everything he was and everything they had were no longer enough for her.

Trying to read her expression only baffled Derrick. Working to maintain some semblance of control, he decided that instead of playing the guessing game of what was going through her mind, he would just ask her. "I would invite you to tell me what's going on, but I've had the pleasure of having firsthand knowledge. Tell me if I've got this right . . . my wife is having an affair with my best friend, and it can't be because she cares about him. Otherwise she wouldn't be screwing him in my own bed. So this must be about me. How you must hate me to want me to see this."

"Don't be so dramatic, Derrick," Charlene said blandly. "I didn't expect you home for hours."

As he waited for something else to come out of her mouth, the room, once again, fell silent. That was it? No explanation? No apology? No asking for forgiveness? No offer to work things out?

Derrick took a hard look at the woman he had pledged his life to, and the anger that had controlled so much of him just minutes ago suddenly turned to sorrow. His home. His wife. His marriage. All three created a place for him that was full of life, full of promise, and full of joy. Now all that had been snuffed out—killed by the woman standing before him as if she didn't have a care in the world. When had she become so cold?

Loosening his fists, that had been clenched since the moment Scott spoke his first words of defense, he remembered the tickets for their vacation and the plan to get his marriage back on track. Sighing in resignation, he understood it was a moot point. Useless. There was no marriage to save.

"If you wanted out, Charlene, all you had to do was ask." Derrick turned on his heel to walk out of the room. It was the last time he set foot in that house.

He'd spent the first couple of months after her betrayal in a haze. Moving into a hotel, he spent his days going through the motions at work and his nights fighting the anger and bitterness that threatened to take over his being. Most nights, the anger and bitterness won.

How could someone who had become his world treat him with such disrespect? That one question swirled in his head day after day, week after week, and month after month. Finally, he realized he might never really know when or why Charlene stopped loving him. She wasn't interested in talking and he was driving himself crazy trying to figure it out for himself. To retain his own sanity, he just had to learn to accept it. He filed for divorce and didn't look back. With any luck, the divorce would be final within the month and he would be able to move on with his life—a life with Natalie.

Just the thought of Natalie caused the tenseness in his body from talking with Charlene to move out of him. When he began dating Natalie, his friends, colleagues, and parents questioned his ability not only to love again, but also to trust again. After what Charlene put him through, to open himself up to be hurt again didn't make sense. Charlene had taken his love and trust and set them aside like old shoes. Didn't he fear being hurt again?

In the months after he discovered his wife's infidelity, Derrick wanted nothing to do with anything related to the opposite sex. His heart had been yanked out and stomped on with a stiletto heel and he had no intention of putting himself in that predicament again. The bitterness of her betrayal lingered in his heart and his naturally warm spirit grew cold and hard.

The relaxed smile and easy nature his patients had become accustomed to had been replaced with a permanent grimace and a complete loss of bedside manner. Some of his colleagues and friends, in an effort to snap him out of it, tried to set him up on several dates. Initially, he refused to go out with anyone. How could he look at another woman and not consider her a liar and a cheat? When he finally agreed to go out on a couple of dates, they were complete disasters.

He was on the defensive and the women picked up right away that he was carrying too much baggage. Though he never shared with his dates why he exhibited such mistrust, they easily realized that he was trying to work through some heavy emotional issues. Neither he nor his dates were surprised when he didn't contact them to get together again. Before leaving L.A., Derrick was well on his way to being an untrusting, bitter man who would be alone for the rest of his life. But all of that changed—thanks to Marlon Hutchins.

At nineteen, Marlon had his whole life ahead of him. A sophomore at UCLA, he was smart, popular, and on top of the scouting list for major league baseball. Late one night, coming home from a campus party, everything in his life changed. A car swerved into his lane, cutting him off and forcing him into the guardrail. Rushed to the hospital, he was told his right arm—his pitching arm—was severely damaged. Although the surgeons worked feverishly to save it, the injury was too extensive.

Derrick had become his doctor after the accident and marveled at Marlon's ability to recover, both physically and mentally, from such a tragic event. The scholarship that was paying for his education was no longer available. Friends who had been a staple in his young life slowly disappeared. The scouts who so graciously courted him during his high school and college life were nowhere to be found. It was a tough situation to live through at any age.

One of the last patients he saw before his move to the East Coast, Marlon made Derrick proud of what he had accomplished since the accident. Just turning twenty-four, he was going to be graduating from college in May. Regardless of losing his scholarship, he had found a way to complete his education. He planned to teach high school and coach the varsity baseball team.

After experiencing so much adversity, Marlon's genuine happiness and overall positive attitude intrigued Derrick. Was it possible to be this satisfied and content with life after it threw him a curve ball? Curious, Derrick asked his secret to maintaining a positive attitude.

Marlon smiled proudly and said words that changed forever Derrick's outlook on life. "Well, Dr. C, sometimes a small speed bump in life could suddenly look like a big mountain—insurmountable. But the reality is—it's just a speed bump. You could either stare at it, hoping it would somehow go away, or you could just go over it, leaving it behind once and for all. I chose to go over it."

Later that evening, as Derrick packed the last of his belongings, he replayed Marlon's words in his mind. Aligning Marlon's philosophy to his situation, he thought about the self-inflicted pain and misery he'd suffered because of his breakup with Charlene. Yes, he'd loved her. Yes, she'd betrayed him. But how long was he going to allow her to dictate how he was going to live his life? How long would he hang on to the disappointment of a failed marriage? How long would he reject loving again?

The speed bump that was Charlene and all the emotional turmoil and trust issues that went along with it had to be left behind. He'd given her the power to steal his ability and desire to love and trust again. He decided to reclaim that power.

Stepping out of the truck and heading across the parking lot, Derrick replaced thoughts of Charlene and his past with visions of Natalie and his future.

Chapter 3

Natalie raced through the front door, tossing her keys and purse on the small bench in her foyer before racing up the steps. Her afternoon workshop had run longer than expected, and she ended up driving home at the height of rush-hour traffic. Always making an effort to stay after a session to answer individual questions, she wanted to make sure the attendees left her workshops with all of the information they needed to keep their businesses on track.

"Financial Health Checkup for the Small Business Owner" was her most requested program. Along with other business associations and organizations, the community college sponsored this workshop at least twice a month. Having made a personal pledge to provide current and timely information that would have a direct and immediate impact on those who came, Natalie kept the number of workshop attendees to under thirty. It was the only way she could give individual attention and recommendations. With the positive feedback the college had been receiving, they were looking to add several more dates over the next couple of months.

Unbuttoning her blouse, she walked into her bedroom and tossed it on the bed. The closer she got to the bathroom, the more clothes she removed. Her pants went on the chaise, her shoes pushed under the bed, and her watch and earrings landed on the dresser. By the time she stepped into the master bath, she had nothing left but her undergarments.

Dubbed her personal sanctuary, this area of the house had been one of the major selling points when Natalie began looking for a place to call home. It not only boasted a huge bath with a lighted vanity area, Jacuzzi tub, and a shower for two with a bench, but a master suite with a cozy sitting area accented by a double-sided fireplace.

With the help of Christine and her interior design firm, the earth tones and subtle lighting provided the perfect place for her to unwind after a hectic day in the rat race. If she weren't going out, she would put on her favorite pair of lounging pants and an old T-shirt, and curl up on the small, but comfy sofa. Lighting the fireplace, she'd pour herself a glass of wine and open one of the many books in her growing stack of "to be read." It was those quiet moments in her house that she relished.

Unfortunately, she had no time to destress this evening. Derrick was picking her up at seven o'clock, which gave her less than an hour to shower, dress, and wrap the gift. With her working, conducting workshops, and being a member of a couple of business associations, Natalie's busy schedule rarely allowed her to indulge in personal social events during the week. The time to hang out with her friends typically happened on the weekends. But tonight was different. This was one party she wouldn't miss for anything.

Natalie stepped under the warm spray from the shower

heads, letting the pellets of water melt away the constant rushing of the day. Lathering with her perfumed body gel, she felt the fresh scent rejuvenating her, giving her a boost of energy. Rinsing, she thought about how far she'd come from the little shy girl in the inner city who was slightly overweight, a little low on self-confidence, and needed glasses and braces. If she had to be categorized, she would probably fit into the cool nerd category—never quite in the "in" crowd, but not completely out. How different she and her life were today.

When she was growing up, there had been no spacious ranch-style home on two acres in the suburbs to spend her days and nights in. The small apartment where she had lived was in the heart of the nation's capital. In a building filled with lower-income families mostly made up of single parents or the elderly, the two-bedroom apartment, with its small kitchen and living room/dining room combo, couldn't boast of a gourmet, eat-in kitchen, a personal gym outfitted with the latest equipment, or an entertainment room with comfortable theater-style seating with a large, pull-down screen. As a matter of fact, the master suite in Natalie's current home, with its separate sitting area, walk-in closet, and oversized bathroom, was bigger than that entire apartment.

A matchbox was what Margaret Donovan called it. She hated living there and wasn't shy about telling Natalie just how much. Every other day, Margaret would talk about what they didn't have in their life or couldn't afford. With no college degree, a young daughter to raise, and limited resources, Margaret blamed everyone around her for her current situation. The few people who wanted to help her were quickly alienated by her sour demeanor and ungrateful attitude.

Working two jobs, trying to make ends meet, was the only life her mother knew. The urban neighborhood, the lack of living space, and the absence of any luxury, had continually chipped away at her mother's hope until she was left with nothing but resentment and antipathy. Natalie had been more than a latchkey kid. She had practically raised herself, both physically and emotionally.

Any time her mother went into one of her tirades about how bad her life had become, Natalie couldn't help but shoulder some of the blame. If her mother hadn't had an extra body to feed and dress, maybe she wouldn't be so miserable. Because of that, Natalie constantly tried to ease her mother's pain. She figured if she could be the perfect child, life would be better for her mother.

Doing chores without being asked, making the honor roll, staying out of trouble, making sure she got into college, were done to somehow make up for the life of gloom her mother seemed to have. But none of her efforts were enough. Her mother's disposition remained unchanged.

Hanging out with her friends whose financial situation was similar to hers, Natalie noticed that they didn't seem to have the same overwhelming desire to please their parents. Natalie, with her melancholy moods, looked, at times, as if she carried the weight of the world on her shoulders. Her friends filled their days with school and play, unaware of the challenges that Natalie faced on a day-to-day basis. As time passed, Natalie began to realize the differences between Margaret and other moms.

Margaret always blamed her unhappiness on external things—money, dropping out of college, her boss, and Henry. With her friends' families, Natalie witnessed a closeness and happiness that no amount of money could buy.

There was joy, contentment, and love just because they had each other. But that wasn't the family life that Natalie had grown accustomed to. With an absent father and a mother filled with resentment, she had little left to create positive childhood memories. Margaret was too busy working and complaining.

That's why Margaret drilled into Natalie the importance of being able to stand on her own two feet. According to her mother, that was her major mistake with Henry. He was a smooth talker and had Margaret eating out of his hand. Thinking she had found the love of her life, she gladly let him dictate everything about their relationship. The faith and trust she put in him, he took and used it to his advantage. It wasn't until Margaret was pregnant and alone that she realized how much it had cost her to put her life in his hands. The last thing she wanted her daughter to do was repeat her mistakes and end up like her.

Pushing the knob in her shower, Natalie cut off the water and her trip down memory lane.

Natalie stepped onto the cool ceramic tile and focused on her night with Derrick, her family, and her friends.

Reaching for a towel off the warmer, she heard the phone ring. "It never fails," she mumbled.

Giving herself a quick once-over to prevent water from dripping everywhere, she made a mad dash for the bedroom.

"Hello," she said breathlessly—too late.

Placing the receiver back on the cradle, she glanced at the caller ID—Florida.

With time ticking, she was down to twenty minutes before Derrick would arrive. There was no way she could call her mother back. Besides, Natalie had to mentally prepare for a conversation with her mother. There was no telling what new, unimportant rampage she would go off on. Two months ago, she tracked Natalie down in a seminar to let her know that she couldn't decide which comforter set to buy for her bed. Last month, she couldn't find her long dress coat. After Natalie finally had a chance to take her call, she reminded her mother that she didn't need that coat in the Florida sun. But that didn't make a difference to Margaret.

In her fifties, Margaret wasn't senile or losing her mind, she just missed her daughter. For so long, it had been just the two of them and even though Margaret believed the best decision she made was moving to Florida, that didn't stop her from reaching out almost daily to her baby girl. Natalie didn't really mind the constant calling. It was just the topic of conversation that her mother always raised on just about any call.

Margaret wouldn't allow more than a few days to go by without quizzing Natalie about the state of her relationships with men. Margaret called it her "check-in." She wanted to make sure that Natalie wasn't letting her emotions get the best of her when it came to dealing with the opposite sex. Proud of what her daughter had accomplished so far in her life, she didn't want to see her lose it all over promises made by someone who ultimately couldn't be trusted.

Having learned a long time ago to let her mother rant and rave, Natalie found out early on there was no use in arguing with her mother. On more than one occasion, she tried to convince Margaret that her experience wasn't necessarily going to be Natalie's experience. That while Henry treated her badly and left her alone, that didn't mean that that's the route that all men would take.

Having witnessed the successful marriages of some of her friends, Natalie believed that there were plenty of men who loved, cherished, and took care of their families. However, Natalie's words fell on deaf ears. Margaret wasn't interested in hearing any positive statements about men or relationships.

So now Natalie just let her talk, rarely offering anything of substance to her mother about her dating or the men in her life. She had yet to share any of the details about Derrick with her mother. It hurt Natalie at times that she had finally found a man who touched her at every level and she couldn't share this experience with her mother. So many times Natalie caught herself before she would say something about him. His success, his good looks, his kind nature, and his ability to make her laugh had all been on the tip of her tongue at one point or another. But she didn't want to deal with the repercussions of such personal revelations to her mom. She should have been shouting with joy with her mother, but this was one topic that she couldn't share.

Margaret would fill her daughter's head with negative comments and doubts, questioning whether she was putting too much faith in Derrick. Margaret would verbalize her concerns about spending too much time with him, letting him do too much for Natalie, and letting him dictate what would be happening in their relationship and in certain areas of her life.

Walking back to the bathroom, she decided against calling her mother back. Natalie wasn't willing to have anything—or anyone—ruin her upcoming evening. She decided to give her mom a call tomorrow.

The doorbell rang just as Natalie slid her feet into her black, sexy heels. Turning out the light in her bedroom, she raced down the steps, careful not to trip. Not completely comfortable wearing such high shoes, she didn't want to end up on the floor. As she opened the front door, her eyes drank him in and a warm glow flowed through her. The man looked fantastic.

One of the first characteristics Natalie had noticed the moment she met him was his eyes. A mixture of brown and gray, their uniqueness made them captivating and intriguing. When you added beautiful lashes, a strong jaw, and luscious lips, it was a package that any woman would be proud to have.

Stepping into the entryway, Derrick lazily perused her from head to toe. His bold and brazen stare took in all of her, and a ripple of excitement traveled through his entire body. "You look absolutely gorgeous."

Natalie beamed at his compliment and did a model's turn to show off the emerald-green silk charmeuse dress. With its thin straps, straight bodice, and two-layered flowing skirt that skimmed the top of her knees, it flared freely in the air. The dress had been a fashion stretch for her. Her accounting background wasn't just a reflection of her intellect, it also reflected her style of dress. She had more business suits and pumps in her closet than she could count. Between work, conducting workshops, and fund-raising, just about all of her time outside her house was spent in professional attire. That's why she decided to go all out for tonight. With her hair pinned up in a French roll, her meticulous makeup, and her sparkling jewelry, she felt sexy and alive. Judging from his response, she felt her efforts were well appreciated.

Before she could thank him for his flattering remark, he lowered his gaze and her words were swallowed as his lips crushed against hers—capturing hers fully and completely. Eagerly responding to the electricity that crackled between them, Natalie opened her mouth and freely accepted the warmth of his tongue. Offering no resistance, she willingly relinquished control and allowed him to have his way. His arms, stretched fully around her waist, coaxed her closer until not even a ray of light could pass between them. As their kiss deepened, his hands slid lower, cupping her butt. Delirious with a raw yearning, she felt his desire grow strong and hard against her body.

Derrick delighted in the sheer pleasure that having her in his arms provided. The instant their lips connected, every crazy part of his life drifted into nonexistence. The moment she had walked out of that café, he unconsciously counted the hours until he would see her, touch her, and feel her. There was such peace with her, such contentment. Being with her eliminated all that he was dealing with. There were no divorce settlement, no lawyers, and no Charlene. The constant battle of ending the chapter of his life that had existed in California could overwhelm him at times, but it was moments like this that banished it all. It was in this place, with her, that he found solace.

Sliding his hands up the sides of her dress and then to the front to cup her breasts. The material of the dress didn't hide the tautness of her nipples pressing against the thin silk.

Just as they were about to reach the point of no return, Natalie took a step back. Breathless and overpowered by the swirl of emotions wreaking havoc in her, she needed a moment for words to come out. "That was some greeting."

Derrick's eyes smoldered with fire as they watched the concentrated rise and fall of her chest. With a mischievous grin, he closed the distance between them and stroked her cheek with the back of his left hand. "How important is it to go to this party?"

Shaking her head from side to side, Natalie turned to walk into the living room to get her coat. "Oh, no, you don't. Christine has been planning this dinner party for Damian's birthday for a month."

Her words didn't have the power or firmness she'd hoped and Derrick followed her, choosing to ignore them. Standing directly behind her, he clasped his arms in front of her. Nuzzling her neck, he felt her body start to relax. "How about if we're just a tad late?"

Stepping completely out of his touch, Natalie stared at him with a curious, deep longing. "You're not playing fair, Derrick. You remember our deal."

Raising his hands to surrender, Derrick let her step out of his embrace. "I remember the deal, but that doesn't mean I have to like it."

Grabbing his hand, she pulled him toward the door. "Come on, baby. Let's go to a party."

The cocktail hour was in full swing by the time Natalie and Derrick arrived at the home of Christine and Damian Ware. As they parked in the stone-paved circular drive, the number of cars in front of them told they were the last to arrive. Greeted at the door by the birthday boy, Natalie gave him a huge hug and handed him his gift. "Happy birthday, Damian."

Planting a kiss on her cheek, Damian thanked her.

"Happy b-day, man," Derrick said, patting him on the back.

After hanging their coats in the closet, they stepped into the opulent two-story entrance. The marble floor, spiral staircase, and antique crystal chandelier that hung from the ceiling set the tone for the entire house. With Christine's keen eye for décor, the foyer, grand in style, gave a sense of welcoming.

Following Damian down the hall, they entered the family room where the other guests had already gathered. The high ceilings, comfortable seating, and roaring fire provided the perfect backdrop for the evening's festivities.

Damian, never one for big parties, wanted his birthday celebration to be shared with close friends and family. Christine, famous for planning full-blown surprise parties, had been put on notice by her husband. He didn't want a house full of colleagues, business associates, or family members that he'd only seen once or twice in his life. This day, his fortieth birthday, he wanted to relax, enjoy, and reflect on all that he'd accomplished and what was still to come. That could only be done with people who truly meant something to him.

Thankfully, Christine had listened and given him exactly what he wanted. The group was small, but it contained those who were closest to his heart—Brandon, Tanya, Danielle, Xavier, Stephanie, Nathan, Derrick, and Natalie.

His younger brother, Brandon, stood in the corner of the room playing bartender for the evening. A successful attorney, he had married the woman of his dreams, Tanya Kennedy, a little over six months ago. Tanya had worked for Damian's construction company when she first met his brother. Because he had a reputation as a playboy, Tanya had no interest in giving Brandon the time of day.

Chasing her for months, he was determined to show her that even a playboy bachelor could change his ways when the right woman came along. It was only through his tenacity that he finally convinced Tanya to give him a chance. Unfortunately, Brandon got scared when his feelings for Tanya began to grow. In true player form, he panicked, causing their relationship to hit extremely rocky roads, almost losing her for good. Finding out that it was harder to live without her, he faced his selfishness and stupidity. Having learned from his mistakes, he worked double time to get Tanya to forgive him and take him back.

Convincing Tanya that he was someone she could love and trust again was the hardest battle he ever fought—in or out of the courtroom. But it was all worth it. Their lovely nuptials had taken place last summer, and it had been the happiest day of his life. He was content and satisfied beyond what he ever thought possible, and they now planned to start a family.

Danielle, Tanya's sister, sat on the sofa chatting with the other women. Dressed in a dark blue fitted dress that stopped just above the knees, large chandelier earrings, and a sophisticated updo, she looked every bit the supermodel she had once been. In high demand at the height of her career, she had inhaled life in the fast lane, enjoying the spotlight and everything that came with it. During that time in her life, no one in this room would have considered her family or a friend.

The hottest supermodel in the industry during her late teens and early twenties, she demanded that she be treated like a queen and that everyone around her put up with whatever she dished out. She epitomized every negative connotation associated with the word *diva*. Failing to appreciate her success, her friends, associates, family members, and other professionals in the business when she was at the top of her game, she headed for the inevitable fall.

Her reputation for being unreasonable and hard to work with began to overshadow her beauty. As a result, her bookings, endorsement deals, and finances took a nosedive. When she went looking for help from all the people she'd treated wrong, no one cared. Alone and broke, Danielle finally came to her senses. For most of those who knew her, the epiphany of wanting to make things right was too little, too late—until Xavier Johnston.

If there was any person who doubted her ability to become humble and grateful, it was Xavier, having witnessed her wicked attitude and treatment of people when she was at the top of her game. She had been blackballed from ever working in fashion or television. When she was at the end of her rope, Xavier agreed to give her a second chance.

As a television studio owner and producer, Xavier had the means to give Danielle back the career she had carelessly thrown away years ago, but when she began to go back into the world of entertainment—the world that had so easily kicked her out—she realized that it wasn't all it was cracked up to be. Deciding to take a different path, she opened Danielle's, an upscale women's clothing boutique located in the city. She and Xavier had been married this past New Year's Eve.

Stephanie and Nathan Hollister made the flight from Atlanta to be with Damian on his special day. Stephanie and Christine had been friends since college and there were rarely any major events that went on in either of their lives that they weren't there for.

Christine stood beside Stephanie about a year and a half ago when she said her "I dos" to Nathan on the most romantic day of the year—Valentine's Day. Months later, Stephanie came back to the D.C. area to spend several weeks helping Christine after she had Brianna, an adorable baby girl who slept peacefully in the nursery, one floor up.

Christine planned to return the favor in four months when Stephanie gave birth to her first child.

As a server walked the room with small trays of crab balls, shrimp skewers, and mini spinach puff pastries, the mood was festive and light. Typical at most small gatherings, the sexes began to divide. The men congregated around the stocked bar in the corner of the room, and the women sat around the coffee table.

"So how does it feel to be another year older?" Brandon asked his older brother. "Have you had a chance to pick up your reading glasses or walking cane?"

Laughter broke out in the group and Damian punched his brother in the arm. "You're not far behind me."

"Hey, I'm far enough," Brandon said, thinking of the age difference.

"You guys shouldn't be treating your elders like this," Damian said with a playful smile on his face. "You should be taking advantage of this time to glean from my knowledge and learn from the wisdom that I've gained over the years."

"You know," Nathan said, stroking his beard in jest, "Damian may be onto something. Please, oh wise one, give us some words of wisdom."

Damian squared his shoulders and stuck his chin out. "I'm so full of wisdom, I just don't know where to start—especially since you guys need so much."

"Oh, you're full of something, all right," Brandon said, nudging Xavier. "I'm just not sure if wisdom is what we'd call it."

"I wouldn't be so quick to laugh," Damian said, glancing at each man. "If it wasn't for me and my infinite wisdom, you guys would be a bunch of grumpy and *lonely* men."

The group went quiet at his statement.

"What are you talking about?" Nathan asked, his curiosity piqued.

"Let's start with you," Damian said, facing his brother. "You messed things up so bad with Tanya that she had absolutely no intention of ever being in the same room with you again, let alone marrying you. If it wasn't for my intercession on your behalf, she would never have found it in her heart to give you another chance."

"He's got you there," Xavier said, remembering the stories he heard about Tanya being so mad at Brandon, no one was allowed to speak Brandon's name around her.

"I got you, too," Damian said, turning his attention to Xavier.

"Now, wait a minute," Xavier said, raising his hands in defense. "I didn't know you when I got together with Danielle."

"That may be true, but it was my tough love for her when she was down and out that started her turnaround to becoming the woman that we know and love today," Damian gently reminded him. "And you know she's come a long way."

The four men nodded their heads in agreement. Danielle used to be a terror in stilettos. No one could stand to be around her for more than five minutes because she usually insulted people or dismissed them as irrelevant and insignificant. She had definitely changed her ways and become someone her family and friends no longer despised

"What about Nathan?" Brandon asked. "You had nothing to do with him and Stephanie getting together."

"Not directly," Damian said with a sly grin. "But my wife, having experienced love with me, encouraged Stephanie to set aside her fears about commitment and accept the love that Nathan offered."

No one said a word as they tried to think of something to say to knock that cocky grin off Damian's face.

Nathan was the first to speak. "But what about Derrick? What pearls of wisdom do you have for him?"

All eyes turned to the doctor as he took a sip of his beer. Without missing a beat, Derrick looked Damian square in the eye. "If you can figure out a way to get Natalie Donovan to marry me—I will consider you the wisest of all men."

Derrick's tone couldn't hide some of the frustration that had been haunting his relationship with Natalie. It was as if he was playing a guessing game about what she wanted from him.

"I'll see if I can work my power."

The fellas laughed and Derrick joined in. No use in having his sour attitude ruin it for everyone else. Deciding that this was neither the time nor the place to worry about that, he focused his attention back on the conversation, which had now turned to sports. This was a celebration, and he intended to enjoy himself.

Chapter 4

"You said no again?" Tanya asked, eyes wide with disbelief. After hearing the story of what happened that morning at the café, she couldn't help but wonder how Natalie could keep doing this. Each time he asked the question, Natalie would find a way to avoid answering. Tanya wasn't sure, if their roles were reversed, she could be so indecisive.

Tanya set her wineglass on the table and took off her black cropped jacket to reveal an off-white top with flared sleeves tucked into black pants. They'd just gotten through their normal greetings of hugs and kisses when the subject of marriage proposals came up.

"Isn't this like the third time he's asked you?" Christine asked, wondering how long Natalie was going to keep putting him off. It seemed as if every time they got together, Natalie was relaying another story that involved a question and a ring.

"I didn't say no—I just didn't say yes," Natalie said, shrugging nonchalantly. "It's actually the fourth . . . but who's counting?"

"I'm sure he's counting," Danielle said, trying to hide her amusement at the situation. "You must be killing his ego."

Holding out her wineglass to be filled, Natalie laughed along with her friends. "That man is starting to sound like a broken record—marry me, marry me, marry me."

"It's so easy to see why you keep turning him down," Tanya said, a playful sparkle in her brown eyes. "Who in their right mind would want a six-foot-two doctor with gorgeous eyes, a killer smile, a caring heart, and a willingness to do anything to make his woman happy?"

"Anything *except* get rid of a certain someone I like to refer to as his wife," Natalie answered with just a hint of resentment in her tone.

Natalie watched the three women cut their eyes at each other, knowing they were treading on a touchy subject. When Derrick first came into her life, there was instant attraction. But she quickly cooled when she found out he was married. Once it became clear to her that his soon-to-be ex-wife was on the other side of the country and there was no chance for reconciliation, Natalie still had her doubts about getting involved with him.

Sharing her concerns with the women sitting in front of her this evening, Natalie was encouraged to follow her heart and do what she believed was right. After Natalie talked to Derrick, he agreed to take things slow. Now, one year later, their relationship had grown into so much more. And here she sat, once again in front of her friends, looking for advice and guidance.

It was hard to believe that just four short years ago, none of these women were in her life. But all that changed the day she found out she had a half sister, Christine Davenport Ware. After getting over the initial shock and all of the emotional turmoil that came with uncovering the lies and deceit of their parents, Natalie and Christine not only developed a strong bond. They also shared an inheritance worth millions of dollars.

With her supersharp short haircut, skin the color of Hershey's chocolate, and a kind spirit, Christine brought joy to Natalie's life when she became a part of it. It was through Christine that she met Tanya, Danielle, and Stephanie.

Tanya was the most giving person Natalie had ever met. With her shoulder-length cinnamon hair and perfectly round brown eyes, she epitomized the word *friend*. When she and Brandon were having problems, Natalie had been there to help her make some tough decisions about what she wanted out life and *if* that life included Brandon. No one could have been happier for Tanya and Brandon when they finally tied the knot in an amazingly romantic ceremony last June.

"Hasn't he been separated for almost a year?" Danielle asked, thinking back to when Natalie and Derrick started dating.

Danielle Olivia Kennedy Johnston was the only person Natalie could claim that she ever hated in her entire life—and that was before they met. Natalie had heard through Christine and Tanya how ruthless and full of mischief Danielle was. Her reputation preceded her and the only thing Natalie wanted to do when she finally came face-to-face with Danielle was punch her in the nose. At the time, many would have applauded her.

A supermodel with the height, body, bone structure, and a million-dollar smile, Danielle also came with traits that made most people hate her on sight. Egotistical, self-centered, arrogant, and downright nasty, Danielle had destroyed so many professional and personal relationships, it baffled Natalie that anyone had yet to knock her out. Her snooty, better-than-anyone attitude alienated her from family, estranged her from her friends, and frustrated her business associates. When she finally hit rock bottom, the cheers could be heard for miles.

Her helping of humble pie was probably the biggest slice ever served. No one wanted to believe that someone like her could truly change her ways. But Danielle, determined to show others that she was no longer the superficial, shallow, and hard-to-get-along-with person she used to be, proved herself over and over again. Natalie and Danielle had forged a friendship based on mutual respect and Danielle had come to understand what was truly important in life—family, friends, and love.

"Last time I checked the dictionary," Natalie said, "separated and divorced meant two different things.

A married man is a married man, no ifs, ands, or buts about it. Margaret Donovan made sure her daughter fully understood this concept. Until a marriage had been officially dissolved, he still belonged to another woman. On many occasions, her friends expressed their opinion that Natalie's view was a little old-fashioned and out of sync with the world's view, but Natalie just couldn't see herself wearing the ring of a man who was legally tied to someone else.

"I thought his divorce was supposed to be final by now."

Natalie scrunched her face in disgust. "That makes two of us, Stephanie. But, apparently, Miss Thang out in sunny L.A. isn't happy that her philandering ways may have cost her in the negotiations of splitting up the assets, so she's fighting like an alley cat to get more of Derrick's money."

"Well, Miss Thang might need a visit from me and my black belt."

Everyone laughed at Stephanie's way of solving conflict. She was a sista who had your back no matter what the situation. Even six months pregnant, she remained full of life and with a penchant for adventure. Ready for anything, she was always dragging one of them to jump out of a plane, climb a mountain, or tour ancient burial grounds. Hanging out with Stephanie promised never a dull moment. Her zest for life was contagious and it was because of her that all of them had done things they never would have considered, including bungee-jumping, hang gliding, and parasailing.

Stephanie also knew how to be caring and supportive in times of need. Her compassion for others could be matched by no one. No matter the time or day, she'd be there. She truly cared about all of them.

"Let me make your flight arrangements!" Natalie said, holding her hand to her ear as if making a phone call.

"Oohh, Natalie, you should be nice!"

"I'm all out of niceness when it comes to that woman, Christine. This has been dragging on for months. I'm just getting a little impatient."

They could hear in her voice that she was telling the truth. Natalie had hesitated to date Derrick, regardless of how attracted she was to him. With all of his baggage, she planned to give him space to work out the situation with Charlene. But the more time she spent with him, the more she got to know him, care about him, and love him.

"So how long do you think it will be before your man is a *free* man?"

"Your guess is as good as mine, Tanya," Natalie confessed.

Reflecting on her current situation, Natalie realized that they could talk about this issue all night and it wouldn't change one thing. "Enough about me. We're here to celebrate—have a good time. Let's move on to the next subject."

As the conversation moved from her relationship to the latest fashion trends, Natalie turned her attention to the men. As if he could feel her, Derrick turned away from his group to look at her.

Dressed casually in a pair of black Armani pants and a striped gray shirt, Derrick could have been a model, right alongside Danielle. His athletic build, sincere smile, and sexual magnetism drew women to him. However, his caring heart and sincere desire to do the right thing separated him from being just another pretty face.

Raising his glass to her, he offered a smile that didn't quite reach his eyes. It might not have looked out of the ordinary to her friends, but Natalie picked up on it right away. Something was on his mind. Whenever he dealt with a tough decision or serious situation, his dark eyebrows slanted downward and his jaw became tight and tense. She had seen the expression many times, including the day they met.

Derrick had come to Natalie and BSI when his parents' dry-cleaning business was heavily in debt after his father became ill. The minute she laid eyes on him, the physical reaction charged every sexual part of her. Each individual cell in her body became acutely aware of him. Her heart fluttered and her breathing became slightly erratic. Normally confident in her professional element, she felt her palms suddenly sweating and her mouth going dry.

Over six feet tall, he stared at her with sexy, unique eyes.

His expensive suit, his sweet-smelling cologne, and his obvious concern for his parents captured Natalie's full attention. For the first time in her professional career, she was at a complete loss for words.

Since his parents refused his offer of money to bail them out of their financial crisis, Derrick worked closely with Natalie over the next couple of months to restructure his parents' finances, consolidate some of their debt, and work out deals with suppliers until they were fully operational and profitable.

Once the business transaction between them was complete, their attraction for each other could no longer be denied. What started out as casual dating had quickly turned into something more. Derrick integrated into every area of her life—the growth of her business, the development of her friendships with the people that surrounded her, the ups and downs in dealing with her mother, and everything in between. It wasn't hard for anyone to see that she had fallen totally in love with him. But with all the turmoil between them, she wondered if all they had would be enough.

Giving Derrick an encouraging smile, she raised her glass to him.

Natalie dropped her keys in her purse and put the small evening bag in the closet. Kicking her shoes off and putting them on the steps to be taken upstairs, she made her way down the hallway to the kitchen. Turning on the light, she pulled coffee beans and the grinder out of the pantry.

It was almost midnight, and they'd just gotten home from the Wares'. Both managed to set aside their situation and join in the laughter and fun shared by the group. Conversations ranging from children to cars, movies, politics, and entertainment kept it lively. No one at that house would have guessed the kind of tension between Natalie and Derrick that hovered just below the surface.

On the drive home, Derrick had gotten uncharacteristically quiet, barely saying more than a few words. Attempts on Natalie's part to engage him failed. Remembering his somber expression from earlier, she was determined to find out what had him so out of sorts. "Would you like some coffee?"

He leaned against the entrance to the kitchen with his coat on and his keys dangling in his hand. "No, I think I'm just going to head home."

Natalie shut the pantry door and took a deep breath. They'd always been able to talk to each other regardless of the subject. She refused to lose that aspect of their relationship. "Are you going to tell me what's bothering you before you go?"

Pushing off the wall, he made no effort to remove his coat. "The party was great, but it's been a long day and I have patients scheduled early tomorrow."

His nonchalant manner incensed Natalie and she stopped making coffee; she turned and stared at him.

"What?" he asked when she didn't open her mouth.

"Don't try that with me," she said. "We've known each other too long and we know each other too well for me to accept that cop-out."

"Please, Natalie. I'm not in the mood for this tonight. I'm tired and I want to go home. End of story."

"Have we reached the place in our relationship that we no longer trust each other to share when something's on our minds? Are you going to keep pretending that you're not bothered by something? Is it the party? Did you not have a good time?"

"No," Derrick said, a little mockingly. "I had a great time with all of our *married* friends."

Now they were getting somewhere. "What does their marital status have to do with this? Is this about your proposal?"

"Let's just say that between you and Charlene, it's been one hell of a day for me."

Natalie's expression remained unchanged except for the small vein that popped out on the side of her neck. Just hearing that woman's name made her blood boil to a dangerous level. Catfights over a man had never been Natalie's style, but if she ever caught that woman in a dark alley, there was no jury that would hold her responsible for her actions.

Her ill feelings didn't stem from the fact that Derrick once loved her or that he was married to her. Natalie despised that woman because of how she treated him—without respect, like he didn't matter. Charlene took their wedding vows and threw them carelessly back in his face. From all that Derrick had told her, Charlene showed no remorse for how things turned out—never offering an apology or an explanation of her actions. How could a woman be so cold and cruel to someone she professed to love? If Charlene wanted out, she should have packed up her suitcases and left. "What did she want?"

Derrick threw his hands in the air. "The same thing she always wants—to fight, to argue, to basically piss me off."

Natalie took note of his rigid position and his raised voice. Then she thought of his solemn mood at the party. That conversation with Charlene had to have taken place over twelve hours ago. Was that why he couldn't fully enjoy himself at the party? How could Charlene still affect him this way? Unable to suppress her annoyance at that fact, she said, "It looks like it worked."

Derrick stared at Natalie and tried to read the meaning behind that statement. "What's that supposed to mean?"

Natalie wasn't looking to start a fight, but for a woman who lived three thousand miles away, Charlene managed to constantly show up right in the middle of their lives. "It means she got what she wanted. You're pissed off."

Derrick could hear her snappish tone and wanted to explain to Natalie what he was feeling. Stepping fully into the kitchen, he dropped his keys on the table and leaned against the back of a chair. "I just want it to be over."

Placing her hands on her hips, she tilted her head to the side, her eyes questioning. "Is that so?"

The question, asked accusingly, caught Derrick off guard and he leaned forward, defensiveness taking over. "Excuse me?"

Natalie could tell that he was doing everything in his power to maintain a calm voice. They rarely raised their voices at each other and Derrick appeared as if he wasn't about to start now. "You say you want this to be over?"

"That's right," Derrick said emphatically. He had walked out of that house over twelve months ago. That chapter of his life needed closure.

Natalie thought about her next words carefully, but decided to just spit them out. "I don't believe you."

The statement was said with such confidence that Derrick wondered how she could doubt his intentions. "After everything you've watched me go through this year, how can you say that?"

"Easy," Natalie said, not the least bit deterred by his challenging demeanor. "Because it's not over."

"Believe me, Nat," Derrick said, pushing up off the chair, "if I could wave a magic wand and have Charlene and everything that has to do with her disappear, I'd do it."

"That's exactly my point, Derrick," Natalie said, trying to make him see her position. "You do have the magic wand. All you have to do is use it."

"What are you talking about?" Derrick said. "I've got a team of lawyers at outrageous fees working to get me out of this. What more can I do?"

Natalie hesitated before she spoke the next words, but she was in too far to stop now. "Give her what she wants."

His eyes widened in surprise and he immediately shook his head at the absurdity of the statement. "Did you just say what I think you just said?"

"If getting this over with is so important to you," Natalie reasoned, "all you have to do is give her what she wants."

"It's not that simple, Natalie," Derrick said, trying to remain calm. "You have no idea what it takes to work this situation out. I've had more conference calls, e-mails, and faxes than I know what to do with."

Natalie couldn't believe that he was missing the crux of her statement.

"You're fighting over what?" Natalie said, trying to keep her voice even. "China? A painting? A golf club membership?"

Derrick didn't respond right away. He just didn't know what to say to make her see where he was coming from.

"Derrick," she said belligerently, "do I need to remind you? You don't live in California anymore. How would you play that course anyway?"

The high energy of this conversation no longer allowed him to stand still and Derrick began to pace. A mix of emotions ran rampant through him. Anger, frustration, and impatience all fought for control. These weren't directed so much at the woman standing a few feet from him, just at the predicament he faced. "I built my practice and made a good life for us. She floated from job to job, practically starting a new career every year. She's selfish, self-centered, and doesn't deserve to take what I worked so hard for."

His words, harsh and clipped, gave a hint at how wound up he was.

After about a minute of silence, Natalie turned her attention back to the coffeemaker. "Fine."

Taking a deep breath, Derrick regrouped. This time when he spoke, his voice was lower and calmer. "Don't do that."

"What?" she said, not turning around.

"Shut down," he said. Moving toward her, he reached out to her and turned her to him. "One of the best things about our relationship is that we can always be straight up with each other. If you have something else you want to say, say it."

Leaning against the counter, she folded her arms across her chest. "You started this day by asking me to marry you. We're ending this day by arguing about a woman you claim to want out of your life."

When he didn't respond, she continued. "You can't have it both ways."

"Both ways? What are you saying?"

"You can't want to marry me and still hold on to her."

Inhaling deeply in disappointment that she saw things that way, he folded his hands in front of him, hoping to relax his body. "That's ridiculous. The last thing I'm doing is holding on to Charlene. I don't love her. I don't want to be with her."

"I'm just calling it like I see it. You need to make a choice."

Derrick's eyes caught and held hers at the meaning of her last statement. "That sounds like an ultimatum."

Natalie just shrugged, letting him take it any way he wanted to. "Call it what you want. It is what it is."

Without another word, Derrick snatched his keys off the table. Heading down the hall, he didn't say good-bye. The only sounds she heard were the closing of the front door and his car pulling out of the driveway.

Chapter 5

The popular downtown seafood restaurant was operating at its peak, serving the lunchtime crowd. Natalie scanned the dining room a couple of times before she located her date. Weaving in and out of the tables, she made it to the booth near the side window and slid in, glad she opted for a black pin-striped pantsuit instead of a skirt. "Thanks for meeting me today."

"You sounded like you had something on your mind," Christine said, looking chic in a pair of jeans and a casual off-the-shoulder sweater. It was hard to believe she had had a baby just a little over a year ago.

The waiter arrived and after a quick scan of the menu, Christine ordered the grilled chicken. Natalie ordered a cheeseburger with the works and a large order of fries.

"Uh-oh," Christine said, handing the menu back to the waiter, "I haven't seen you go for grease in a while."

Growing up, Natalie had found it hard to connect with other women. She'd forged many professional relationships over the years but didn't allow herself to truly open up and allow a good friend in her life. That all changed with Christine.

When Christine's mom died, the family connection the two of them shared came to light. They shared the same father—Henry Davenport.

Henry had not only abused Christine's mother, but had cheated on her with Natalie's mother. In the mess that followed, including a fight over an inheritance, Christine and Natalie somehow managed to look beyond the craziness and strife that had been created among their parents and forge a relationship that had turned into true sisterhood. In fact, they dropped the "half" part months ago and just referred to each other as sisters. "Before we talk about me, what's the latest on my little cutie pie, Brianna?"

Christine's eyes lit up and her smile reached from ear to ear. Reaching in her purse, she pulled out a set of pictures. "I just printed these off the digital camera this morning. We went to the park last week. Isn't she the most beautiful little girl you've ever seen?"

Pride and joy reverberated in her voice and Natalie had to agree as she stared down at her niece. "It's hard to believe how much she's grown."

"Thirteen months and counting."

Christine and Damian had to be the poster couple for living happily ever after. Married for almost three years, they still seemed to be on their honeymoon. Their happiness could give anyone hope in finding a love that would last a lifetime. Could she have that with Derrick?

Thinking of him brought to her mind their conversation last night and her reason for calling Christine. The smile that was on her face just a few short seconds ago faltered.

Christine noticed her change in mood and put her pictures back in her purse. She focused her attention on her sister. "What's going on with you, Nat?"

Unrolling the napkin and placing it in her lap, Natalie took a sip of her water.

"Are you going to keep stalling, or are you going to tell me what has you so worked up that you're eating all your allowable calories for the week in one meal?"

Taking a deep breath, she said, "I think I pushed Derrick too far."

"Too far?" Christine said, reaching out to hold her shaking hand. Whatever was going on between the two of them was evidently quite upsetting. "We just saw the two of you last night. He seemed fine."

"I'm talking about what happened after the party." Natalie replayed the conversation and all the emotions began to take shape again. Hearing it herself in this setting, she began to question her position. Divorce was never easy. Should she have added to Derrick's emotional stress by making it seem as if he was holding on? Did she have a right to judge how he was handling the situation?

Christine listened intently to Natalie and wondered if there was more to this story than she was willing to admit—or even knew. "Why haven't you said yes to his proposal?"

The question caught Natalie off guard. She thought they were talking about Charlene and his pending divorce. "What does that have to do with Derrick finalizing his divorce from his wife?"

"I'm not saying it has anything to do with it," Christine said, noticing her self-protective response. "I was just curious."

"You know the answer to that question," Natalie said, not sure why this turn in the conversation was making her so uncomfortable. "My mother slept with a married man under the impression that he was leaving his wife—you know what happened with that story."

"You're right. I do know the story. But we're not talking

about Henry," Christine pointed out. "We're talking about Derrick. A man who lives three thousand miles from his soon-to-be ex-wife. A man who hasn't shown the least bit of interest in a reconciliation."

Everything Christine said was true, but Natalie couldn't get past the fact that he was still married. "Until the final decree is signed, he belongs to someone else."

"What about when the divorce is final?"

"Then we talk about next steps."

Christine still didn't mention that she still hadn't heard the word *marriage.*

"Do you love him?"

Natalie's expression softened and her voice lowered. "Yes, I do."

Squeezing her hand for encouragement, Christine said, "So what are you afraid of?"

Natalie exhaled lightly and leaned back in her seat. Up until that moment, she hadn't thought of her resistance as fear. Trying to come up with an answer, she drew a blank. "I'm not sure."

"Come on, Natalie," Christine said, surprised at the vulnerability she heard in her voice. "You know Derrick loves you. I've seen the way he looks at you. I've watched the two of you together. This is the real deal." Leaning closer, she lowered her voice to a whisper. "And not to get too much in your very personal business, but I bet you feel it when the two of you make love."

The waiter arrived with their food and Natalie removed her hands from Christine's, avoiding eye contact.

The motion didn't go undetected by Christine, and once the waiter left, she thought carefully about her next words. "Are you telling me you don't feel it?"

"No, not exactly," Natalie said, with a hint of mystery in her voice.

Caught off guard by her response, Christine fell silent as their meal went untouched. She worked her mind to decipher whatever code Natalie was speaking in.

The expression on her face told Natalie that her sister was struggling to make sense of her statements. Deciding to just put it out there, Natalie picked up the ketchup bottle and opened the top. "We haven't . . . we've never . . ."

Christine fought the urge to clean out her ears with her fingers, because there was no way she just heard what she thought she heard. Momentarily speechless, she searched for the appropriate response. "But you've vacationed together. You've stayed at each other's homes. Are you trying to tell me that you and Derrick have . . ."

"Never slept together," Natalie said, finishing her sentence as she poured the ketchup over her fries.

Dumbfounded, Christine wasn't quite sure how to respond. She said the first words that popped into her head. "But you're not a virgin."

Natalie nervously glanced around the restaurant at the other patrons nearby. "Could you keep your voice down?"

"Sorry," Christine said, finally getting over the shock of this latest revelation. "It's just so hard to believe. You guys have been a couple for almost a year."

"And he's been married every bit of that time," Natalie reminded her.

Her explanation brought it back to the fact that he wasn't divorced. "I'm trying to make sense of this, Natalie. I really am. But to be honest, I don't understand. Derrick is committed to you. He loves you. The papers may not be signed, but his marriage is over. He hasn't seen that woman since he walked out of the house. He hasn't been back to California since you met him and he is trying to get you to take a ring. What is the problem?"

Natalie couldn't fault Christine, or anyone else, for being completely taken aback about her way of thinking. Even Derrick, who agreed with her request not to have a physical relationship, didn't fully understand. Respecting her position, regardless of whether he understood it or agreed with it, made Natalie love him even more.

"Christine, you have no idea what it was like growing up with my mother. Having to hear almost daily about how her life was destroyed by her involvement with a married man. She preached the Gospel that married was married—any man in that situation was not available, period."

Sympathizing with her situation, Christine tried to think of a way to help Natalie see that she didn't have to hold on to her mother's theories. Christine had met Margaret on several occasions and it was no secret that Margaret couldn't stand the sight of Christine. Christine's eyes, her complexion, and her determined attitude reminded Margaret too much of Henry.

Margaret found it next to impossible to see Christine for the individual she was. Instead, she chose to forever brand her as part of the family that Henry refused to leave to be with Margaret. If this was the kind of garbage that Natalie had to listen to growing up, no wonder she had these hang-ups about Derrick. "After how Charlene treated him, do you really think Derrick is interested in getting back with her—or with anyone else?"

"My mother's life was almost destroyed because she slept with a married man. I just can't do it."

"But these are two completely different situations," Christine said, trying to reason with her.

"I know it doesn't make sense," Natalie readily admitted. "It's a twisted philosophy. But it's how I feel."

"How has Derrick taken all this?" Christine asked. "He's got to be the most patient man on the face of the earth."

There had been many close calls over the last year when it came to their lack of a sex life. She couldn't count the number of times they'd let their emotions and passion take them to the brink of ending the agreement. But just as Natalie had done last night before the dinner party, she'd done on many occasions—pulled back—stepped away. She'd even left the room. She never claimed that this was easy—she just claimed that she felt it was right in her heart. "In spite of not sleeping together, we've become such good friends. Our relationship has developed on so many levels. When we make love, it will add to our relationship, not define it."

Christine nodded at the heartfelt words. She recalled the first time she made love to Damian. They had shared so much of themselves before that it was the sweetest, yet most powerful, night. "How can you keep turning down proposals from a man like this? Understanding. Patient."

"I wouldn't be turning him down if he wasn't already attached."

Christine watched Natalie pick up a fry and take a bite. She wasn't quite convinced that once Derrick's divorce was final, all of Natalie's hang-ups would magically disappear. Hoping to open the door to exploring that opinion, she said, "It sounds to me as if you may have some concerns beyond his divorce."

Picking up her burger, Natalie disagreed. "His divorce is the stumbling block for us. This brings me back to last night. I want to make things right. Get us back on track."

"You have to talk to him," Christine said. "To apologize."

"I tried," Natalie confessed. "I called him this morning and on the way to meet you. He hasn't returned either call."

"Maybe he's been busy with patients," Christine offered. "We both know how time can get away from us. We have the best intentions, but we somehow get around to it later than we planned."

Natalie smiled at her lame attempt to make her feel better. "We've never had a problem catching up with each other. He's ignoring me."

"Maybe a call isn't the way to go," Christine said. "If you have a few minutes, why not stop by his office? He wouldn't have a choice but to talk to you."

"That's a great idea," Natalie said, beginning to think about her afternoon schedule.

"Natalie," Christine started, still searching for the right words.

Hearing the seriousness in her voice, Natalie stopped eating and waited.

"We both had challenging childhoods. Our parents instilled some strong views into us about relationships. Ninety-five percent of those views do nothing to serve us now. I went through so much drama with Damian before we got married because I got hung up on how my parents' lived their lives. Don't do the same thing."

"I hear you, Christine," Natalie said. "We both ended up with some seriously deficient parents. But what I'm going through with Derrick isn't about them. It's about his divorce. As soon as those papers are signed, sealed, and delivered to the California Superior Court, we can move forward."

Christine had a feeling that Natalie's problem with accepting Derrick's proposal went far beyond his divorce. She just hoped that whatever it was, the two of them could work it out.

After saying good-bye in front of the restaurant, Natalie headed back to the office. She had a couple of meetings scheduled but should be able to head to Derrick's office by three o'clock. If he didn't want to return her calls, she'd have to take matters into her own hands.

Walking through the doors of BSI, Natalie greeted Jea and picked up the mail on the corner of her desk. Making her way through the small, but functional, office suite, she felt pride at what she and the people who worked with her had accomplished. Armed with a small personal investment and an even smaller grant, she had opened her doors almost two years ago.

She'd helped many people start a business, grow a business, and taught them how to sell it or dissolve it. However, her main focus, and her passion, was assisting small business owners who had the skill and the know-how to run the operations, but found themselves in financial trouble because of lack of information or investment in qualified financial advisers.

Over the years, it wasn't uncommon for Natalie to work with the IRS to develop a payment plan for back taxes or to contact suppliers on behalf of business owners to structure a business option that would keep the supplies coming so the owners could stay in business while making payments that would allow the suppliers to meet their financial goals. It had been rewarding work for Natalie, especially since many of her clients were minorities.

Last year, she received a half-million-dollar grant and was able to expand. With that money, she hired additional CPAs to assist her, as well as started hosting training programs to assist potential business owners in structuring their businesses for success prior to opening, with the goal of not needing her services somewhere down the line.

After working for a huge, highly respected public accounting firm where her clients were paying close to a million dollars a month for services, she felt good to be helping the little guy. It's the small companies that truly sustain the workers and families in this country.

Opening the door to her office, she tossed her blazer to the side and listened to her voice-mail messages on speakerphone.

"Natalie, baby, where are you? You are just too busy for your own good. Give me a call."

Discarding the message, Natalie took a seat. With all that was happening between her and Derrick, she hadn't had a chance to call her mom back. After she had listened to five other messages, all of which were business related, her heart sank. She'd left two messages for Derrick and he had yet to return one of her calls.

"Natalie, your one-thirty appointment is here."

The voice of her assistant buzzing her on the phone reminded her of her tight schedule. No time to wallow in personal problems when duty called. "Can you put them in the conference room? I'll be right there."

With eight minutes before she would officially be late, she picked up the phone and dialed. Experience had shown her that there was no such thing as a "quick call" with her mother, but there was always the off chance that this would be the day.

After several rings, Margaret's voice mail came on. "Mom, I'm giving you a call back. Sorry it's taken me a couple of days to get back to you, but give me a call at the office."

Replacing the receiver, she grabbed her files and headed for the conference room.

* * *

Derrick finished writing notes in the patient's file and set it on top of the nurse's desk for filing. It had been nonstop action since he arrived. He was double booked for most of the morning and everyone showed up. He barely had time to catch his breath. Which, today, was a good thing. If he had any downtime, there was no doubt he'd spend it thinking about Natalie and the state of their union.

At almost three o'clock, his grumbling stomach reminded him that he had yet to eat lunch. He'd skipped the morning ritual of Carla's Café and was living off a cup of coffee he had almost six hours ago. With another patient scheduled for 3:30, he decided to make a quick run to the deli across the street.

"You look like you're having a rough day."

Derrick turned to the voice and curved his lips into a friendly smile.

Suzanne Spencer stood a few feet from him holding a bag with the deli emblem on it. "I thought you could use this."

"You're a lifesaver," he said, taking the bag out of her hands. "You must have been reading my mind. I was just about to make a quick run to pick up some food."

"You've been so busy seeing patients, I didn't think you had a chance to eat."

Heading for his office, he thanked her again. "What would I do without you? Not only are you a top-notch office manager, but you also manage to keep me from passing out."

Following behind him, she held up another bag. "Do you mind if I join you?"

Derrick usually used his lunchtime to update patient files from the morning. Rarely having time to write everything down before seeing the next patient, he liked to get them done while the information was fresh in his mind.

Catching the hesitation in his body language, she added, "I've been so swamped with inventory and ordering supplies that I haven't had a chance to eat either."

He motioned to the chair in his office. Chatting with his staff had always been done in passing. It couldn't hurt to get to know them a little better.

He opened the blinds on the window behind him, and the bright afternoon sun streamed in. When he had joined this practice, he made a point of decorating his office in a way that encouraged relaxation and comfort. Doctors' offices could be intimidating enough to patients. There was no need to add cold, stiff colors and furniture. He was forever grateful to Christine and her design company for creating that atmosphere.

Taking a seat behind his desk, he opened the bag and pulled out a sandwich. "Turkey sub with lettuce, green peppers, pickles, and mustard. You know me too well."

Shutting the door, Suzanne took a seat and reveled in the compliment. As the office manager, she had the job of taking care of all four doctors who owned this practice, but she always paid special attention to Dr. Carrington. Mainly because he was the nicest man she'd ever gotten to know. Not only was he was handsome, but he had such love and care for his patients. How could any woman not be attracted to him? And those eyes! What she wouldn't do to have just one night with him. "After working together for almost a year, I've picked up quite a few things about you."

"Oh yeah?" Derrick said, surprised at that bit of information. "Like what?"

"Let's see . . . you like your coffee black. You're the only doctor I know that tries his best not to keep his patients waiting for more than fifteen minutes. You love the Dallas

Cowboys, and you keep to yourself when you have a lot on your mind . . . like today."

Derrick raised a brow at the end of her statement. Suzanne's description of him was on point—even about him being preoccupied. With thoughts of his conversation with Natalie running through his mind most of the day, he didn't realize how noticeable it was.

Last night had touched a nerve in him that he just wasn't ready to deal with. That's why he hadn't returned Natalie's call. He had no idea what he would say.

Watching the play of emotions across his face, Suzanne knew she hit the nail on the head. Ever since Dr. Carrington joined this practice, she'd gotten to know his moods and his demeanor so well that she could almost anticipate his next move. She would have made a move on him sooner, but he began dating Natalie right after he started.

Hoping that it would be a short fling that would leave him wide open for her, Suzanne had been greatly disappointed when it appeared that he and Natalie were growing closer and closer. She had a strange inkling that if she ever wanted to see if there could be something between them, she had to act—and act fast. Her plan of action was to step up their friendship, become someone he could depend on, talk to, trust completely.

"How did you know that?"

"You're normally a little friendlier to the staff. You talk to your patients more about what's going on in their lives outside of their health. You didn't do any of those things today."

"Oh," Derrick said, not realizing his behavior was that easily read.

"If you want to talk about it, I'd be more than willing to listen. Even if I can't help, just sharing it can sometimes make you feel better," she said casually, removing her smock to reveal a tank top that hugged her body in all the right places.

Derrick slowed his chewing as he took note of her—five feet three, with a short bob cut that framed her bronze face. Derrick had never paid much attention to her body, but that option was now unavoidable. The borderline-professional top exposed her cleavage and the seductive swell of her breasts, capturing his full attention. He moved his eyes back to her face.

The beginning of a smile tipped the corners of her mouth. "I promise I'm a good listener."

Forcing his mind away from her body, he focused on her words.

"Many of my family and friends use me as their sounding board," she continued, pleased that he saw something he obviously liked. "When you talk things out with someone not directly involved in the situation, you could get another point of view that might help."

Derrick thought about his present situation. He definitely couldn't talk to Natalie. That would only lead to another argument. Talking with the fellas at Damian's birthday party hadn't yielded any results. Maybe Suzanne was right. Maybe he did need someone to talk to.

He'd been trying to figure things out on his own and it was making him crazy. Between dealing with Charlene and their divorce and Natalie's constant rejection of his marriage proposals, he could use some advice.

Setting his sandwich aside, he replayed Suzanne's words in his mind—a sounding board, someone to talk to. Could that be what he needed? Would it help him find a way out of his current dilemma?

Having worked with her for almost a year, Derrick

never thought of Suzanne as anything other than a colleague, but the more he thought about it, the more he realized he had learned quite a bit about her.

She'd been divorced about three years from her high school sweetheart and had a four-year-old daughter, Delilah. Derrick recalled that when she decided to go back to school and get her degree, her husband felt neglected and took that as an opportunity to cheat on her. In that sense, Derrick and she shared a commonality. While Suzanne didn't know what Charlene had done to him, she could probably tell he was the one who had been wronged in that relationship.

Derrick commended Suzanne for moving on with her life after her breakup. At thirty years of age, she'd bought a town house earlier in the year and had recently decided to further her education with a master's degree in health administration. He admired her tenacity and ability to work full-time, raise a daughter, and go to school.

Having removed the uniform coat that all the staff wore, she sat before him more of a friend than a coworker. Even though he didn't linger on her body, he was sure that she would turn a few heads from the opposite sex.

If he was honest with himself, she'd just turned his head. But physically attractive women were a dime a dozen—what he had with Natalie was so much more. Taking a few minutes to think over her offer, he decided opening up to Suzanne might not be the best route to take. When you cross the line from professional to personal, it's almost impossible to go back. His life had gotten complicated lately. There was no need to make it worse. Talking about his personal life with her could ultimately cause more damage than good.

"Thanks for the offer, Suzanne, but . . ." he said, glancing at his watch, "my next patient is due any minute now. I better finish my sandwich."

Keeping her expression unchanged, Suzanne stood up and nodded in understanding. She heard his words, but she also watched his actions. There was no doubt in her mind that he was affected by her physical attributes. The eyes never lie, and his eyes had definite interest in them. He might not have wanted to admit it, but he liked what she was offering. The hesitation in his voice was probably due to catching him off guard. But now that she'd put an offer on the table, it might make it easier for him to accept another offer.

Not ready to throw in the towel just yet, she picked up the remnants of her lunch and headed for the door. Facing him before opening the door, she widened her smile. "Your last patient is scheduled for four-thirty. If you'd like, we could grab a drink after work. Delilah is with her dad and I don't have class tonight."

Derrick paused at her tone. If her intentions were unclear a few minutes ago, she made them crystal clear with that statement. Ten seconds ago, he could have considered her a concerned coworker. Now she'd crossed over to *interested* coworker. What she asked sounded too much like a date, and even though things were up in the air with Natalie, he had no intention to take Suzanne up on her offer. "I don't think that's a good idea."

Thinking about her next words carefully, she decided not to hold back. "I know you've been dating Natalie, but I also know you well enough to know that something is going on with you. Since she's called twice and I don't think you've returned her call, my guess is that it probably has something to do with her. Just remember, you have options if things don't work out."

Opening the door, she turned to leave and bumped smack into Natalie.

Natalie glanced from one to the other before focusing her attention on Suzanne. "Good to see you again, Suzanne."

"Likewise," she answered in her most professional voice. Natalie usually made an appearance at the office once a week, meeting Derrick for dinner dates or movies. She rarely popped by in the middle of the day.

Suzanne's curiosity got the best of her and she wondered what was going on between them. "I was just enjoying a late lunch with Dr. Carrington. Gives us both a chance to take a break from our hectic days."

Natalie didn't answer right away and stared at the woman. The smirk on her face told her more than her words did. Having been in enough situations with women to know when the claws were coming out, Natalie knew Suzanne was ready to scratch.

Giving a half smile that lasted a quick second, Natalie walked past Suzanne into the office. Without looking her way, she said, "You can shut the door on your way out."

Once they were alone, Natalie turned her attention to Derrick.

"So," Natalie said, plopping down in the seat Suzanne had just vacated. "How long has Miss Susie had her eyes on you?"

Finishing his food, he tossed the wrapper into the trash. "I'm going to ignore that question."

"Why?" she said.

"Because it doesn't require a response."

Natalie had a hard time believing Derrick could be that blind. And if he wasn't, why was he protecting her? "That woman practically rubs it in my face, letting me know that the two of you huddled up in your office is a common occurrence, and you're telling me it doesn't require a response."

"First of all," Derrick said, realizing that Natalie was not going to drop this, "we were not 'huddled up,' we were having lunch. Secondly, she was concerned."

That word perked Natalie's ears up. "Concerned? About what?"

"Me."

The word was said with such simplicity, it defied how complicated this situation was rapidly becoming. "What is that supposed to mean?"

"It means that we've worked together long enough for her to recognize when I have something on my mind," Derrick said, hating the position that Natalie was putting him in. She was making Suzanne out to be the problem, when it was the two of them that had the problem. "She offered to be my sounding board."

Natalie swallowed, deliberately trying to keep her tone relatively civil, in spite of her growing agitation. Counting backward silently from ten, she spoke when she reached number one. "Let me make sure I understand what's happening here. I've been trying to reach you all day to talk about us, and you've been with Miss Office Manager because she was so concerned about you."

Rubbing his hands over his face in frustration, Derrick leaned back in his chair, trying to make sense of how this conversation got so out of hand. "I didn't call you back because I wasn't ready to talk. You called me out on some pretty heavy things last night."

Natalie leaned forward, placing her hand on his desk. "You weren't ready to talk to me, but you were all set to tell it to your personal sounding board?"

"Suzanne and I are professional colleagues—that's it," Derrick said.

"And what are we, Derrick?" Natalie said, feeling her emotions about to take over. "Are we so close and personal that you can't even talk to me? How is it that one minute, you're pulling out a ring box and the next minute you can't decide if you want to take my phone calls?"

"You're the one who can't seem to make up her mind about what you want," he said, completely exasperated.

"I can't make up my mind?" Natalie repeated. "You're the one that vacillates between a wife and me."

Instead of responding, Derrick opened the top left drawer of his desk. He picked up the ring box and held it out to her. "I know what I want. Marry me."

Natalie stared at his hand but didn't move. "Get a divorce."

"*I am,*" he practically screamed. Realizing this situation was getting out of control, Derrick took a deep breath and regrouped. "All I'm asking is that you tell me you'll be my wife. Just say yes."

After several seconds of silence, he dropped the ring on the desk in frustration. "I've just proven my point."

He waited a few seconds for a response—but still nothing. "I've got patients to see." Before she could stop him, he was gone.

Natalie didn't move from her spot for several minutes after he left the office. Why didn't he understand her position? Why didn't he comprehend that she couldn't give him the answer he wanted right now?

Picking up her purse, she made her way down the hallway toward the waiting area. Just as she passed the front desk, Suzanne seemed to come out of nowhere.

Natalie ignored her, but just as she reached the front door, she heard her call after her. Realizing she was being petty, she stopped and turned around. "What is it, Suzanne?"

Putting on her most sympathetic look, Suzanne said, "I couldn't help but overhear you and Derrick. I couldn't make out the words, but it sounds like things aren't going so well between the two of you."

"Did you want something?" Natalie asked, refusing to discuss anything with this woman.

"Just to tell you to have a nice evening," she said. "I'm sure everything will work out."

Her fake smile and pompous attitude grated on Natalie's nerve. "Thanks, Suzanne. You have a nice evening, too."

Chapter 6

Saturday night, Derrick sat at the end of the bar drinking his second beer, casually dressed in a pair of blue jeans and a dark blue button-down cotton shirt. It had been four days since his blowup with Natalie at his office and neither made a move to contact each other. They were officially at a standoff. After seeing his patient, he returned to an empty office. He didn't expect her to hang around and wait after the way he stormed out, but he was still disappointed that she was gone.

Packing up for the evening, he contemplated whether to call, stop by her house, or find another way for them to reconnect. Still upset by her accusations, he decided to do none of the above. He needed time to think, to find a way that could possibly get them back on track.

After Natalie left, he said nothing to the staff or other doctors about their argument, but judging by his brooding attitude the rest of the day, it was apparent to them that it hadn't gone well. Every person in that office probably knew that Derrick and Natalie were in the midst of a serious challenge.

Besides the other three doctors, there were four nurses,

two administrative assistants, an insurance claims adviser, and a receptionist. Over the past year, they'd all developed a good working rapport, and he prided himself on keeping his staff motivated and satisfied with their work life. They'd celebrated birthdays, births of children, and a wedding. There was a general sense of what was going on in everyone's life. While no one said anything to him, every last one of them knew that there was a problem.

Heading out the front door, he noticed a light on in Suzanne's office. Knowing it was past her quitting time, he stopped by to say good night. When he stuck his head in the door, she offered up a friendly smile, giving him another chance to accept her suggestion of getting a drink.

Not ready to have another round with Natalie and not in the mood to spend an evening at home thinking about her, he felt Suzanne's invitation to be quite appealing. She was offering friendship and an ear and wasn't looking to make judgments about what he was, or was not, doing about his impending divorce. It might be exactly what he needed—a nice evening out, no hassles, no chance of it ending in an argument like his past few dates with Natalie.

Natalie. Thinking about her caused him to second-guess the road he was traveling. There was already one woman in California wreaking havoc with their relationship. After the run-in that Natalie had with Suzanne in his office, would it be worth it? Derrick didn't think so. Bidding Suzanne good night, he headed down the hall to a long and lonely evening.

Suzanne stood, offering to walk him to the door. "I want to make sure the security system is set since I'll be here alone."

When they reached the lobby, Suzanne lightly touched him on his arm. "Derrick, I want to say something about my actions earlier today. It's obvious that you're going through a rough time right now with Natalie. You haven't been your normal, cheerful self. I just want you to know that I meant what I said. I truly am concerned about you—as a friend."

Her words caught Derrick off guard. After making her position very clear at lunch, he thought there would be awkwardness between them. But based on the sincerity with which she spoke, Suzanne honestly seemed to be concerned about being his friend more than anything else. And she had a point—one could never have too many friends.

"The offer still stands if you ever want to talk. We can have dinner, drinks, whatever."

Nodding, Derrick thanked her. "Good night, Suzanne."

Now, days later, he was no closer to working things out with Natalie than he was when he walked out on her. In the past, they'd always been able to talk about their issues, work through their situations. But this time was different. They weren't disagreeing on something that didn't matter. They were on opposite sides of the galaxy on an issue that was fundamental to their relationship. How could they work through this if they weren't speaking to each other?

At his wits' end, he found his attempts to make sense of how their situation had spiraled so much out of control utterly fruitless. They'd already overcome so many challenges in the past year, including his pending divorce, yet they still managed to fall in love. Even when she told him she couldn't sleep with a married man, he agreed to be patient and told her he respected her position.

Initially, he found it hard to believe that after everything he shared with her about Charlene she would consider him "married. Her having told him a few tidbits about her childhood helped in his attempt to understand, but regardless of whether he understood it or not, if that's the way she wanted it, that's the way it would be.

As the weeks turned into months, he actually found it refreshing. They'd spent so many nights talking, sharing, and getting to know each other that he felt he'd had a glimpse into her soul. He'd never been as close to any woman as he had become with Natalie.

But none of that mattered now. They weren't on speaking terms. Those poignant, special moments of their courtship seemed like a distant memory—and he desperately wanted to make things right again. Yet he didn't have a clue as to how to accomplish that. That's when he began considering Suzanne's advice and her offer. She may have been onto something when she volunteered to hear him out—to be his sounding board. Facing facts, Derrick decided he did need someone to talk to. If doing so didn't render any answers, he would probably feel better for just having talked it out.

"I hope you haven't been waiting long."

Turning to the voice, Derrick smiled in relief. "Thanks for meeting me."

"No problem. I hope you don't mind, but I brought reinforcements."

Looking past Damian, Derrick saw Brandon. "I can use all the advice I can get. Let's get a table."

Lenny's was operating at full capacity. One of the most popular restaurants in the D.C. area, it was a hot spot for singles, couples, and networking professionals. The food was southern cuisine and Derrick loved the down-home flavor. This had become one of his and Natalie's favorite spots.

Once settled, Brandon started things off. "My wife tells me that things aren't going so great between you and Natalie right now."

"Your wife is a liar," Derrick said, finishing off his beer. At their confused expressions, he elaborated, "Things are downright horrible between us. I have no idea how we went from talking about marriage to not talking at all."

"That bad, huh?" Brandon said, signaling for the waitress.

"Worse."

A sudden chill hung in the air at his one-word answer.

"Christine said that Natalie had gone to your office to talk things out with you. What happened?" Damian said.

"If the purpose of that visit was to work things out, then we missed that objective by a mile." Derrick relayed the entire scene, from the moment Natalie spoke to Suzanne to when he stormed out of his office.

As he replayed it again, a shadow of annoyance crossed his face, along with his confusion. It seemed as if he and Natalie were on two different planets. One minute they were happy and content. The next minute they were disagreeing about marriage, and now—they were fighting about a woman who meant nothing to him.

The waitress brought some menus, giving an appraising look to all three men. Whenever they were together, their height, combined with their style, class, and confidence, commanded appreciative looks from the opposite sex. But since two of the three were sporting platinum wedding bands, the waitress turned her attention to Derrick. Offering him a small, shy smile, she paid special attention to him, promising to return in a few minutes to take their order.

Derrick hardly noticed as he continued to focus on his current problems with Natalie.

"What's the deal with Suzanne?"

"There is no deal, Brandon," Derrick said. "Why does everyone insist on reading more into it than was there? We were having lunch, in my office. That's it."

"I've met Suzanne," Damian said, remembering the last time he met Derrick at his office to head to a Washington Wizards game. "As I recall, the sista had it going on. Cute face, nice body."

"Yeah," Derrick said, thinking about her physical features. He'd never thought of her that way until she put it out there.

Damian and Brandon cut their eyes at each other at his response.

"Is there something going on with you and this Suzanne woman?" Brandon asked. He hated to ask, but he had to know.

Derrick's eyes hardened at him. "Are you out of your mind? I can't even make sense of the relationship I'm in. Why would I complicate it with another one?"

"So what was that look about?"

Derrick responded honestly, "Damian was right. The woman is fine. But that's the extent of it. I see beautiful women practically everywhere I go. Outward beauty doesn't faze me at all. I'm one hundred percent committed to Natalie. She's the most beautiful woman I know—inside and out."

It was obvious to both of them, Derrick meant every word he just said.

"But right now," Derrick continued, "I have to admit, she's driving me crazy."

The anguish in his voice brought them back to the

purpose of this gathering. "It seems to me like you're letting your soon-to-be ex-wife come between you and Natalie."

"Now you're starting to sound like Natalie," he said. "And if this was the night of your party, I would agree. But this thing with Suzanne threw me for a loop."

"How?" Brandon asked.

Over the last four days, Derrick had had a chance to reflect on where he stood with Natalie. Something just wasn't adding up. "When Natalie turned down my proposals, I thought it was because my divorce wasn't final. But now I'm not so sure."

"What do you think is going on?" Brandon asked.

Running through the last few conversations he'd had with her, he started to understand that Natalie's issues might run much deeper than Charlene or Suzanne. "It's almost as if she's afraid to make the commitment."

Damian and Brandon turned to stare at each other before cracking smiles that quickly turned into laughter.

"A woman . . . afraid of commitment?" Damian said, trying to catch his breath. "That's practically unheard of."

"You would think," Derrick said, joining in the laughter. "I don't think I've ever run into a woman who wasn't looking to have her dating turn into something permanent."

"I find it hard to believe that if your divorce was final she wouldn't readily accept your proposal," Brandon said, his laughter becoming a soft chuckle. "That woman isn't interested in anyone else but you."

When they all calmed down, Derrick continued, "I hope you're right, but lately it's like she's looking for an excuse. First, the divorce . . . now Suzanne."

"You know she loves you, man," Damian said, all trace of his laughter gone.

Derrick relaxed his posture and released a knowing smile, reviewing their time together—the late-night talks, the vacations, the dinners, the movies, the quiet evenings they spent together. Of that, he had no doubt. "She loves me."

"And you love her?" Brandon said.

"No question," Derrick said, without delay.

"When two people love each other, they should move mountains to make it work," Damian said. "So what mountain is standing between you and Natalie?"

Derrick recalled everything that had transpired between them in recent weeks. "If I had to sum it up in one word—Charlene."

"Sounds to me like you know what you have to do," Damian said, looking at his brother, who nodded in agreement.

Natalie's eyes began to blur from staring at the same page for at least the last twenty minutes. Obtaining grants was the lifeline of BSI. Without them, program expansion would be nearly impossible. That's why she could ill afford to waste time reading the same paragraphs over and over again without any comprehension. As a nonprofit, BSI could provide services only with money received through grants, or private and corporate donations. Early on, that made things tough.

Her first office space housed her original small staff of two—her and Jea, who was part-time. Heavily dependent on volunteers, Natalie often became perturbed that there just weren't enough resources to meet all of their needs. Over the past year, thanks to an increase in donations and a huge grant, their budget significantly increased and she was able to hire more accountants, lease a larger space, and help more people and their businesses.

This grant was vital because it would allow them to consult with people as they went through the process of getting a loan from the Small Business Association. If she didn't get this grant reviewed and couriered over to the SBA by the end of the day, BSI would miss the deadline and a chance for three hundred thousand dollars. But with the nonnegotiable deadline looming, she found it hard to concentrate. Thursday afternoon—it had been over a week since she was left standing in Derrick's office, and they had yet to make contact.

Christine and Tanya had been sympathetic but could offer no details about Derrick's meeting with their husbands. Brandon and Damian would only say that Derrick was upset yet very much in love with Natalie. Both women encouraged Natalie to call him. But Natalie vehemently opposed that idea.

Derrick had walked out on her. He was the one who hadn't returned her phone calls that day. He was the one who had that woman hanging out in his office, looking for more than just a professional relationship. There was no way the ball was in her court. If anybody needed to make the first move, it was him.

She'd been preaching that sermon all week to herself and it initially came out with force and conviction. As time passed, her confidence started to wane. What if he never called her? Could she let him go? Give him up? Let him disappear from her life?

The knock on the door snapped her out of her haze. "Come in."

The words sounded harsh and she immediately apologized for her tone of voice.

"No problem," Jea said. "I know how hectic and on edge things can get around here when there's a grant due."

Natalie didn't deny the explanation for her foul mood. If Jea thought it was because of the grant proposal, then so be it. It wasn't a secret that Natalie could get a little short-tempered when putting the finishing touches on a proposal.

"I know you're pressed for time, but you have a visitor," Jea said. "I didn't think you'd mind the interruption for this person."

The automatic smile on her face completely gave her away. If someone didn't have an appointment, Jea would rarely let them get to Natalie. That could only mean one thing—Derrick.

So happy that he came, Natalie dismissed all the chastising she'd wanted to do to him. How they treated each other that day suddenly became neither here nor there. If she was being honest with herself, she had completely overreacted about Suzanne. They'd been working together for a while and it never bothered her before. She'd obviously created that scene because she was already on edge. Even though he walked out on her, it was clear that she owed him an apology.

Barely able to contain her excitement, she unconsciously straightened her hair. "Send him in."

Jea watched her boss do a little primping and realized her mistake. Natalie hadn't said anything directly, but it was clear to her and everyone in the office that things weren't going so well with her and Derrick. His calls typically came through the main switchboard, and, according to the receptionist, he hadn't called one time all week. Add to that Natalie's somber mood and it all added up to one thing. Natalie and Derrick were in the midst of a major crisis.

"Umm . . ." Jea started, shifting uncomfortably from one foot to the other. "It's not a him. It's a her—Christine."

Maintaining the same expression, but dying from embarrassment on the inside, Natalie nodded. "Then send *her* in."

Jea nodded, kicking herself for making such a stupid mistake. Natalie had been on edge all week and her periodic questions of whether she'd missed any messages clearly showed that an end wasn't in sight. Having watched Natalie and Derrick's relationship develop over the past year, Jea was really pulling for them to make it.

When Jea entered her freshman year of college, she met Jeremy Walker. Dating all four years, they made plans to spend the rest of their lives together. Then a case of cold feet attacked him with a vengeance. He soon began standing her up, not returning phone calls, and being too busy to talk to her whenever she stopped by. That's why she was determined to enjoy her singleness. After being soured on the whole love thing, she thought it would be nice if Derrick and Natalie worked it out—just to restore her faith.

"Also," Jea said, pointing to the phone, "your mom is on line three. She said she was returning your call."

Natalie hadn't caught up with her mom since she left that message for her about a week ago. Actually, this was the first call she had received all week. Had her mother really gone more than several days without calling? "I don't have the time to talk with her now. Tell her I'll call her tonight."

Jea put her hands on her hips and gave her boss a stare that said *I don't believe you.*

Feeling scolded, Natalie said, "I promise, Jea. I'll call her."

"I'm going to hold you to that," Jea said before leaving.

Christine breezed in and didn't bother with any pleasantries. "Still being stubborn, I hear."

Natalie didn't need an explanation of what she was talking about, and all thoughts of apologizing to Derrick went out the window. Her guard went up and she refused to take complete blame for this one. "Thanks for stopping by in the middle of my busy workday. Are there any other insults you'd like to throw my way before you leave?"

Christine heard more sarcasm than anger and sat in the chair opposite Natalie's desk.

"Please," Natalie said, realizing Christine was determined to have her say. "Have a seat."

"You still haven't called him." It was a statement, not a question.

"He left me standing in the middle of his office!"

"That's right," Christine said. "But as I recall, that was after you turned down his marriage proposal and then accused him of having a thing with his office manager!"

"I accused him of being blind to that woman's advances," Natalie corrected. "Any person could see that Suzanne wants my man. *We were just having lunch. Derrick and I work so well together.* Please, give me a break."

"The only one who has a problem with Suzanne is you. Derrick is not the least bit interested in her. He loves you," Christine said, trying to get Natalie to focus on the real issue. "How long do you think he's going to be your man if you keep treating him like this? How much do you think he's going to be able to take before he gives up?"

Standing, Natalie pushed down her feelings of guilt and shrugged nonchalantly. "Tell him to call me."

"Why are you being so inflexible about this?" Christine asked. "Damian said that Derrick is torn up about this."

"I'm not the inflexible one," Natalie declared. "He's the one who keeps pushing for marriage."

The phrase caught Christine's ear and her eyes narrowed, a puzzled look crossing her face. "*Pushing* for marriage? I thought this fight between the two of you was about his divorce?"

"It is," Natalie answered emphatically.

Christine wasn't buying it. "Then why did you just say—"

"Look, Christine," Natalie said, cutting her off and picking up some papers on her desk. "I'm not trying to be rude—"

Christine cleared her throat loudly.

"OK," Natalie said, releasing a grin, "maybe I am, but I do have a grant to get out the door today."

"You're avoiding this, Natalie," she said. "You're not talking to the man you love to work out your problems. That's defined as avoidance."

Picking up the documents that she had been reviewing before she was interrupted, Natalie held them out to her. "I've got to have this date- and time-stamped by this afternoon if I want to have a chance at getting this money. I'm not avoiding anything—I'm working."

Even though she wanted to continue this conversation, Christine understood how much grants meant to the success of BSI. Standing, Christine picked up her purse. "This conversation isn't over."

"Great," Natalie mumbled.

"Can we get together later—maybe dinner?" Christine asked. "Damian is having father-daughter night with Brianna, so I'm free."

"I'll call you," Natalie said, leading her to the door.

Christine followed, but eyed her suspiciously.

Natalie laughed. "I promise, Christine. I'll call you tonight and you can psychoanalyze me all you want."

Giving her a quick hug, Christine stepped into the hallway and headed for the door. "I just want you to be happy."

"Thanks, Christine. I really do appreciate your concern. It means a lot to me." She reached out to give her sister a hug.

The seriousness of her tone told Christine that she meant it. "I'll talk to you later."

Natalie shut her door and forced herself to concentrate on the task before her. She had to get Derrick, divorce, and marriage off her mind if she was going to meet her deadline. Sitting back in her chair, she picked up the papers and started reading.

One hour later, Natalie placed the grant proposal in a manila envelope and buzzed Jea. "Can you call the courier and tell him our package is ready to go?"

"Sure," Jea said. "Someone should be here within the hour."

With that taken care of, Natalie's thoughts immediately went back to Derrick. Her emotions had been on a roller-coaster ride all day. One minute she was feeling guilty and taking the blame and the next, she couldn't believe he had the audacity to defend Suzanne and walk out on her.

Pushing out of her chair, Natalie walked to the window and stared onto the streets of the nation's capital. Closing her eyes, she inhaled deeply, feeling her lungs fill up. This technique usually helped her relax when she was feeling the stresses of life. She hadn't had a good night's sleep in over a week and her body was starting to wear down. Maybe dinner with Christine would be good for her. Or maybe she could have dinner with Derrick.

"Natalie?" Jea's voice boomed over the intercom.

"Yes, Jea?"

"You have a call on line two . . . it's Dr. Carrington."

Natalie stared at the blinking red light for almost a minute trying to calm the butterflies in her stomach. "Natalie Donovan," she said in her most professional tone.

"How are you?"

The moment she heard his voice, the battle resumed—guilt and anger. The anger won out. "You'd already know the answer to that if you'd bothered to call."

"I didn't call to fight," he answered calmly.

Natalie relaxed—immediately regretting her words. Inhaling deeply, she admitted the truth. "I'm sorry. I didn't mean that. The phone lines work both ways. I don't want to fight either."

Relieved that they finally agreed on something, Derrick said, "I want to come by tonight. What time will you be home?"

"Seven," she said with no hesitation. She'd missed him so much she didn't know if she'd be able to make it through one more day without seeing him.

"I'll see you then."

Chapter 7

Natalie checked her makeup just as the doorbell rang. After standing in her closet for almost twenty minutes trying to decide what to wear, Natalie was acting as if this were a first date. After discarding a pair of blue jeans and tan cargo pants, she finally settled on a pair of black roll-waist pants and a burgundy cotton shirt with a boat neckline.

"Hi," she said, motioning for him to enter.

Stepping inside, he was powerless to keep from reaching out to her. It felt as though they hadn't been together in years. When she walked willingly into his embrace, he gently brushed her lips. The taste of her sent awareness straight to his core and it confirmed that nothing had ever been as right as the two of them together.

Since they'd started dating, they had never gone this long without seeing each other unless one of them was out of town. He made a silent promise that they would never be apart this long again. "I've missed you."

Natalie fully embraced the feel of his body against hers. Reveling in the comfort she received, she wondered what could be so important that it would keep her from feeling like this every day of her life. "Me too."

For several minutes, neither of them moved. They stood in the foyer holding each other until their heartbeats seemed to come in sync.

"I meant what I said on the phone. I don't want to fight," Derrick said into her ear.

Following her into the living room, he took his jacket off, revealing a pair of khaki pants and a loose-hanging pullover shirt. When he sat on the couch, she took a seat beside him. They'd spent many nights in this room. With the comfortable cushions and entertainment center, they often cuddled to watch a movie, play cards, or just talk. "Thanks for agreeing to see me. I'm not so sure I would have after the way I stormed out of my office."

Sitting next to him, she kicked off her shoes and pulled her feet underneath her. "I actually want to apologize to you. I had no right to make accusations about you and Suzanne."

"I didn't come here to talk about Suzanne or our fight." Reaching in his pocket, he pulled out a piece of paper and handed it to her. "This is what I came to talk to you about."

Confused, Natalie took the paper. "A FedEx receipt?"

"I stopped there on the way over here," he said. "Check out the recipient address."

It was addressed to Logan, Petry & Williams. "Los Angeles?"

Folding his hands in front of him, he stared directly into her eyes. With all of the turbulence they've had over the past several weeks, there was still love reflecting back at him. Without a doubt, he knew he had made the right decision.

"I don't understand." She said, not connecting a receipt to what was going on between them.

Derrick took a deep breath. Ever since he'd met Natalie, he'd been waiting for this moment. Regardless of how wonderful their relationship had become, there was always a cloud hanging over them. There were many times when the sun peeked through, but the cloud always remained. He hoped that what he'd done would remove that cloud once and for all. "I signed the settlement agreement and the divorce papers. I sent them back overnight to be filed with the court first thing in the morning. The divorce is final."

Natalie opened her mouth to speak, but nothing came out. She swallowed deliberately, hoping her voice would come back. Was this really happening? After all this time, was it finally a reality?

"You were right," he continued. "I let my vengeful state of mind prevent me from moving on. I couldn't let go. But your words the night of Damian's party struck a chord with me. What was it that was keeping me tied to Charlene and our marriage? Possessions. Things. Suddenly, I realized that those *things* just weren't important to me."

Holding her hands in his, he continued. "And they definitely weren't more important than you."

Finally finding her voice, Natalie said, "But the paintings . . . your club membership . . . your furniture . . ."

"Are not essential to my life."

"You worked hard for what you had."

"True." He had given more to that marriage in every way. "But I decided that it wasn't worth it anymore."

Natalie looked at the receipt again. When he had called earlier today and asked to meet with her, Natalie tried to predict how the evening would go. She was already prepared to apologize but didn't know if that would be enough to get over the hurdles they faced. Never would she have guessed that this was the news that he would be sharing. "How did you manage to get it done so quickly?"

Derrick's lips curved upward as he thought about the constant discussions between him and Philip. His attorney always gave the client final say after offering the best possible advice, but Philip couldn't believe the compromises Derrick was willing to make to get this settled quickly. He'd checked with Derrick three times before he had the final papers drawn up. "When one person is truly cooperative, it's amazing what can be accomplished."

Natalie sat back, letting his words sink in. It was almost too good to be true. After all this time? After all they'd been through?

"Is it really over?" Natalie whispered, afraid to say it out loud. "Are you officially a single man?"

"According to the stack of papers I signed in triplicate, I am."

Natalie tossed the receipt on the table and leaned into him, feeling his strength as he wrapped his arms around her. "How do you feel?"

Derrick took several seconds before he responded. He spoke the first word that flashed in his mind. "Free."

Giving him a kiss on the cheek, she stood and reached for his hand. "This calls for a celebration. How about dinner at your favorite restaurant—my treat?"

Derrick shook his head from side to side, his arms going around her waist and pulling her back down on his lap. "Not in the mood to go out."

"How about we order something in—Italian, Chinese?"

Caressing her arms with the tips of his fingers, he gave her a teasing smile. "I'm not hungry."

Natalie heard the seductive tone in his voice and realized where his mind was headed. "I've got a great bottle of wine in the kitchen."

The sparkle in his eyes told her that she was getting warmer. "That's a good start."

Derrick got two glasses out of the cabinet while she got the corkscrew. Having eaten many meals in this room with her, he went to the refrigerator knowing she'd have fresh fruit. Placing strawberries and grapes in a small bowl, he put everything on the center island.

Natalie popped the cork and filled each of their glasses. Raising hers, she offered a toast. "To freedom."

Clinking his glass with hers, Derrick pressed the contours of his body to hers. He took a sip before leaning forward to kiss her lips. "You have the sweetest lips I've ever tasted."

Setting his glass aside, Derrick traced her lips with the tip of his tongue.

The hairs on her body stood up and she opened her mouth, intertwining her tongue with his. They'd shared kisses, but this time the tenderness and sensuality of this kiss were laced with anticipation and expectation. These created a sense of urgency for what was to come.

"I'd like to discuss our previous agreement," he said between kisses.

"I'm listening," she said, barely breaking contact.

Placing a soft kiss on her forehead, he hugged her close. "You didn't want to have a physical relationship with a married man."

"Uh . . . uh," Natalie said, closing her eyes as his lips moved to touch the tip of her nose.

"My signature on those papers releases me from all ties."

Natalie reached up and stroked the nape of his neck. "Go on."

Picking her up, he spun her around and sat her on the

island. Stepping between her legs, he moved a piece of hair out of her face, his burning eyes capturing her full attention. "I love you, Natalie."

"I love you, too."

He'd waited so long for this moment of his life to come—free from his marriage, free from Charlene, free to move forward into his future—a future he planned with the woman resting in his arms. "Are we still tied to that understanding?"

Leaning forward, Natalie placed her lips on his and silently answered his question by moving her hand to his belt buckle.

The moment she unhooked it, all the pent-up need and wanting that had been suppressed over the last year came gushing forward in an uncontrollable flow.

"Let's take this upstairs," he said, helping her off the island.

"I'll race you," she said, jumping off the island to get a head start.

Discarding clothes as they raced up the steps, Natalie entered the room in her bra and panties, and Derrick had on his pants, but no shoes, socks, or shirt. Natalie clicked a button on her universal remote and smooth jazz sounds came through the hidden speakers. Stepping to him, she ran her fingers across his bare chest, and his sharp intake of breath told her she was pushing all of his hot buttons.

Without regard for her wanton behavior, she lowered her other hand down his pants and stroked him.

"Ohh, baby," he said, leaning his head back with his eyes closed. The gratification that she was giving him was rapidly becoming all-consuming.

Taking joy in hearing the erotic moans coming from

his lips, she continued to stroke him, feeling him grow and harden.

The sweet torture of her touch was driving him to the brink of insanity. Each time she touched him, stroked him, kissed him, the heat inside him rose ten degrees. He wasn't sure how much more he'd be able to endure.

Taking matters into his own hands, he led her to the bed where he laid her down before him. Standing above her, Derrick thought of all the memories they'd made together—the many mornings at the café, the laughs, the long walks, the easy talks, the good times they'd shared with friends, and the special moments with just the two of them. They, together, defined love.

He often wondered if he would ever find someone else he could trust his heart to. After Charlene, he hadn't been sure. While he liked to think that he'd not allowed Charlene's treatment of him to affect his ability to love again, the reality was that he had never been 100 percent sure—not until today, not until her. "You are more beautiful than I ever imagined."

Not wanting to rush this moment but unable to contain the burning fire that craved to make every part of him a part of her, he lay beside her. Running his fingers through his hair, he wanted to pay tribute her body. Gently massaging her scalp, he worked his hands down to her neck and to her shoulders, rubbing and kneading. Replacing his hands with his lips, he kissed her chest before unhooking the latch in the front of her bra. Freeing her breasts, he immediately cupped one while kissing the other. Each touch branded her with his symbol of love—making her his, one inch at a time.

Natalie almost forgot to breathe as the touch of his hand and the heat of his tongue singed her skin. As she arched her back toward him, hot, burning passion prevailed over her entire being and her heart hammered. All the bad dates, the broken hearts, the disappointments, and the heartache were all necessary so that she could completely give herself to this night, to this man.

She would never have imagined that she could find such contentment, satisfaction, and peace. Derrick Carrington provided all of that for her. He gave her joy. He gave her happiness. He gave her love.

Her need and want of him took over her senses and she reached for his pants and helped him wiggle out of them. With one small piece of clothing left between them, she watched him retrieve a small foil packet from his pants and step out of his underwear. When she removed hers, it took less than a second for him to come to her, fully aroused, with love in his eyes and in his heart.

The moment he entered her, time stopped. All that was her became him and all that was him became her. The rhythm of their motion fell in sync and Natalie wrapped her legs around him, determined to push him deeper and deeper into her. With each stroke, their bond became stronger.

Their breathing became one. Their bodies became one. Their hearts became one.

"You are my everything," he said.

With a deep, satisfied breath, Natalie's entire body shook with delight and fervor and she moaned aloud with indescribable pleasure. Powerful passion ruled her body and she was helpless to stop it. She screamed his name, her body trembling in sweet release.

Overcome with the complete connection Derrick experienced with her, he felt his emotions overwhelming him. How could he ever have claimed to love when he had never claimed her? And in this moment, he claimed her—mind, body, and spirit. Content in that, he exploded with his own release.

Neither moved as both tried to regain some semblance of control. In the silence of the room, their heavy breathing soon returned to normal and Derrick sweetly kissed her lips. "You are my world, Natalie. I love you."

Wrapped in his embrace, Natalie felt comfort and peace from his words. There was no other person in the universe who could give her this. "I love you, too, Derrick."

Natalie lazily stretched her body and turned over, wallowing in the comfort of her bed. Opening her eyes, she squinted at the bright sunlight dancing through her palladium windows. Feeling more relaxed and more alive than she could ever recall, she wished she could bottle this moment and keep it with her forever. Peeking at the alarm clock on her nightstand, she felt the euphoria she was just soaking in starting to lift.

"Oh my God. That can't be right!"

Was it after eleven o'clock? She should have been at work hours ago.

Panicked, she sat straight up, trying to think of the last time she had overslept. College? Turning to her left, she noticed the empty pillow. The note on top was addressed to her. Immediately, her body relaxed.

Good morning, sweetheart,

I called Jea and she was able to reschedule your appointments for today. Meet me downstairs for breakfast, Derrick.

P.S. You look absolutely amazing when you're asleep—and satisfied.

Natalie's cheeks reddened at that last comment. *Satisfied* was too mild a word to adequately define what last night had done to her. Time and time again they had turned to each other, uncontrollable desire racing through their veins, deepening their affections for one another. The insatiable hunger chased them all night but could never be satisfied completely. By the time they finally drifted off to sleep, wrapped tightly in each other's arms, the sun had begun to make its appearance.

Curling her knees to her chest, a small smile creasing her face, she thought about the men who had been in her life. There had been lots of dates, some steady boyfriends, and one or two serious relationships, but nothing came close to this.

Pushing the covers back, she stepped out of the bed and headed to the bathroom. After taking a few steps, she slowed her walk considerably. Every muscle in her body was sore—some she didn't even know she had. But Natalie didn't mind. Last night had been the best workout she'd ever had. After a long shower, she followed the smell of fresh-brewed coffee.

Derrick sat at her kitchen table reading the day's paper. When she walked in wearing just an oversized T-shirt, he set the paper aside. "Look who finally decided to join the rest of the world."

"Very funny," she said, going for the coffeepot.

"Oh no," he said, walking to her. Kissing her on the lips, he gave her a wicked grin. "You must be exhausted from last night. Have a seat. I have a surprise for you."

After holding out a chair for her to sit, he opened the oven door and the aroma wafted through the air.

"Tell me you didn't?" she said, but hoping that he did.

The warming plate was set on the table with four cinnamon rolls, icing dripping down the sides.

Unable to help herself, Natalie grabbed one and took a big bite. "Oooohhhh. This stuff has to be laced with an illegal drug. Nothing legal can be this good."

"Nothing?" Derrick asked, lowering his eyes to her body.

"OK, I'll admit, there is one thing better."

Before she said anything else, she dusted off one roll and reached for another. Seeing Derrick's stare of amazement, she explained, "I worked up quite an appetite last night."

He just laughed. "I figured as much, so I snuck out to Carla's Café while you were sleeping. By the way, your snore has gotten worse."

Natalie almost choked on her food. "Has not."

"Oh yes, baby," he said, imitating her sounds, "it has."

"You were saying?" she said, deciding that wasn't a subject she wanted to pursue.

"When I placed the order, Carla, in not-so-polite words, told me my breakfast for two had better be with you."

"She's a trip," Natalie said, secretly glad that someone was watching out for her. "You would think that with all the customers that woman serves in her restaurant, she wouldn't be able to keep up with everyone's business."

"Don't tell Carla that," Derrick warned. "She considers it a great gift to hand out unsolicited advice."

"I'll remember that," Natalie said. "Thanks for calling Jea."

"That was another person who was extremely pleased that you were taking the day off and spending it with me."

"What about your patients?"

"I called my office and Will and Sherisse agree to see

my patients for today. I'm sure I'll pay dearly for it when one of them wants time off, but it's worth it."

Natalie couldn't believe all he'd managed to get done while she slept the morning away. "Thank you, baby, for going out this morning to get my favorite pastry."

She was halfway through her second one when Derrick watched a small drip of icing ooze down the side of her mouth. It reminded him of the many mornings when they shared breakfast in the café. At that time, he couldn't do anything about it. This time, he leaned across the table and licked it for her.

"Ummm," she said, turning her lips to his. Forgetting about breakfast and cinnamon rolls, Natalie got up from her chair and walked around the table. Not breaking physical contact, she straddled his legs and felt his arms move under her T-shirt and pull her closer.

"You don't have anything on under this shirt," Derrick said, feeling the heat when connecting his skin to hers.

"Is that a complaint?" she asked, teasing him by leaning away from him.

"Not in the least." Lifting her, he carried her in his arms. "Back upstairs?"

"Uh-uh," she said, "I can't wait that long."

"Neither can I."

Laying her on the table, Derrick pushed the plate of rolls to the side, getting icing all over his hands.

Natalie removed her shirt and Derrick wiped his hands all over her body, trailing his fingers around her breasts, down her stomach, and finally to her core. Sliding his finger inside made Natalie let out a soft sigh of pure delight.

Tracing the trail he left behind with his tongue, he nibbled on each breast, leaving no remnants of the sticky treat. Going lower, he licked and tasted her stomach before moving even lower. He reached up to caress her breast while moaning at the sugary taste of her.

Natalie gripped the side of the table and cried his name in pleasure. After what they had shared last night, she would have sworn to anyone who would listen that there could be nothing that could take her to greater heights. But how wrong she would have been. The wicked things he was doing to her body today rivaled anything he had done to her last night. Just when she thought she couldn't stand the bliss one more second, her body burst into a million pieces. Derrick kissed the inside of her thighs and she loosened her grip. What was she thinking, making this man wait?

"That takes care of the bedroom and the kitchen," Derrick said. "Why don't we hit the living room next?"

Natalie laughed at his plans for the day but didn't object. If she was going to play hooky, she might as well do it up right. "Let's not forget the sunroom."

Hours later, as the sun began to set, Natalie and Derrick lay in bed eating Chinese food right out of the cartons. Having just got out of the shower, Natalie put on a T-shirt and Derrick threw on some shorts.

"Do you know we've only done two things today? Eat and—"

"I know," Natalie said, putting some broccoli in his mouth. "Not a bad way to spend a Friday."

"Or a Saturday or Sunday for that matter," he said, thinking of all they would do on the upcoming weekend.

"We've got to leave this house at some point," Natalie said, but not really wanting to believe it.

Thinking of their lives outside this house, Natalie set her food aside. "Derrick, I want to apologize again for the other day. I had no right to judge how you handled your divorce."

"No, you didn't," Derrick said sternly, before breaking into a relaxed smile. "But what you said had some truth in it. I was being unreasonable when it came to the settlement—trying to pay Charlene back for what she did to me. The truth of the matter is that I didn't own enough stuff to take from her that would make up for her sleeping with my best friend."

"So you gave in to her to get that part of your life over?" she asked, still not quite believing that it was really a done deal.

"I wouldn't necessarily call it giving in," he said, remembering the countless calls with his attorneys. "I call it negotiating in good faith."

Curious, Natalie asked, "Which means?"

"Which means I won't be eating any food off that ugly china. I won't have to stare at blobs of neon colors on canvas that some have referred to as artwork. But next winter," he said, pulling her closer, "we'll be taking a ski vacation in Vail."

Natalie snuggled closer. "I like the sound of that."

Saturday morning, Natalie awoke again to an empty bed. She'd slept like a newborn in Derrick's arms, and even though they'd only spent two nights together, she couldn't imagine sleeping without him. The note on the pillow asked her to meet him in the sunroom instead of the kitchen. Just thinking about what they had done in that room after closing the retractable blinds yesterday sent shivers up her arms.

After a quick shower, Natalie put on a pair of capri pants and a tank top. She stopped short when she entered the room. The glass garden table was filled with the makings of a great brunch. Fresh fruit, scrambled eggs, and waffles were laid out before her.

"You're going to spoil me."

"That's my plan," Derrick said, dressed in a pair of sweatpants and a T-shirt. They'd done so much over their year together, he had clothes, shoes, and personal items already at her house.

"I talked to my lawyer this morning."

Natalie slowed her chewing at the tone of his voice—serious and staid. "He confirmed the filings of my papers. The judge signed the order," Derrick said.

Natalie relaxed and took another bite of food. "I can't tell you how happy I am to hear that. I know it's been a long road for you, but you've finally reached the end. You can move forward."

"Moving forward is what I had in mind for today—as well as a few other things," Derrick said lightly.

"Can I at least finish my breakfast first?" Natalie playfully pleaded. "I'm going to need my strength."

Standing, Derrick walked around the table until he was directly in front of her. "You won't need much strength for this."

Kneeling, he pulled the small ring box out of his pocket, opened it and held it up to her. "You know what question comes next."

Natalie sat back in her chair and her eyes moved from his face, to the ring, and back to him. "Derrick—"

"Aaaah," Derrick said, sounding like a buzzer from a

game show. "While we are looking for a one-word answer—that's not it."

Slightly smiling at his humor, Natalie reached down and clasped her hands around his. "Are you—"

"Aaaah," Derrick said again. "That's two words, not one. Let me help you out . . . Yes. That's the word we're waiting for."

Natalie leaned away from his touch and her smile disappeared.

Derrick watched her actions and felt his heart sink. He stood.

She got out of her chair and walked to the large windows that overlooked the patio and garden. Natalie could feel his eyes staring into her back. Turning to face him, she searched for the right words.

Her unspoken words and body language were abundantly loud and clear.

"You're not going to say it, are you?" The disbelief in his voice echoed around the room.

"Listen to me, Derrick," Natalie started compassionately.

"Unless the next word out of your mouth is 'yes,' I don't want to hear it," he said, his breathing becoming short as his annoyance rose.

Natalie could feel the shift in the room—it was charged with joy and love just a few short minutes ago, but dissent and tension began to creep in. "I just want you to think about what you're asking. You just got out of a marriage—less than twenty-four hours ago. Maybe you need to take some time to adjust."

He couldn't believe what was registering in his ears. Was she actually turning down his proposal—again? Snapping the box shut, he tossed it on the table like a cheap trinket instead of a twenty-five-thousand-dollar ring.

"Adjust?" Derrick said, offended and annoyed at her attempt to put this on him. "I walked out on an adulteress wife over a year ago, never having any desire to go back. I think that's been plenty of time to, as you put it, adjust."

"You walked out a year ago, but you just broke ties yesterday," Natalie said.

"What is up with you, Natalie?" Derrick said, feeling frustration rise from the pit of his stomach. "You said you couldn't accept my proposal because of Charlene. Now that I've handled that situation, you come up with a brand-new excuse."

"It's not an excuse, Derrick," she said, walking toward him. "You know that. But you just closed an emotional chapter in your life. Are you really ready for this?"

Exasperated, Derrick wasn't buying any of this. "Let me get this straight. Three weeks ago I proposed to you and you put me off because I'm still attached. I become unattached, and you still won't marry me because you think it's for my own emotional well-being?"

Natalie hadn't meant to mislead him, but that's exactly how he was taking it. "I just don't want you to do anything that you'll regret."

Nodding in the affirmative, Derrick gave a slick smile. "Oh, I regret something . . . falling in love with you."

The words, spoken with such conviction, pierced Natalie's heart. When she hadn't answered his proposals over the past several weeks, she couldn't picture herself wearing his ring because of Charlene. Once his divorce became final, she had honestly believed she would not hesitate to accept his ring.

Now that he was a free man, these new concerns rose up in her. How could someone come out of a marriage where he had been treated so badly and be ready to commit to someone else so soon? She couldn't lie to herself, or to him, and deny what she was feeling.

Reaching for his hands, she raised them to her mouth and gently kissed them. "We just shared some amazing nights together. Nights filled with our passion and our love. Can't we just enjoy this moment, spend the weekend together, and talk about this later?"

"No," Derrick said, snatching his hands out of her embrace. "I'm tired of talking about this. There's a question on the table and I want an answer."

"Now who's giving ultimatums?" she asked, hurt that he rejected her touch and losing patience with his inability to see her point of view.

"You can call it what you want, honey, but I meant what I said. If you don't want to marry me, just say so."

Natalie remained silent as confusion ran rampant in her mind. "It's not that simple, Derrick."

"That's where you're wrong, Natalie. It's very simple. Simple as yes or no." Without another word, Derrick took the ring off the table and left the sunroom. Following him upstairs, Natalie watched him gather his belongings and throw them into a gym bag.

"We can't talk about this?"

"What is there to discuss?" he said, disappearing into the bathroom before coming out with his hairbrush and shaving items.

"Those things have been here for months," she said, watching him gather other items that had made their way to her house over the course of their time together.

Derrick didn't respond. Zipping the bag, he searched around the room one more time to make sure he was leaving nothing behind.

"So you're walking again?" she said, accusation laced in her voice.

"Last time I walked out, it was out of anger and haste. This time, it's a rational decision and I'm fully aware of the consequences."

"Which are?" she asked, walking a few feet behind him as he made his way down the stairs.

At the bottom of the stairs, he turned to face her. Standing on the bottom step put her eye to eye with him. "I'm not playing this game with you anymore, Natalie. I know what I want. I love you and I want to marry you."

Without a kiss good-bye, he opened the front door. Right before walking through, he faced her one last time. "Give me a call when you figure out what you want."

Natalie stood on the steps shocked at the dramatic turn of events. How could she have everything one minute and lose it all the next? Sitting down on the bottom step, she stared at the closed door as seconds turned to minutes and minutes crept toward an hour. The heights they had soared to these past couple of days gave her a high that no drug could possibly come close to. But the pit that she was rapidly sinking into tore her up inside. Resting her head in her hands, she didn't try to fight it. She let her tears fall freely.

Chapter 8

Natalie sat at the corner table of Carla's Café attempting to appear as if she wasn't watching the door. Monday had typically been one of the days she and Derrick would meet for breakfast. It was a long shot, at best. They hadn't spoken since he left her sitting in her hallway. The words that he spoke before leaving had been said with such finality, she held out little hope that he would show up.

She spent the remainder of her weekend on the couch. The scent of him was everywhere, in her bedroom and, especially, in her bed. She was unable to bring herself to sleep in it because the memories of what they shared were too strong.

Barely eating, she refused to answer the phone when she realized it wasn't him, essentially cutting herself off from the outside world. The only reason she managed to pull it together this morning was that she had two important meetings scheduled with clients who desperately needed her help. Not in the mood to focus on her appearance, she had opted for a magenta suit, skipping the accessories and makeup.

She'd lost count of the number of times she picked up

the phone and started to dial. But each time, she hung up before the call was completed. What would she say? How could she explain how she felt? Was there any way to make him understand? If she did have the words, would he be willing to listen? He made it quite clear that until she answered his question, they had nothing to talk about. By showing up at the café today, she hoped that he would do the same. At least they'd be face-to-face and have the chance to begin dialogue between them.

Refilling her coffee cup for the third time, Carla noticed the anxious look on her customer's face. "Are you ready to order or do you want to wait for Dr. Carrington?"

Natalie heard the chimes over the door and leaned to the side to see around Carla. It wasn't him. "I'll wait a few more minutes."

Noticing the crestfallen expression on her face, Carla looked to the front door and then back at Natalie. "The puffy eyes, watching the door, turning down my fresh rolls—what's going on? He was just here on Friday, happier than I'd ever seen him, surprising you with breakfast. He said that you two were better than ever. How did things get so bad between you two?"

Natalie thought about the cinnamon rolls he brought to her on Friday and Carla's inquiry to make sure they were for her and wondered the same thing. How could they go from being blissfully happy one day, to on the brink of never seeing each other again? Masking her inner turmoil, she shrugged. "I'm not sure."

Whenever Carla watched Natalie and Derrick argue, she could tell they still had love and respect for each other. Taking a closer look at Natalie today, she could tell this was no ordinary disagreement. From the look on Natalie's face, this could be the final straw. Her heart went out to her. "Hang in there . . . I'm sure everything will work out."

The half smile Natalie gave as a response didn't offer much hope that she believed her. Derrick made it clear that if there was to be any talking between the two of them, she would first have to answer his question. Remembering the hurt in his eyes when he left, she had little doubt that he meant it. If he showed up this morning, maybe she'd find the words to explain why she couldn't answer.

Being dumped by the married man who had gotten her pregnant devastated Natalie's mom. Young, pregnant, and broke, she had to drop out of college and live with her brother until she could scrounge up enough money to live on her own. Her parents, ashamed and embarrassed by her behavior, wanted nothing to do with her, and they died without really making peace with their only daughter.

Years went by and Margaret, though hurt and filled with pain over how Henry treated her, always had a little part of her that held out hope that he would someday come back for her and give her the love he'd so easily held from her. It didn't matter that he treated her like dirt, or that he had a wife and another child. The memories of the good times they had were what Margaret clung to, held steadfast to. Even with all signs indicating that she and Henry would never be together, her feelings remained. She couldn't turn them off.

That's what Natalie was trying to explain to Derrick. Regardless of how Charlene treated him, they built a life together. He cared for her and loved her. Could all those emotions get turned off because a little time had passed and the court papers had been signed?

"Well, look who's here—alone."

So deep in her thoughts, Natalie failed to see Suzanne

approach, dressed for the office in her uniform whites, her hair pinned back in a ponytail.

Natalie took a slow sip of her coffee, hardly acknowledging her presence.

"I almost didn't recognize you," she said with a smirk. "The red eyes and lack of makeup are not a good look for you."

Returning the fake smile that was given first, Natalie set her cup on the table and folded her hands in front of her, refusing to spar with her. "Hello, Suzanne."

Taking note of the empty chair at the table, Suzanne gave Natalie a sympathetic look. "You're at a table for two . . . yet you're sitting by yourself."

Natalie didn't dignify her comments with a response. She wasn't in the mood for playing games with someone as insignificant as Suzanne Spencer.

Not the least bit deterred by Natalie's lack of participation in the conversation, Suzanne pulled out the empty chair and sat.

"Please join me," Natalie said, not hiding her sarcasm or rising irritation.

"I'm waiting for my order," Suzanne said, flashing the receipt with her number on it. "When I saw you, I just had to come and say hello."

"How considerate of you, Suzanne," Natalie said, too sugary to be sincere. "Now that you've said it, why don't you practice saying another word—good-bye?"

Leaning forward, Suzanne lowered her voice. "I hope you're not waiting for Derrick. He's already at the office. I actually came over here to get us breakfast. He'll appreciate this gesture on my part. His first patient isn't due for another hour, so we'll just enjoy a leisurely breakfast in his office. Just the two of us—alone."

Natalie held words on the tip of her tongue and decided not to fall into her trap. She wouldn't give Suzanne the satisfaction of getting a rise out of her.

"I didn't even have to check with him to see what he wanted. I know exactly what he likes—and how he likes it."

When there was still no response from Natalie, Suzanne shrugged her shoulders and placed her chin in her hand as if in deep thought. "He seemed so preoccupied this morning. I wonder what could be on his mind. You two seem close—do you have any idea?"

The urge to reach across the table and wrap her hands around Suzanne's neck was suppressed as Natalie remained calm on the outside. She'd been counting backward from ten in her head ever since Suzanne made her approach, hoping it would help keep her calm. But the more that woman talked, the more Natalie realized that the only way to shut her up would be to put her fist in her mouth.

"Don't you two usually meet for breakfast?" Standing, Suzanne pushed the chair back under the table. "Well, I guess Derrick's looking to change a few things about his life."

Natalie's foot lightly tapping on the floor was the only outward indication that her patience was waning fast.

"Oh well," Suzanne said, tossing her hands in the air. "No use trying to guess what's going on with him. We've become so close lately. It's as if he's realized what a good friend I am for him. When you spend as much time together as we do, it's inevitable that the working relationship becomes so much more. I'm sure whatever's on his mind will come out during the special, cozy breakfast time we'll share this morning."

Suzanne heard her order number called. The syrupy

ADRIANNE BYRD
LINDA Hudson-Smith
Above the Clouds
Gwynne Forster
ARABESQUE
ALICE WOOTSON
Aloha LOVE
YOU'LL GET 4 SELECT ROMANCES PLUS THIS FABULOUS TOTE BAG!
ARABESQUE

smile that laced her face throughout the conversation disappeared and was replaced with a determined stare. "Just in case you're not smart enough to read between the lines, Natalie, I'll spell it out for you. Derrick looks like he needs a friend and I'm willing, and more than able, to meet that need." She paused before she continued, "And any other need for that matter."

Without so much as a flinch, Natalie finally decided it was time to speak. There was enough going on her life that she didn't need little Miss Office Manager thinking she had an inside track to Derrick. Her voice was even, but lethal. "Let me spell a few things out for you, Suzanne. You can live in your little delusional world if you want and pretend that you and Derrick have something more than a professional relationship, but that's where it will stay—in your own little fantasyland. And, just for the sake of argument, if he does need something, he's too smart to go slumming in back alley trash cans to get it."

Suzanne's confidence wavered and Natalie could tell she touched a nerve.

Trying to pull herself together, Suzanne just shrugged. "Well, I'm off to spend the day with Derrick."

Natalie watched her walk out the door before she released a frustrated grunt. Rage burned at the audacity of that woman. If there was ever a doubt that Suzanne had a thing for her man, it was completely erased with this one conversation.

"I didn't know the devil wore dresses."

Natalie genuinely smiled for the first time in days and felt some of her agitation go away as she watched Carla set a cinnamon roll in front of her.

"I figured you could use this—on the house."

Natalie watched Suzanne exit the café and get in her

car. How could any man be attracted to someone who was obviously so desperate? Focusing her attention back on Carla, she thanked her for the food. "Is there any conversation in the café you don't hear?"

"Not if I can help it."

"Well," Natalie said, "you always have an opinion—so go ahead. Let's hear it."

"Oh, this is an easy one," Carla said. "You should stop talking to me and call your man before that little you-know-what makes it back to the office with his breakfast."

For once, Natalie decided to heed Carla's advice. Before she had a chance to talk herself out of it, she pulled out her cell phone and called his.

Derrick sat in his office staring at the wall. He'd been up since the early morning hours. Giving up on getting any sleep, he decided to just come in. The walls of his house felt as if they were closing in and he couldn't imagine spending one more minute in it.

After storming out of Natalie's house, he could hardly see through the anger that propelled him to get away from her. Getting in his truck, he had driven around for hours with no particular destination in mind. Finally, he found himself headed to the one place that always gave him peace.

The single family house located in a Virginia suburb had been his home since he was ten years old. With its brick front, wraparound porch, and nice backyard, there were many fond memories of family gatherings and playing with friends. Using his key, he opened the front door and called out for his parents.

"Derrick? Is that you?"

His mom stood at the top of the stairs. Looking much younger than her sixty years, her silver hair cut short, she was dressed for comfort in a pair of tan casual pants and a cotton shirt.

"Hey, Mom," he said, shutting the door behind him.

Meeting him at the bottom of the steps, she gave her only son a hug. With her five feet six, his six-foot-two frame towered over her, but she didn't care. There was no better feeling than holding your son, no matter what his age.

"Where's Dad?"

"Working at the store," she said, letting him go. "The plan that Natalie put together for us has been working like a charm. Not only have we greatly reduced our debt, but we're in a great position to sell. We can't work forever, you know."

At the mention of her name, Derrick headed toward the kitchen. He wasn't in the mood to hear what a great job Natalie had done with restructuring his parents' business. "Something smells good."

"It's my famous jambalaya," she said, following him. "It's just about ready. Hungry?"

The brunch that Derrick had prepared for Natalie was untouched when he left the house. Now, late in the afternoon, his stomach was starting to growl.

Elise fixed their plates and watched her son eat most of it before she asked, "Do you want to tell me what's wrong?"

Setting his fork down, he said, "What makes you think—"

"Don't even try that with me, Derrick." From the moment he had walked in the door, she knew something was on his mind. "You haven't stopped by here unannounced on a

Saturday afternoon since you returned from L.A. You usually spend your time with Natalie."

The flinch in his face was so subtle that someone who didn't know him might have missed it. But Elise Carrington knew her son better than anyone. "What are you two fussing about this time? Can't decide what restaurant to eat in? Can't agree on who has the best basketball team?"

Finishing the last of his food, Derrick got up and rinsed his plate in the sink. Facing the window, away from his mother, he dropped his head and shoulders. If only this were as simple as a place to eat or a sports team. What was happening between him and Natalie at this moment was worse than anything he'd ever experienced. He was so angry with her and their situation that that emotion had completely taken over, leaving no room for any other emotions. But standing in his mother's kitchen, he felt some of that anger subsiding, allowing sadness, grief, and disappointment to rise.

Walking to her son, Elise turned him around and saw a tear in the corner of his eye. "Talk to me, Derrick. What's going on?"

"It's over . . . that's what's going on."

Elise had never known her son to shed a tear over any woman. Even when he shared the breakup with Charlene, he didn't cry. "Derrick, you guys have had tough times before and you've bounced back. I'm sure if you two just talk it over, you can work it out. It's obvious you still love her."

A vision flashed in Derrick's mind—him on his knees, professing his love and holding out a ring to her—only to have her throw everything he was offering back in his face. Drying his eyes, he stiffened his back and the anger pushed its way back to the top in full force. "Thanks for your concern, Mom, but unless that woman makes some major adjustments, we won't be seeing each other anymore."

Derrick's thoughts came back to today and he turned away from the wall to face his desk. He'd come in early, so he might as well try to get some work done.

When his cell phone rang, the number flashed and Derrick debated. After several more rings, he pushed the button to take the call.

"Derrick, it's Natalie," she said, after he answered on the third ring.

"What do you want?"

The venom in his voice momentarily stunned her. It was a tone she'd never heard from him before. Taking a deep breath, she couldn't completely blame him. Derrick thought she was playing games with his heart. "I want to talk to you."

"Talk."

Natalie cringed at his short words and wondered if she'd made the right decision in calling. Maybe she should have gone to his office. "Not now," she said, hoping to make arrangements for later when they wouldn't be interrupted. "How about Lenny's? Seven-thirty? You love their food."

"Why, Natalie?" Derrick said, rubbing his temples. He was tired, irritable, and not in the mood to go at it again with her. "I'm not interested in meeting just to replay the same old conversation between us. Are you going to say yes to my proposal?"

How did their entire relationship get reduced to one question? "Is this an all-or-nothing situation, Derrick? Isn't there some place in the middle we could meet?"

Derrick was tired of trying to find the middle ground. It was too exhausting of an exercise. "What do you want from me, Natalie? We fell in love, I asked you to marry me, and you turned me down. Seems pretty all or nothing to me."

The harshness with which he spoke set her off balance and, for the first time it hit Natalie that he was ready to walk away from her—from them. "All I'm asking is that we talk this out."

"Sorry, Nat. But I'm all out of words," he said with finality.

"But—"

"Gotta go," he said, cutting her off before she could finish her sentence. "My breakfast is here."

Before she could respond, the line went dead.

Natalie stared at her phone for several minutes. He sounded so distant and cold, she wondered how that could be the same man who had made love to her just a few short nights ago. Was this how her relationship with him was going to end?

Natalie set her phone on the table and stared at it. He hung up on her. She was in the middle of speaking and he ended the call. Had she pushed him so far that he couldn't fathom talking to her? Not caring that she was in a very public place, she didn't try to stop the small tears that escaped from the corner of her eyes.

"Here you go."

Glancing up, Natalie took the napkin out of Carla's hand and wiped her face.

"I guess the call didn't go well."

Natalie sniffled and sighed. "He won't even talk to me."

"Whatever is going on between you, it just might take a little time for him to calm down," Carla said, "to be ready to talk and work things out. Give him some space. I'm sure he'll come around."

"You didn't hear him, Carla. I don't think he's interested in working things out," Natalie said, recalling that void of emotion in his voice.

Carla thought about all the times she'd seen them together. They'd fuss, but there was never a hint that their spats would ever be big enough to come between them. But whatever was going on between them now was different. Something in their relationship had changed over the last several weeks and Carla wondered if it had to do with his proposals. When she saw Derrick on Friday, it appeared as if they had worked it out. Now they could be headed to a place where working it all out might no longer be an option. "I'm not going to ask you to share what's going on between you two, but if it has anything to do with that ring he can't seem to get you take, you need to think long and hard about what's important to you before you contact him again."

Natalie nodded in agreement. "*He's* important to me."

"I'm not the one you need to convince."

Carla left Natalie to think about her next move. Should she go over to his office? Drop by his house tonight? Give him some time to cool off? Everything had gotten so bad, so quickly, she was at a complete loss.

Maybe she needed someone to talk it out with. Her mind went to Christine, Tanya, and Danielle. Her circle of friends had been the strongest, most supportive base anyone could ask for. They always had her back and she could count on them for anything. However, this situation weighed so heavily on her heart, Natalie wasn't convinced that they could help.

This was new territory for her. She'd always prided

herself on being independent and able to handle anything that came her way. But at this moment, she was baffled at what to do next and was starving for some guidance. Her mother's face came to her mind and Natalie wondered if she should confide in her.

Natalie had always held her mother at arm's length when it came to her relationships. Margaret could be so opinionated about men and how women should never put their complete trust in them that Natalie often found it not worth the effort. But this situation was different. Derrick was different. Natalie loved that man and it was all falling apart. The vulnerability and the helplessness regarding how to make this work between them were a totally new experience for her. How was she supposed to be in control of her life when she couldn't get through the day without crying?

At not quite eight o'clock in the morning, she scrolled the Rolodex in her phone until the Florida number came up. Pushing the Call button, she tried to recall a time when she wanted so desperately to talk to her mother. She couldn't think of one.

On the third ring, disappointment settled in as Natalie thought the call was going to go to voice mail. She'd put her mother off for weeks, and now that she wanted to talk to her, open up to her, she wasn't going to be able to. As she was preparing to leave an urgent message, the call was finally answered.

"Hello?"

Natalie pulled the phone away from her ear and looked at the preprogrammed number. It was her mother's, yet the voice on the other end definitely did not belong to Margaret Donovan. "Who is this?"

"Who, may I ask, is this?"

"You may not ask," Natalie said, getting indignant. "Let me speak to Margaret."

"I'm sorry," the male voice said, politely, "she's unavailable at this time. Is there a message?"

Unavailable? "I don't know who this is, but there is no reason why a man should be answering my mother's phone. Put Margaret on the phone in five seconds, or I'm hanging up and calling the police."

"Your mother?" the male voice said cheerfully. "This must be Natalie. It's so nice to finally meet you—sort of. Your mother talks about you all the time."

His jovial tone did nothing to influence Natalie's position on the situation. "Well, I haven't heard one word about you and your time is ticking—four, three, two."

"No, no," the man said, suddenly panicked. "Hold one minute. I'll get her for you."

One minute turned into two and Natalie was just about to hang up and carry out her threat when she heard her mother's voice.

"What's all this about calling the police on Samuel?" Margaret said, sounding a little winded. "I had to jump out of the shower to get to the phone."

Jump out of the shower? "Mom, who exactly is this Samuel person and why is he there at this time of morning while you take a shower? Is he the landlord? A repairman? A neighbor?"

Margaret laughed at Natalie's assumptions. "He's none of the above. Samuel's here because he spent the night—with me."

Too startled to answer right away, Natalie let the phone go completely silent. Once the words registered in her head, she stood up, almost knocking her chair over. "He did what?"

Several patrons turned their attention to Natalie and she remembered where she was as she glared at them to mind their own business. Sitting back down, she lowered her voice. "Mother, what is going on with you? How long have you known this man? Why haven't you said anything about him?"

"If you would ever return my phone calls," Margaret politely reminded her, "you'd know all about him."

Natalie thought back over the last couple of months, trying to remember the conversations they might have had. There hadn't been many, and those that they did have were usually short because Natalie was always on the go. They hadn't had a real talk in quite a while.

Remembering her mother's statement about just jumping out of the shower, Natalie decided not to worry about the past and focus fully on the here and now. She wanted to know exactly what was going on with the two of them. "Is he still there?"

"Of course he is," Margaret said, indicating he might be there quite often.

"I hope you have on a towel or a robe—something," Natalie said, feeling completely uncomfortable at this strange turn of events.

"Neither," Margaret said boldly. "I didn't have time—thinking you were in the process of calling the police."

Natalie was momentarily speechless.

"Natalie, let me call you back."

Remembering why she called, she said, "No . . . Mom, I want to—"

Margaret's laughter interrupted Natalie's last words.

"Mom?"

The giggles in the background continued.

"Mother?" Natalie said, a little louder, hoping to regain her attention.

"I'm sorry, honey, what did you say?"

"What is so funny?" Natalie felt as if she were left out of a private joke.

"Samuel, stop," she said halfheartedly.

Natalie could barely hear her. Did she set the phone down?

After a couple of seconds, Natalie could hear her mother picking up the receiver again. "He knows I'm ticklish."

The vision caused Natalie's face to scrunch up and she wondered if her mother had been drugged, lost her mind, or both. "Mother."

When she didn't answer right away, Natalie called out again, "*Mom*, are you listening to me?"

"Listen, Natalie, I really am going to have to give you a call back. We'll talk later. Love you."

"Wait . . . Mom . . . don't hang up . . ." But it was too late. For the second time that day, Natalie was left talking to a dead phone.

Chapter 9

Derrick sat in his office reviewing test results for Otis Fleming. The good news was that the test he ordered on his kidneys came back negative. He'd just called him with the news and the man thanked him profusely. The bad news was that it was only 2:30 in the afternoon. The day had been dragging, and with patients booked throughout the afternoon, he couldn't skip out early.

Even in the most stressful moments of his profession, he couldn't recall a time when he felt like this—no desire to work, no energy for his clients. His spirits had never sunk this low, even after his breakup with Charlene. For Natalie to take away the joy he gained from his work meant that she had become more to him than he ever could have imagined.

For as long as he could remember, becoming a doctor had been his dream. His interest in medicine never wavered, and all of his studies starting in junior high school had been geared toward medicine. When his parents saw his desire, they worked to make sure his dream would come true. Completing his undergraduate studies at Duke University and attending medical school at Stanford had made Derrick's parents, Carl and Elise Carrington, the proudest parents in the world.

The medical profession had changed since his college days. With the escalating costs of malpractice insurance, the complications and expense of health insurance plans, and dealing with the pharmaceutical companies who wanted to shove all their products at you, being a doctor just wasn't what it used to be.

But even with all of that, Derrick couldn't imagine making a living any other way—helping people, taking care of people, treating people, educating people, that was his purpose. To serve and to heal were a fundamental part of who he was.

It was those same qualities that brought him to seek out Natalie Donovan and BSI. His father had become ill, causing Derrick to come to the East Coast to help him get back on his feet. Helping his mom with their business while his dad recovered, he realized they weren't as solvent as they had led him to believe. His father's medical bills were piling up and the debt against their business was growing. With their having just upgraded to new equipment, the option of securing another loan was next to impossible.

Over the years, he had provided money to assist his parents in their personal lives. He'd paid off their home and cars and set up investment plans to assist in their retirement. But he had had no idea how much their business finances were in disarray. His mother refused to accept his money to help them out, so he did the next best thing. When a friend told him about BSI, he immediately went to find out more about their services.

The moment Natalie walked into that conference room, he was hooked. Striking. Stunning. Beautiful. None of those words did justice to her physical features.

Honey-brown skin, light eyes, and dark hair were a lethal combination. The conservative suits and pumps she wore couldn't hide her slim frame and the curves of her body. When she began to discuss options for helping his parents, his positive impression skyrocketed as he realized there were brains that went along with that beauty.

Over the next several months, she evaluated their tax returns, bank statements, and inventory. She reviewed every loan and supplier contract. Contacting the IRS and several creditors, Natalie devised a plan that not only got his parents back on track, but had kept them operating in the black ever since.

Walking out of her office the first day they met, Derrick had realized there was something truly special about her. The immediate draw to someone was unfamiliar to him. He had never experienced that, not even with Charlene. Deciding to maintain a professional relationship until his parents' business situation got resolved, he didn't act on his attraction. But fate had a funny way of stepping in and taking over.

Just a few short weeks after their first meeting last year, the D.C. area had one of its worst snowstorms. On his way to the hospital to assist with a shortage of doctors, Derrick's truck stalled. When he trudged through the foot of snow to the closest house to use the phone and get warm, he couldn't contain his shock when the person who opened the door was Natalie. They were both startled by his sudden appearance at her door. Natalie was skeptical of his intentions but finally agreed to let him in her house before he caught pneumonia or frostbite.

For a brief moment, they had both just stared at each other and Derrick felt his bones warming up—not from the heat inside the house, but the reaction his body was having to the woman standing in front of him. Finding his voice, he smiled. "I have to admit, five minutes ago I told myself I had the worst luck in the world, but now it appears as if the tides have turned."

She gave Derrick her sexiest smile, but her expression faltered when he sniffed deeply and crinkled his nose. "What's that smell?"

Drawing a deep breath, Natalie wailed. "Oh no . . . my hot chocolate."

Racing to the kitchen, she snatched the pan with the burned ingredients at the bottom off the stove. "I forgot all about it."

Standing in the entryway to her kitchen, Derrick watched her dump what looked to be black tar into the sink. Forgetting for a moment that some of his clothes were wet from his trek through the snow, he turned his attention to the woman cursing at a piece of cookware.

Leaving the pan in the sink to soak, she set a clean pan on the stove.

"Looks like someone likes to make her drink from scratch," Derrick said.

"I can't stand anything instant."

"Everything that's instant is not necessarily a bad thing," he said.

"Are you kidding me . . . instant pudding, instant coffee, ready-to-bake cookies, microwave pasta? Believe me, I'm sure there's not one thing 'instant' you could name that I would consider good for me."

Moving to stand directly in front of her, he asked, "What about attraction?"

Natalie froze in midmotion and turned to face him. "What did you just say?"

"You asked me to name something instant that would be good for you. I offer you attraction."

Sarcastically, Natalie pointed her finger at him and countered, "How wrong you are, Dr. Carrington. Some of my worst experiences started with instant attraction. So you see, I'm more prone now than ever to take the slow, unhurried route in that category."

Reaching around her, he took the cocoa and added it to the pan. "You may want to take the slow route, but sometimes the attraction can be too strong, too potent. Your only option is to react."

Natalie stepped back and realized this conversation had just turned very personal. Watching him gently stir the simmering mixture, she answered, "A sure sign of immaturity is a person unable to control himself. That's why this society of instant gratification and quick fixes will soon reap the results of its juvenile behavior."

Pouring the milk into the pan, Derrick continued to stir and responded without turning around, "So you're telling me that you're adult enough to suppress your feelings of attraction for the sake of maturity."

With a playful laugh, Natalie countered, "Your assumption is that I have an attraction to suppress."

Pouring the steaming drink into two mugs Natalie had placed on the counter, he handed her one. Their hands connected and neither moved.

"Do you, Natalie?" Pausing, he watched her reaction closely. "Do you have an attraction you're trying to deny?"

"Derrick, you have a patient waiting in room three."

The voice over the intercom pulled Derrick out of his thoughts. "I'll be right there."

Not moving, Derrick thought about all the moments like that one he'd had with Natalie over the past year. They'd laughed together, shared their deepest thoughts, and supported and depended on each other like best friends. Why wasn't she willing to accept his proposal?

Standing, Derrick headed for the door. The bottom line was that he was tired of trying to figure things out. If this was the way she wanted it, then this was the way it would be.

When the last patient had left, Will sat in Derrick's office unwinding from a hectic day. Will had watched Derrick all day, and there were definite signs that things were going pretty bad for him right now. He wasn't quite rude, but he'd zoned out a couple of times when one of the nurses was talking to him and his time with patients didn't include his normal banter about stuff other than health.

Will didn't need a degree in psychology to tell him that Derrick was working out some serious issues. "Everything OK?" Will asked. "You've been real quiet today."

Everything was far from OK, but Derrick was not in the mood to rehash the situation with Natalie. He'd been over it a hundred times in his head, talked to his mother, and attempted to talk to Natalie when she called. The only thing any of those attempts to remedy the situation accomplished was to make him angrier than he was before. "Everything's cool."

"We've been friends since medical school. We've shared many late nights and talked about everything from school to women. You're not just my business partner, you're my friend."

Derrick leaned over his desk and placed his head in his hands. Will was right. They had been through a lot together.

Raising his head, he threw his hands up in defeat. "She's driving me crazy and I've just about had all I can take."

"I can tell," Will said, not needing a name to know whom he was referring to. "So are you going to keep moping about it or are you going to do something?"

"That's just it, Will," Derrick said, having asked himself the same question all day long. "When I signed those divorce papers, I thought I did do something about it. But evidently, it wasn't enough."

Will had been an eyewitness to the quandary Derrick dealt with in negotiating the settlement with Charlene. They shared many beers over how long the process was taking, how unreasonable Charlene was being, and the impact it had on his developing relationship with Natalie.

After Natalie called him out on his motives for not having settled yet, Derrick reassessed his position. When it became more important to him to move on with his life than to fight with Charlene, he did just that. Will signed on the witness line when Derrick signed the divorce papers.

Will remembered their time in medical school when Derrick and Charlene were a steady couple. When Derrick told Will that he was getting married, Will thought it was the worst move he could make. Not because Charlene was a bad person, but because that kind of commitment to someone was a major decision. How could he ever be sure that the other person loved him as much as he loved her?

When their marriage fell apart, Will's assumptions about holy matrimony had been confirmed. He hated to see his friend so torn up about it, but it just showed that Will's philosophy of keeping relationships light and easy was always better than the heavy and emotion filled.

When Derrick met Natalie, Will heard the same warning bells going off in his head. The more time they spent together, the more he could see his boy getting deeper and deeper into her. Over time, he watched their friendship turn into something more and he had never seen his friend that happy. Even if falling in love wasn't for him, he was pulling for his friend and Natalie to work it out.

"What did she say when you told her it was final?"

Thinking back to that morning just a few short days ago caused mixed emotions for Derrick. On the one hand, after a year of waiting, they had finally consummated their relationship. The physical and emotional bond that was created between them touched the core of who he was. They were the only two people who existed in the world and it was purely about giving of themselves to each other, about sealing their lives together.

Then there were the anger and frustration at this mountain that had come between them. What more could he do?

"Initially, she was thrilled that I had officially closed that chapter in my life. And after spending two wonderful days—and nights—together, I asked her to marry me."

"She said no?" Will asked, obviously surprised. "I thought that once your divorce was final, she would happily wear your ring."

"Yeah, well," Derrick said, remembering how she left him hanging, "join the club."

"Did she give a reason?"

"Oh, you'll love this. She put it all on me—again."

"How?"

"Wondering if I was completely over Charlene and the pain of our breakup. Questioning whether I was ready to fully commit again. She told me I had just ended one marriage and that I should take some time to think about what I wanted before jumping back into marriage."

Will didn't want to admit it, but he had those same

thoughts. He admired Natalie for putting it out there. "Sounds like a valid question to me."

"Are you serious?" Derrick said, wondering if the whole world had gone mad. "You saw what a wreck I was after everything went down with Charlene. My feelings died for her that day and they have never returned. "

Everything Derrick said was true. Will had flown to L.A. to help move Derrick's stuff out of the house. Derrick refused to step one foot back into that home, and Will couldn't blame him. But the reality of the situation could not be brushed over. "Isn't Natalie the first person you've seriously dated since you separated?"

"So?"

"That makes her your rebound relationship," Will said, "and you know how those typically turn out."

"Exactly," Derrick said, as if Will had just proven his point. "No rebound relationship lasts a year—with no sex!"

"Yeah, man," Will said, digressing a little from the topic. "I still can't believe you agreed to that one."

"Neither do I," Derrick said, thinking back all those months ago when Natalie had explained her position. "That makes my case even stronger—rebound relationships are always about the sex."

Will nodded in agreement. "I just ended a rebound relationship that lasted about three weeks. Believe me—it was definitely all about the sex."

Derrick stared at his friend in bewilderment. "How can you have a rebound relationship if you don't have the real relationship first?"

"What are you talking about?" Will said, appearing offended at what Derrick was insinuating. "I was coming off a real relationship."

"With who?" Derrick said, trying to hold back a smile.

He silently did a quick rundown of the women he'd seen Will with over the last several months. If he had a serious relationship, it must have been kept deep undercover.

"Connie."

"Connie who? Anderson?"

"Yes," Will said, slightly defensively. "Connie Anderson."

"You've got to be kidding me," Derrick said, thinking of the petite dental hygienist Will had met in an elevator a few months back. "You dated for what—two months? And weren't you dating Donna, too?"

"It was almost eleven weeks," Will clarified, "and Donna and I were just friends."

Derrick eyed him suspiciously.

"All right," Will said, correcting himself. "Donna and I were just a little more than friends, but my number-one priority was Connie."

"Oh, well, that makes a difference. Clears everything right up," Derrick said, rolling his eyes. "So, Connie . . . when was her birthday?"

Will hesitated.

"What was her favorite color?"

"Blue," Will boldly declared. "No, lavender."

"Where did she go to school?"

Frustrated at the line of questioning, Will pleaded the Fifth.

"That's what I thought you'd do," Derrick said. "How can you claim a relationship with someone you don't know the most basic things about?"

"The basics are relative," Will said in his defense. "Those things might be the basics by which you judge your relationships on, but I have a different set of basics."

"Oh, I can't wait to hear this," Derrick said, leaning back in his chair and placing his hands behind his head.

"Connie is a perfect example. I might not know when her birthday is or what school she went to, but I do know that she prefers whipped cream to melted chocolate, she has a special spot right behind her left ear, and she can take her tongue and—"

"Whoa . . ." Derrick said, leaning forward from his relaxed state. "That's enough. I get the picture."

Will couldn't stop laughing. "I thought you would."

"Let's just agree that you have your way of measuring what makes a relationship and I have mine," Derrick said.

"If you don't get it together and get things right with Natalie, you won't have a relationship."

The laughter that had just been in the room fell into the background. "Me? I don't have to get it together, she has to get it together."

"You can't discount what she's feeling, Derrick."

"I'm not. I just don't know what to do anymore."

"Maybe you need to reassure Natalie that this is what you really want. That her fears and doubts are unfounded."

"You don't think getting divorced and proposing over and over again is enough?"

"Hey," Will said, hearing the exasperation in his voice. "I just help with the analyzing. I don't provide solutions."

"Very funny," Derrick answered.

Gathering their belongings, they headed for the front door.

"You want to go and get a drink?"

"No, thanks, Will. I'm going to head home."

Passing the front desk area, they both stepped outside into the cool night breeze.

"If it was up to me, I would consider heading over to her house," Will said.

Before Derrick could object, he continued. "All I'm suggesting is a conversation. You can't ignore her forever."

"A man can take only so much rejection," Derrick said, seriously contemplating whether another discussion with Natalie would really solve anything.

"If you've reached that point, I understand," Will said. And he did. The man had gotten down on one knee, for God's sake. Very few men would want to set themselves up for rejection after something like that. "You have to talk to her—if for no other reason than to end it once and for all."

Chapter 10

Curled up in a chair in the living room, Natalie sipped green tea, staring at the telephone. The day had dragged at work and when she picked up her purse and said good night to her staff, she was relieved. Going through the motions of work, she'd managed to get a few things accomplished and be somewhat coherent in her client meetings.

The hustle and bustle of the office helped keep her mind off Derrick, but now that she was alone, there was nothing to compensate for the overwhelming feeling of loneliness. Her pride wouldn't let her call Derrick, but she couldn't shake the disappointment of not hearing from him. It appeared as if they were at a stalemate—again.

Then there was her mother. Getting over the shock of a man answering her phone had been tough. When her mother hung up on her, she wanted to scream. That was completely out of character for her. Natalie's attempts to get back in touch with her mother two more times today had been futile. Each time, the call went to voice mail.

Natalie recalled the last few conversations she'd had with her mother. If her mother had been talking about a man named Samuel spending the night in her home,

Natalie would surely have remembered. This could only mean that her mother was purposely keeping him from her. The immediate question that came to Natalie was why? What was it about this man that would keep her mother from talking to her only daughter about him?

Natalie didn't like this new Margaret—holding stuff back from her, not having time to talk to her. Was this man trying to pull her away from her only daugher? When she finally got in touch with her mother, Margaret Donovan had better be prepared to answer her tough questions.

Rising, Natalie went to the kitchen and dumped the remainder of her cold tea in the sink. Opening the pantry in the corner, she stared at the various food items. Her breakfast that morning had been ruined by Suzanne. Her staff ordered Thai for lunch, but she barely touched her favorite dish. Jea had offered to get her something else, but Natalie declined. With thoughts of Derrick and her mother running circles in her mind, there wasn't any food that she was in the mood to eat.

Now that it was close to nine o'clock, her stomach was demanding immediate attention. Opening the drawer by the stove, she flipped through all the take-out menus, quickly deciding against all of them. Maybe she would just go with a bowl of cereal. That was about as much cooking energy as she could muster.

She was reaching for a bowl when her phone rang. Almost tripping over her feet to pick up the cordless, she exhaled in disappointment. "Hi, Christine."

"Hey, girl, I got your message earlier but didn't have a chance to call you back. What's up? You sounded upset."

Upset was just one of the plethora of emotions swirling around in her body. Derrick walking out on her, her mother hanging up on her, and not hearing from either one of them—how could her life spiral so completely out of control in a matter of days? Once again, her throat tightened and the moisture came to the corners of her eyes. Trying to hold it together, she did a pitiful job. "Where do I start?"

At Natalie's voice cracking, Christine's concern turned to alarm. "Natalie, what is it? What's going on?"

Without warning, all the pent-up confusion, frustration, love, and affection she had experienced over the last few days swelled up from deep in her belly and the pride she took in always holding it together, always maintaining control, evaporated in a second. Everything that was happening with Derrick and her mother had her completely off balance. Nothing made sense anymore. A month ago, everything in her life was just fine. Now it seemed as if she would never get it together. "I . . . Derrick . . . walked out . . . we . . . divorce . . . Mom . . ."

"Don't say another word," Christine said, already putting on her shoes. "Damian's home and can stay with Brianna. I'll be there in less than thirty minutes."

Natalie hung up the phone and relief flooded through her. Sitting alone in her house, she'd been thinking things out on her own, and it was getting her nowhere. Her mother had been the one she wanted to reach out to, but that conversation had abruptly ended. With no one to talk to, the walls were closing in. Until Christine called, she didn't realize how desperate she was for someone to help her through this.

True to her word, Christine stood at the door in a pair of black sweatpants and a light jacket in less than half an hour. When Christine opened her arms, Natalie stepped into them. "Girl, what is going on with you? I've never seen you like this."

Settling into the living room, Natalie rehashed the last several days of her life, from the moment Derrick had presented her with his final divorce papers to when he had walked out of her house without a word.

Her voice cracked and she didn't bother wiping the tears that fell across her cheeks. The hard, confident exterior that had become such a part of Natalie's persona completely crumbled. This woman wasn't the confident, smart-mouthed, know-it-all who blazed her own trail to a successful life. This woman was unsure, uncertain, and insecure. The man she had counted on to be a part of her life might very well have said his last words to her.

Christine listened as her sister relived the past couple of days of her life, and her heart went out to her. It was evident that Natalie was deeply hurt and confused about the turn her relationship with Derrick had taken. When she told Natalie of their last phone conversation, she couldn't believe that he had been so cold and unfeeling.

On all of the occasions that she had been with Derrick, all of his actions, as well as his words, showed that he was fully committed to Natalie. He treated her like a queen and respected her for who she was and what she had accomplished. It was difficult to reconcile that man to the man whom Natalie was speaking of today. Rude? Unwilling to talk? Hanging up on her? That just didn't make sense. "Have you tried contacting him again? It sounds like you guys need to talk."

Natalie didn't want to chance having another blowup with him. "I don't know if I can handle another conversation with him where we end up arguing. The last time we talked, he hung up on me. I'm not interested in reliving that scenario."

Christine had listened to the saga play out over the last

several weeks, and there was one theme that was the common thread. Derrick was trying to talk to Natalie about something that she had no intention of discussing. If she could get Natalie to see that, maybe that would be the catalyst to get the two of them talking again. "Maybe that's because you're not having the *right* conversation with him."

Natalie reached for a tissue and wiped the remaining tears. Not answering right away, she wanted to make sure that she had heard Christine correctly, because she didn't like the way her response put the onus on her. "That sounds a lot like you're blaming me—making this all my fault."

The defensive tone didn't come as a surprise to Christine. If she wanted to have a conversation with Natalie that would make her see things from Derrick's point of view, there was going to be resistance. She wasn't here to upset Natalie more, but she was here to help her figure out if there was something she could do to help her current situation with Derrick. "I don't think we should be worried about placing blame or finding fault, we should focus on the resolution—getting you and Derrick back where you belong—together."

The words sounded good, but Natalie wasn't so sure that Derrick would see it that way. "You didn't see his eyes when he left my house. They were cold, distant, unfeeling. And when I tried to talk to him at his office, his voice was the same way. It was as if he's already put me out of his mind . . . and his heart. At this point, he may not be interested in getting back together."

Christine thought about her next words carefully. Of all the ups and downs Natalie and Derrick had been through the past couple of weeks, it was all because of one thing.

It was time Natalie dealt with it. "Why don't you answer his question?"

Natalie got up and tossed her tissue in the small trash can in the corner of the room. Without answering she headed to the kitchen. "Do you want something to drink?"

Avoidance had never been an issue with Natalie. She was straightforward, to the point, and didn't have time for those who didn't have their act together. That's why Christine was shocked at how she was handling this situation. Following her, she watched Natalie get a glass of water. "You don't want to marry him, do you?"

Natalie, frustrated, raised her voice. "Why does everyone keep asking me that? As if that one question holds the key to whether me and Derrick can be together."

"If you and Derrick are apart because of this . . . it obviously is the one question that holds you two together."

Natalie thought about her words and suddenly realized that they were true. But that didn't change anything. "It's not that simple."

Christine disagreed and told her so. "Actually, Natalie, it is. For some reason, you're making this complicated. The question you need to answer is Why?"

Sitting at the table, Natalie said, "It's just like I told him. He's not ready. He can't be ready."

"How can you be so sure? What has he done or said to make you believe that?" Christine asked. "Because from everything I've seen and from what you've told me, he hasn't hinted at that at all."

"He doesn't have to say or do anything," Natalie reasoned. "The evidence is right in front of him."

"Then please tell me, because I don't see it and it's clear that he doesn't either."

"Derrick just got out of a marriage. Anybody would

need time to adjust. Would you jump into another marriage?"

"We're not talking about me," Christine reminded her.

"I'm just answering your question."

"OK," Christine said, taking a seat opposite her. "For the sake of argument, let's assume that you're right about Derrick. He's emotionally not ready for the next step in your relationship. That only explains why Derrick shouldn't get married. Let's talk about why *you* won't get married. Are *you* ready?"

"Why does everyone keep putting it all on me?" Natalie was tiring of having this same discussion over and over again—same words, different people. "I'm just asking Derrick to evaluate where he is and what he wants in life before making a commitment. How could I be considered wrong for that?"

"No one's faulting you for your feelings, Natalie," Christine said softly. "Whatever is going on inside you, I respect that. I just want to understand where they are coming from."

Natalie smiled at the acknowledgment. It was the first time in all of this that someone actually gave her credit for feeling the way she did and not discounting it. "Men have such a hard time sticking with their relationship commitments. I should be commended for allowing him to take this time to be sure that marriage is really what he wants."

"Men have a hard time with commitment?" Christine repeated. "That doesn't sound like Natalie talking—that sounds like Margaret."

Natalie raised her hand to stop Christine. "Please, don't even say the name. On top of everything that I've been dealing with, I talked to my mother today and she has apparently lost her mind."

Christine hesitated. Was this another ploy to change the subject? "What are you talking about?"

Sitting forward, Natalie leaned in as if she was about to share a juicy piece of gossip. "You won't believe it."

"What?" Christine said, curiosity getting the best of her. What could have Natalie sitting on the edge of her seat?

"I called her this morning to talk about Derrick."

"Whoa, hold up," Christine said. "You called the queen of don't-fall-in-love to talk about Derrick? What got into you?"

"I don't really know," Natalie said. "Derrick had just hung up on me and I was feeling so hurt and angry, I didn't know where to turn. Then my mom's face just popped into my head. I can't explain it. I just had an overwhelming desire to talk to her."

The thought that Natalie would call her mother to talk about something so personal caught Christine completely off guard. In all the time that she had known Natalie, she had barely tolerated a relationship with her mother, but since she had moved to Florida, they had seemed to be getting along better. To call her about Derrick was a big step for Natalie. Having lost her mother a couple of years ago to cancer, Christine constantly prayed that Natalie and Margaret would find a way to have a strong mother/daughter relationship. Hopefully this was a step in the right direction. "What did she say when you told her about Derrick?"

"That's just it. I never got to Derrick."

"Why?"

"Are you ready for this?" Natalie said. "A man answered the phone—not a repairman, not the cable man, not a deliveryman—a *man*!"

"Oohh," Christine said with a wide grin. This *was* juicy. "Your mama's getting her groove on!"

Shivers ran through Natalie's body at the thought. Unable to sit still, she stood and paced the room. "Do you know she had the nerve to be 'jumping out of the shower' when I called?"

"Sounds like you were interrupting a little somethin' somethin'," Christine said, finding the entire situation funny.

"Ugh!" Natalie exclaimed, getting a visualization. "Please don't say that. My heart can't take it."

"What did she say? Who is this guy?"

"That's just it," Natalie said. "She didn't say anything. All I know is that his name is Samuel and he's been spending the night at my mother's house."

"That's it? You didn't get any more info out of her?" Christine found it hard to believe that Natalie didn't give her mother the third degree.

"How could I? She hung up on me because he was tickling her!"

Christine broke out in laughter at Margaret hanging up on her daughter. When she saw that Natalie was not laughing along, she calmed down. "Oh, come on, Nat. Lighten up."

"This isn't funny."

"Oh, yes, it is. Your mother? Dating? I don't know if I've ever seen your mom with a man," Christine said, thinking back over the past couple of years.

"Exactly my point," Natalie said, finally sitting back down. Her mother had never dated anyone for any length of time. After her pining for Henry year after year, the sour taste left in her mouth from that caused her to mistrust the opposite sex, making them almost nonexistent. That was why they both thought this move to Florida would be good for Margaret. She'd make a fresh start—but Natalie hadn't thought she'd be doing it with a man.

No longer consumed with being a single parent, working two jobs to make ends meet, or all the negative experiences that happened in her life, Margaret finally allowed herself to let go of the past and enjoy the rest of her life.

Natalie had taken a week off and accompanied her mother on the drive to Florida, helping her make the transition. The active adult community was perfect for her. Once Margaret moved in, Natalie worried that she wouldn't be happy living so far away from her family, her friends, and her daughter, but her mother was determined to take advantage of her opportunities. Based on the phone calls and the couple of times Natalie has gone to visit, that's exactly what she had done.

Meeting several women within her first few weeks, she always had something to do and someone to do it with. Shopping at the outlets, enjoying all the sites that St. Augustine had to offer, she had even signed up for a Spanish class. She was happier than Natalie had ever known her to be, and Natalie took comfort that her mother had found a way to find fulfillment. And this new lifestyle of fulfillment was supposed to be enjoyed with friends like Julia, Emily, and JoAnn—not a guy named Samuel.

"I think it's great your mom is seeing someone. This could be exactly what she needs. It could be good for her," Christine said. "She's still young and it would be nice to have someone to share her life with."

"How can you say that?" Natalie asked. "What does my mother know about dealing with men? Her experience in that area is so limited. Who knows what kind of guy this Samuel is? He could be a leech, hooking his life-sucking tendrils into my mother."

Christine couldn't hold back her laughter. "You sound ridiculous. I'm sure your mother is quite capable of taking care of herself."

"Yeah, right," Natalie said, wondering what kind of game Samuel was running on her unsuspecting mother. "She hasn't dated in twenty years. She's ripe for being taken advantage of by any smooth-talking, feet-tickling parasite."

"*Natalie,*" Christine said, amazed at how she was carrying on about this. Typically, Natalie would be complaining about how much her mother depended on her. Glad that she made friends so quickly once she moved, Natalie had encouraged Margaret to foster those friendships. Now that Margaret had a male friend, Natalie was off balance. "You're overreacting."

"She hung up on me," Natalie said, as if that would show that she had the right to rant and rave. "This is a woman who calls me three times a day, tracks me down wherever I am, fusses at me if I go more than two days without calling."

"If I had a man who was tickling me when I jumped out of the shower, I'd hang up on you, too."

"You can defend this all you want, Christine," Natalie said, still thinking of what this Samuel guy wanted from her mother. "Something's not right, and I plan to find out exactly what's going on."

Thursday morning, Natalie stood in the middle of her closet in a silk robe and fuzzy slippers. Sleep had been at a premium this week, with her having spent most of her nights tossing and turning. Functioning on less than four hours of sleep over the last several days was starting to take its toll. Dark circles and bags hung under her eyes. Her long hair, usually nice and neat in a bun or ponytail, hung loosely and wildly.

Flipping through the suits that lined the walls, she tried to decide which one to wear today. All shades, colors, and styles, and none of them appealed to her. On the opposite wall were stacked professional-looking shoes in varying heel heights and designs. The task of getting dressed this morning seemed daunting and Natalie wondered if she would be able to muster the energy.

When the rest of the week passed with no word from Derrick, Natalie started to face reality. If she didn't do something, this could be the end of their relationship. Just the thought of not having Derrick in her life caused such overwhelming grief that she leaned against the wall for support and strength.

She had tried to keep a brave front at work—smiling and nodding at all the right times, joining everyone in the conference room for a birthday celebration for John, one of her accountants. But it was hard and she struggled to get through every day.

Jea didn't have to guess what was wrong with her. Derrick hadn't been around and he hadn't called. Jea offered to rearrange her schedule if she wanted to take some time off, but Natalie declined. She was determined to be a trooper. But the more days that passed, the harder it became. Jumping each time the phone rang, constantly listening for the door, going back and forth a hundred times about whether to call him again was driving her insane.

Reaching for her taupe pantsuit with the black trim, she stared at it for several minutes and thought about what she'd have to endure if she went back into the world today. She decided she didn't have the energy. Hanging the suit back on the rack, she slammed the door to her closet on the way out.

Walking back into her bedroom, she kicked her slippers to the side and crawled back under the covers. Dialing her office on the cordless phone, she got Jea's voice mail. "Hi. I'm calling to let you know I'm not feeling well today so I'm taking the day off."

Natalie paused before she continued. "And tomorrow, too. I have three appointments scheduled for today and I think two for tomorrow. Please have John cover for me. Call me if you need me."

Pushing the End button, she pulled the covers to her neck and curled her body into the fetal position. It never entered her mind that by her not answering his question, Derrick would no longer want be a part of her life. But here she was—trying to make it through the days—and the nights—without him.

Christine and Tanya had come by Tuesday to convince her to hit the mall with them, but they ended up leaving without her. Danielle called last night, offering dinner. Natalie said no. Making it to work and being halfway productive had become a challenge. How could she possibly enjoy social events?

Natalie turned over when she heard the phone ring. When the number popped up, she didn't think twice. "Derrick?"

"I'm at Carla's this morning and you're not."

Just hearing his voice caused an automatic smile to appear. "I'm not going to the office today."

"I don't have any patients until this afternoon," Derrick said. "I'm less than twenty minutes from you. Can I come by?"

Natalie glanced down at her wrinkled pajamas and

thought about her hair and face. She would need at least a half hour just to make herself presentable. She hadn't showered or brushed her teeth. "I'm not really dressed."

"This won't take long," Derrick said.

Not sure if she liked the sound of that, she agreed. Once she hung up, she jumped out of bed and ran to the bathroom. After a three-minute shower, she brushed her teeth and ran some cleansing cream over her face. Darting into the closet, she found a pair of jeans and a black pullover with a square collar. Brushing her hair, she clipped it back, leaving a few tendrils to frame her face. Spraying on her favorite daytime perfume, she headed downstairs just as the doorbell rang.

The moment she opened the door, her eyes drank in his amazing looks. Casual, his dark slacks and dress shirt fit his athletic build to a tee. Unable to stop herself, she stepped to him and placed her lips on his. Wrapping her arms around his neck, she reveled in once again connecting her flesh to his. When his arms didn't embrace her, Natalie stiffened. Slowly lowering her arms, she broke contact with him and took a tentative step back.

"Thanks for seeing me on such short notice," he said, stepping inside.

Natalie didn't like the tone of his voice. For having such a personal relationship, he sounded formal and distant. Suddenly, nervous butterflies swarmed in her stomach and she got the sinking feeling in its pit that he didn't come with good news. "You want something to drink—coffee?"

"No, thanks," he said, walking past her. "Can we talk in the living room?"

Taking a seat on the sofa, Natalie felt her heart dropping when he sat in the chair on the opposite side of the coffee table. For all the time they'd spent in this room, they'd always shared the sofa. His quiet demeanor concerned her and she braced herself for whatever he was about to say.

Taking a deep breath, Derrick prepared to recite the speech that he'd rehearsed on the way over. A speech that almost went out the window when she opened the door. The only thing he could think about was how much he missed her and how beautiful she looked. The jeans were hugging her just right, and with her hair pulled back and no makeup, she looked innocent.

When she stepped into his arms, he almost melted and called on every ounce of self-control to keep from taking her right there on the floor. But that would have put them back at square one. He refused to do that. This visit was about moving forward. "When I left here last weekend, I had no intention of coming back unless you asked me to."

"I tried to call you and—"

"I know," Derrick interrupted. "I want to apologize for being so abrupt with you. I wasn't ready to talk. I needed time to think."

"And now that you've had time to think?"

Derrick stood and walked to the fireplace. The mantel was filled with pictures that chronicled their time together—the two of them in New York in front of the Statue of Liberty, a picture taken on the boardwalk in Ocean City. He turned away from it; his emotions couldn't handle it. "Natalie, the moment I met you, my world became brighter. Your wit, your style, your independence. I was hooked from the moment I met you. I've never known anyone who cares so much about other people. You impressed me with your brains and overwhelmed me with your sexy body. You took my broken, wounded, and injured soul and nursed it back to health. I was determined never to love completely again, but you left me no choice. I couldn't stop myself from loving you. You are all that I want, all that I need, and all that I could ever desire."

"I hear a 'but' coming," Natalie said, nervously twisting her hands together.

"But," Derrick said, sitting back down, "I've decided to face the truth. Just as I wasn't enough for Charlene, I'm not enough for you."

"Derrick, you don't—"

Refusing to let her finish her words, Derrick continued to talk over her. "It's OK, really. If I learned anything from my catastrophic relationship with Charlene, it was that it wasn't me—it was her. And so it is with you. We are where we are because this is where you've put us. I've given all I have to give. And for whatever reason, it's not what you need. So—"

"Wait, Derrick, you have to let me say something," Natalie said, fearing what his next words were going to be.

Derrick sat back and gave her the floor.

"I have never loved any man before you came into my life. In my past relationships, I always held something back. I couldn't give myself completely. The day you walked into my office, everything changed. You broke down every barrier, every stone, and every obstacle that was held firmly around my heart." Feeling her emotions take over, she paused. This wasn't the time for tears. "I love you, Derrick."

"If I was all of that to you, why are you going to let me go?" he asked her, wondering if she fully understood where they were headed. "That's what this is about, Natalie. I can't stay in this relationship. There were signs with Charlene, and I ignored them. I'm not going to make that same mistake twice. I deserve to get what I'm giving."

The words were like a brick wall crashing down on top of her. She began to fight her lungs just to breathe. "You can let us go that easily? Just like that?"

"I didn't say anything about this being easy."

"Can't we talk about this?" Natalie said, unable to hold back the few tears that fell down her cheek. "Work this out?"

Derrick fought the powerful urge to go to her and tell her everything was going to be all right. But that was what he had done with Charlene. "You know what I want out of this relationship. I've made that perfectly clear. You're cheating me, Natalie. You just told me that I freed your heart, yet you're still holding back."

"Do you really think you're ready for what you're asking for?"

He had decided before he came that he wouldn't have the same argument again. "The question is not whether I'm ready, the question is, if I mean to you what you say I do, why aren't you ready?"

"I love you, Derrick."

This time, Derrick couldn't stay in his seat. He went and sat beside her, holding her hand in his. "I know you do, Natalie. But I want more than your love—I want every morning and every night, sunrises and sunsets. I want breakfast each day and midnight snacks. I want kids, grandkids, and retirement checks. I want all of you."

Natalie felt the tears warm the corner of her eyes. The world he planned for them was everything she wanted—with him. Her heart screamed for her to say yes, but her mouth couldn't form the word. "I need more time, Derrick."

Derrick let go of her hand and stood. Walking back over to the chair, he picked up his jacket and put it on. "You're right, Natalie, you do. I'm going to give it to you.

I've gotten down on my knees, professed my love to you, and offered you all of me. You've made it abundantly clear each time where you stood. I won't put myself in that position again."

She watched his back as he walked down the hall toward the door. Natalie wanted to run after him, but her feet wouldn't move. *Stop him! Don't let him walk out that door!*

The front door shut and the house fell silent. Replaying the entire conversation in her head, she realized there was no other way to interpret it—he'd just broken up with her and her heart began to crumble.

Making her way back upstairs, she crawled into bed fully clothed. The tears flowed so freely, she didn't bother to wipe them. After a couple of hours, she was finally cried out. Sniffling, she couldn't stand being alone in this place any longer. Picking up the phone, she dialed the number already programmed in it.

Chapter 11

Will sat in Derrick's office after the last patient had gone home, watching him barely hold it together. Will knew that Derrick had gone to see Natalie but hadn't found out what the outcome had been. Judging from Derrick's looks, Will knew it didn't go too well.

Will had only known Derrick to be with two women—Charlene and Natalie. And it looked as though both of them would end up breaking his heart. Charlene had been the world to Derrick and he had done everything in his power to make her happy. Whatever Charlene wanted, she got. Movers and shakers on the social and professional scene, they made a stunning couple. Charlene always made sure she had the latest fashions, the best stylists, and she had turned their seven-thousand-square-foot home into a master showplace. Looking back, Derrick seemed to have been just another accessory for Charlene.

Natalie had been the complete opposite. Beautiful, smart, and talented in her own right, she wasn't pretentious or caught up in appearances to the outside world. She ran a successful business, had a magnificent home, and had a closet full of designer clothes. But those things didn't define her—nor did things define her relationship with Derrick.

The times that Will had been around Charlene and Derrick, they always seemed "on." That was the atmosphere that Charlene thrived in, but Derrick never seemed comfortable in that role. With Natalie, everything came naturally. He hadn't seen Derrick that relaxed and happy in years. But the man sitting in front of him today was far from that. With his tight jaw, darkened eyes, and overall foul mood, the last thing anyone would think about Derrick Carrington was that he was relaxed or happy. "You want to tell me what happened?"

Derrick set a stack of patient files to the side to be returned to the front desk. Folding his hands on the desk, he simply said, "It's over."

"You say that as if you're not bothered by that."

"What should I do?" Derrick said, thinking of all he'd already done. All week he'd come to work, making it through the day on autopilot. Not wanting to go home only to sit and think about her, he hit the gym—hard. He worked every muscle in his body until he couldn't take it anymore. Once he got home, he zoned out with television, hoping that the gut-wrenching pain he was feeling would subside. "Do you want me to yell? Scream? Hit the wall?"

"I don't care what you do, but you can't tell me this is how you're gonna let this story end. You've got to find a way to get you two back together."

Derrick stood, took off his white coat, and hung it on the hook behind him. "Forget it. I've done all I can. She's made her feelings crystal clear."

Will thought back to all their conversations about Natalie

and couldn't recall one time they had talked about her crystal-clear feelings. "Which are?"

Derrick hated to say the words, but if doing so would shut Will up, he'd say them. "She doesn't want to marry me."

"Funny," Will said, staring toward the ceiling in thought. "I never heard her say that—and I would bet money that you haven't heard her say those words either."

Derrick shook his head with a half grin. "You're playing word games, Will."

"It's not a game, it's the truth."

"Whatever you want to call it, it all leads to the same place. We want different things."

"What do you want?" Will asked.

"I want it all," Derrick said. "No offense, man, but I've watched you go through women like nothing. It seems like each month it's somebody new. I thought I'd have to do the same thing after Charlene to find someone who I could love and build a life with. The idea of that scared the hell out of me. But I came back to D.C., walked into BSI, and there she was."

Will felt slightly uncomfortable at Derrick's assessment of his personal life. It was true. He did date quite a few women. Not because he was trying to find Mrs. Right, but because he wasn't interested in finding her. He enjoyed the dating scene and avoided the relationship trap. A psychologist would probably say he was afraid of commitment from some deep, childhood trauma, but that would be a gross misdiagnosis. His parents had been married for almost forty years, his younger brother had been happily married for the past two years, and his baby sister was engaged. Strong couple commitments were all around him.

He just preferred to keep things simple. Will didn't have

commitment problems because he didn't make commitments. It was a powerful strategy that had worked quite well for him. It was the only way he could see living his life. Long-term commitments weren't his style, but they were definitely Derrick's, which added to the confusion of the way he was treating Natalie. "What does she want?"

"I have no idea," Derrick said.

"How can you walk away without finding out?"

"It's not for lack of trying that I don't know," Derrick said, reliving some of the frustration he'd experienced with Natalie. "I swear, man, I've asked that woman a hundred times in a hundred different ways what she wants. If she knows, she's not telling and, frankly, I'm tired of playing the guessing game."

"Maybe this isn't about you," Will said. "Maybe you've just been looking at this all wrong."

"Who else would it be about?"

Will had joined Natalie and Derrick on many occasions, and there was no denying their affection for each other. "I've seen the two of you together. That woman adores you. I find it hard to believe that she doesn't want the same things you want and that you two can't find a way to be together."

"Yeah, well," Derrick said, "there is a way."

"So that's it," Will said, trying to make Derrick see the finality of his actions. "You're never going to see or talk to her again."

Derrick refused to think about "never." The only thing he could do was take it one day at a time. "Will, this has been the hardest week of my life. I told the woman I love that I couldn't see her anymore."

"Have you ever considered that maybe she has some

other hang-up about marriage? Maybe she's been hurt before."

Derrick had thought about that but didn't believe that was the case. "I've shared my deepest feelings with her. We've become closer than I could ever imagine two people becoming. How could she think I would hurt her?"

"Did you think Charlene would hurt you?"

Derrick paused at the question. If anyone had told him one day before he caught Charlene and Scott together that his wife was cheating on him, he would have laughed in their face. The good times they shared, the plans they were making for a future, and all they had invested in each other, there would have been no way his wife was stepping out on him.

Will could tell that his question touched a nerve. "Maybe you should give Natalie the benefit of the doubt."

Derrick didn't look convinced.

Will offered another approach. "What about her independence?"

"What about it?"

"Didn't you say she was the most controlling, independent person you know?"

Derrick's laugh was genuine and it felt good after such a hard week. Thinking of all the battles over who would pay, who would choose the movie, and who would pick the restaurant. It drove him crazy—and he missed it. "And?"

"She's been on her own for a long time," Will said. "You told me she was raised by a single mother, no father figure in her life. She's a business owner, a home owner, and she's been keeping the oil changed and the tires rotated ever since she got her driver's license. That's a long time to be flying solo. Maybe she doesn't know how to relinquish some control, to compromise, to give and take."

"Or she could not want to get married. Or she could not love me as much as she says she does," Derrick said. "We could sit here all night and try to figure out what is going on in that pretty little head of hers, but I'm just not going to do it. I'm exhausted by that exercise."

The conversation was going nowhere and Will didn't know what else to say to help bring Derrick around. "You think she'll contact you?"

The weekend his divorce became final flashed in his mind. The bedroom, the kitchen table, the sunroom floor, and the shower. The connection between them existed on every level. His heart and mind, along with his body, were given wholly to her. Never had he been privileged to have someone give everything she had. It was the moment in their courtship that he believed she had completely given all of her to him. But now he just wasn't so sure. "I hope so."

"Sorry for the interruption. I came to get those files."

Both men turned to the door as Suzanne walked in.

Glancing from one man to the other, she could tell that something serious was being discussed. At times, the office could become melancholy when one of their patients got bad news about a health problem, but those situations were usually known by the entire staff. This didn't appear to be patient-related.

Derrick had been uncharacteristically quiet the past couple of days, and she wasn't the only one who noticed. Both nurses on duty and the receptionist asked if everything was OK. Suzanne also noticed that Derrick had been arriving at the office earlier than usual, which meant he wasn't meeting Natalie for breakfast as he usually did. When she did a quick check with the receptionist, she confirmed that Natalie hadn't called in several days. If she added all those things together, it could only mean one thing—the relationship of Dr. Derrick Carrington and Natalie Donovan was officially over.

That bit of deduction caused Suzanne to smile slightly. "I wanted to get these filed before I went home."

"Thanks, Suzanne," Derrick said.

Walking around his desk, she picked up the files and curved her lips upward. Just inches from him, she wanted to reach out and touch his shoulder, his arm, any part of him. But now was not the time or the place. Dr. Proctor was just a few feet away and when Suzanne made her move, she wanted to position herself so that it would be next to impossible for Derrick to turn her down. Patience and timing were the name of this game. If she played it just right, she and Derrick would soon be a couple.

"You better watch that woman," Will said after Suzanne shut the door behind her.

"Suzanne?" Derrick said. "She's harmless."

"Oh, please," Will said, not hiding his surprise. "Are you trying to tell me that you don't know she wants you?"

"I'm not trying to tell you anything," Derrick said, remembering her offer a couple of weeks ago. "She made a move, I turned her down. End of story."

"Yeah, right," Will said, "everyone in this office knows she has it bad for you."

"I think you've been working too hard. "

"You better hope she doesn't find out that you and Natalie are having challenges. She's going to be all over you."

Derrick picked up his keys to head home. "I'm sure you have better things to do than focus on my life. I'm sure you have a date tonight."

Will checked his watch and nodded. "Yes, but I have plenty of time before I have to meet her."

"Meet her?" Derrick said mockingly. "You're not going to do the gentlemanly thing and pick her up?"

"Since when have you known me to be a gentleman?"

Derrick looked to be in deep thought before smiling. "You're right, Mr. Love 'Em and Leave 'Em, I've never known you to be a gentleman."

"It's not such a bad way to live," Will said. "Not every man can find his soul mate."

"Look at you, you don't even have the decency to be ashamed of how you treat your women."

"What is there to be ashamed of? I'm just interested in enjoying the company of a woman without having to worry about a relationship." His words were spoken with complete honesty.

"There's nothing wrong with having a girlfriend for more than a couple of months," Derrick countered, thinking that Will must have dated at least fifteen different women last year, including his self-declared courtship with Connie Anderson.

"Are you serious?" Will asked incredulously. "Look at where having a girlfriend for more than a couple of months got you."

Thinking of his current situation with Natalie, he had to admit that Will had a valid point. "Still, don't you miss having someone to talk to on a deeper level, to have someone you can depend on?"

"Nope."

Derrick smiled at his answer. Will had been this way ever since they met. Medical school didn't allow him too much time for long term-relationships, so he didn't even try to develop them. Once he graduated and started his private practice, that pattern of dating continued. The amazing thing was that Will managed to find women who didn't try to change him. They seemed to go along with his philosophy of short-term affairs with no strings attached. "So who's the lucky woman this month?"

"Brooke Tyler."

"That's a new one," Derrick said, waving good night to Suzanne as they walked through the lobby and out the front door.

"Just met her two weeks ago at a fund-raiser for Trinity Hospital."

"Vitals?"

"Five feet seven, skin as smooth as a baby's bottom, and a body that makes me scream."

"Well, I would tell you to have a good time, but I already know you will."

Will thought about all his friend had been through the last couple of days. Even though he'd put up a brave front at work, going home alone had to be the worst part. Suddenly, being with Brooke wasn't that important. "Actually, if you want, I can cancel and we can go grab a beer or something."

Derrick paused and stared at his friend. It was an offer that he'd never heard Will make. His rule was never to give up a night with a woman for a night with the guys. "If that's a pity offer, forget it."

"Not pity," Will said. "It's just that if you want to talk some more, I'm here for you."

"I appreciate the offer, man, but don't worry about me. I'll be OK."

Having reached his car, Will clicked the button on his

key chain and his Jaguar doors unlocked. "You can always give Natalie a call. Try to work things out."

Tossing his briefcase in the backseat of his SUV, Derrick didn't have to contemplate that advice. "I don't think so. Not right now. Have a good time tonight."

Christine sat on the edge of the bed watching her sister fall apart. With her swollen eyes and melancholy expression, Natalie was experiencing pain like never before. But the wound was self-inflicted. "You just let him walk out of your life?"

There was no mistaking where Christine stood on this subject. Propping herself up on a stack of pillows, Natalie clarified the situation. "I didn't *let* him do anything. He came here with his mind made up."

"That's not what it sounded like to me," Christine said. Seeing the exasperated look on Natalie's face, Christine continued. "If you called me to have a pity party, you called the wrong person."

Natalie balked at her words. "He told me that he didn't want to go on this way. He wanted out."

"That's not what I heard," she said, reminding Natalie of the conversation. "I heard a man come to tell you how much he loves you, cares for you, and wants you to be a part of his life. He only walked out when you didn't return his feelings."

"That's just it, Christine," Natalie said. "I did return his feelings. He had me. I was his. I've never loved any man as much as I love him. He took that love and walked away from it."

Christine put her hand on Natalie's forehead. "Girl, are

you delirious? What is going on in that brain of yours? You can't seriously believe that."

Natalie slapped her hand away. "It's true. I watched him walk out that door and away from what we had."

Christine shook her head in complete disagreement. "You are trippin'. That man asked you to marry him, Natalie—several times. Each time, you tossed his question aside."

"He was already married," she said, raising her voice.

"*Was*, Natalie," Christine said. "That man gave up God knows what in his settlement—for you!"

Natalie remained silent.

Taking her voice down a notch, Christine reached out to her. "Take a minute and be honest with yourself. What are you afraid of?"

"Me? I'm not afraid," Natalie answered. "I just want Derrick to be sure about what he really wants. Love and marriage are two different things. If anyone should know that, it should be him. His ex-wife treated him so badly. Do you honestly think he could be ready for another marriage?"

"I didn't know you could be this stubborn, this hard-headed, and this stupid. How many times do I have to tell you that this isn't about Derrick and whether he's ready or not? This is about you. Natalie Lynette Donovan, answer the question—are *you* ready for marriage?"

When Natalie didn't respond, Christine continued. "You want to know what I think?"

"No, I don't," Natalie said. And she meant it. The way this conversation was going, Christine was going to tell her that this whole thing was her fault. That the reason she and Derrick were not together was that she couldn't seem to get it right.

"You are so strong, so independent. That's how Margaret raised you." Softening her expression, Christine continued. "You're smart, you're confident in your profession, and you created a life that any woman could be proud of."

Natalie basked in the compliment. "Thank you, Christine. I really needed to hear that. To remind me that I've done well."

"What you've done," Christine said, "is made yourself one-dimensional."

Natalie paused at the description she used. "What does that mean?"

"It means you always have to be the one in control, the person in charge. You got that role down pat. It's the other roles that you seem to have dismissed. Where's you ability to lean on someone? Where's your vulnerability? When do you let someone all the way in?"

"I've let Derrick in."

"Have you, really?" Christine said. "That man has opened up his soul to you and laid it all on the line. Have you done the same—or are you vacillating back and forth—one day giving him your all, the next day holding back? Derrick is asking you to lean on him a little more—not because you're weak, but because you can."

Natalie thought about her words. "I'm no more independent than you or Tanya or Danielle."

"Oh, yes, you are," Christine said with a chuckle. "And you're stubborn, too. We all had our challenges to overcome before we could commit to our men. I was dealing with the death of my mother and Henry's betrayal, Tanya was dealing with a crazy ex-boyfriend, and Danielle was dealing with her own ambition. But that didn't take us away from our men—it drew us closer to them."

"I hear you, but—"

"We also don't refuse to consider the opinions of

others—like you are right now," Christine said, grinning from ear to ear.

The joke broke the tension and Natalie couldn't believe she actually smiled after all that she had been through today.

"So now what?" Christine asked. "If this relationship is going to be saved, it has to come from you."

Truer words had never been said, but Natalie didn't have an answer. "I don't know, Christine. I don't know."

Standing, Christine picked up her purse. "I give up. You're hopeless."

"What?"

"You know what, Natalie. You know what you have to do. You just don't want to have to deal with it."

"Derrick . . ."

Christine shook her head from side to side. "I'm not talking about Derrick. I'm talking about that messed-up junk about marriage that your mother filled your head with."

"My mother?" Natalie said, completely thrown by the change in subject. "What are you talking about?"

"I'm talking about the fact that your mother raised you with the fear of hell if you fully gave yourself to a man. If she filled you up with that, maybe, now that she's found a man, she can help you get over it."

Giving her sister a hug, Christine headed for the bedroom door. "I'll let myself out and call you tomorrow. Promise me you'll think about what I said?"

"I promise," Natalie said.

After Christine left, Natalie found the energy to fix herself something to eat, then crawled back into bed. At almost nine o'clock, she didn't want to watch television and there wasn't one book in the pile beside her that she wanted to pick up. Eyeing the phone, she thought about calling Derrick. There had to be a way she could explain her point of view.

Hesitating, she thought about the conversation she had tried to have with her mother. Maybe if she talked to her mom first, she'd be able to face Derrick.

Margaret and Natalie had never nurtured the close mother/daughter relationship that most young women experienced. That especially held true when it came to the boys and men Natalie dated over the years. From her first crush in the fourth grade to her first boyfriend in the tenth to her college relationship that lasted almost three years to Derrick, there were few details that she had shared with her mother.

It was a conscious decision on Natalie's part because, no matter what, the conversations would always end up the same way. Whenever Natalie wanted to talk about her developing feelings about a man or broached the subject of becoming serious or falling in love, her mother would warn her about putting too much trust in a man. The message that Margaret was sending was that it was OK to date, spend time with, and even have feelings for a man, but never give herself completely over. If she did, the results would leave her hurt and alone. The funny thing about it was that she was now hurt and alone.

Natalie thought of Derrick. Early on, she knew he was different from all the rest. He had a certain way of making her feel that caused her to be a better person when she was with him. Once he waltzed into her life, she couldn't get him out of her head. He made constant appearances in her mind at the craziest times—in a meeting, giving a presentation, or hanging out with her friends.

When things began heating up between her and Derrick, she debated sharing their budding relationship with her mother. But one phone call from her mother helped her make her mind up early in their dating. Sharing anything about Derrick with her mother was out of the question.

Last year, with the city blanketed in snow, her mom had called from Florida to check on her and tease her about the great weather she was having.

"I'm glad you're enjoying the sun. Meanwhile, I'm buried under almost a foot of snow."

"I'm sure you'll be fine, Natalie. You're a trooper. Always have been. Always will be." The pride in Margaret's voice could be heard loud and clear. "I always knew you would do something with your life. I may have made the mistake of putting my trust in a man who claimed to love me, but, thank God, you didn't make the same mistake."

Natalie remained quiet, waiting for the words that always followed a statement like that. Margaret took full advantage of any conversation that lent itself to reminding Natalie about letting a man get her off track.

"You have a great job with your nonprofit organization, and you did it all without the help of anyone from the male species. Trust your mother on this, baby, you'll always be better off without a man."

What a strange turn of events. The same woman who had spoken those words a year ago was now involved with a man who had her laughing, giggling, and sharing her home and bed.

Maybe this would be a good time to call her mom and talk to her about Derrick. The phone rang several times before someone finally answered.

"Hello."

Natalie breathed a sigh of relief that Samuel hadn't answered the phone. She didn't like the idea of him hanging around her mother so much. "Mom, it's me."

"Oh, hi, sweetie," Margaret said.

"I'm calling because—"

"One second."

Natalie held the phone while her mother set hers down. She couldn't make out the conversation, but she definitely heard a man's voice. Natalie was hoping that her mother was in the process of saying good-bye.

"Look, honey, I can't talk right now, Samuel and I are headed out. He says he has a surprise for me."

The disappointment was immediate. "Mom, please. I was hoping we could talk."

"Don't have time right now. I'll call you later."

Before Natalie could get another word out, her mother was gone. "I don't believe this!" Not replacing the receiver, she dialed again—within minutes everything was taken care of.

Derrick crawled into bed, exhausted. He'd stopped by the gym on the way home and practically run a marathon on the treadmill. By the time he hit the weights, his body was about to give out on him. That suited him just fine. When he got home he wanted to be able to sleep and not think about Natalie.

But his plan wasn't working. His body was fighting for rest, but his mind was in overdrive thinking about her. Maybe Will was right. Maybe there was something more to her reluctance to marry. Should he have given up so quickly? Was she afraid of being hurt? Too independent?

Checking his watch on the nightstand, he saw it was almost midnight. Picking up the phone, he listened to the dial tone until a woman's voice came on asking him to make a call. He set the phone back down.

What more could he say? He had practically begged her to open up to him, to share with him why she hesitated to answer his proposal. He had nothing else to say. Turning over, he prayed for the impossible—a decent night's sleep.

Chapter 12

The line for a rental car was snaked around the ropes and Natalie impatiently checked her watch. Her plane had landed almost two hours ago, and she had yet to leave the airport. After waiting almost twenty minutes for her bags to come around the carousel, she got to the rental car area where she'd been standing ever since.

She had chosen an 8:00 a.m. flight because she wanted to arrive in time to have lunch with her mother, but those plans were scratched, as it was already after twelve. At this rate, she'd be lucky to make it from Jacksonville to St. Augustine by early evening.

Arriving at the rental car counter, Natalie gave the woman her name and watched her peck on her keyboard for several minutes.

"I'm sorry, Ms. Donovan, but I don't have a reservation for you."

"That's impossible," Natalie said. "I called last night."

"Do you have your reservation number?"

Natalie thought about all the information she had written down for her travel arrangements. The sheet of paper was still on her kitchen counter. "No, I don't. Do you have my name in your system?"

The woman checked again. "I don't see anything."

Tired from getting up early to make it through security at a Washington, D.C., airport, Natalie felt her patience waning and she was getting crankier by the second. Handing over her license and credit card, she pasted on a polite smile. "Fine. Forget the reservation. I'll just take whatever you have available."

The clerk clicked a few more keystrokes before she raised apologetic eyes to her. "I'm sorry. We're completely out of cars."

Natalie stared at the woman as if she spoke another language. "That's impossible. I know you have at least one car—the one I reserved."

"I don't see—"

Natalie glared down the front of her blue and white uniform at her name tag. "Marsha, it is just after noon. There will be flights arriving at this airport all day. Are you trying to tell me that you won't be giving any cars out for the rest of the day?"

Turning around to face the twenty or so people waiting in line behind her, she raised her arms to them. "All these people are waiting for cars and you're telling me you don't have cars for them?"

"If they have reservations, ma'am, we have a car for them."

Natalie faced her again, all of her patience gone. "That's interesting—I have a reservation and you don't have a car for me."

"Can I help with something?"

Natalie watched the manager ease Marsha aside to deal directly with this irate, loud customer.

"You're damn right there's a problem. I flew to this Sunshine State to get away, to relax, to destress. I have a lot going on in my life right now and this minivacation was supposed to help me take my mind off things. Then Marsha informs me of some news that defeats all the reasons I chose to come to your city."

"She didn't have a reservation," Marsha whispered in her manager's ear, refusing to take the blame from this potentially volatile situation.

"I heard that, Marsha, and I *did* have a reservation!"

The manager stared at Natalie and she at him. Finally, he blinked.

"Marsha, why don't you tend to the next customer? I'll help Ms. . . ."

"Donovan," Natalie said.

"I'll assist Ms. Donovan personally."

Finally finding parking slot number forty-six, Natalie threw her bags in the back of the Pontiac. Curtis, the rental car manager, had personally walked Natalie over to a competitor and secured a vehicle for her. He apologized for the mix-up and offered her 20 percent off her next rental.

Pushing her shades up on her nose, she adjusted her rearview mirror and shifted into Drive. After showing her paperwork to the man at the gate, she was finally on her way.

Opening the sunroof, she felt the sun beaming in, warming her body. Inhaling several deep breaths, Natalie finally started to relax. Over the past week, she had walked the fine line of crying herself dry to picking up the phone to call him to blaming herself and to blaming him. Then there was the topic of her mother—and that man. Just how much time were they spending together? What if he was taking advantage of her? Natalie had read countless stories of men who preyed on older women, only to use them and take advantage of them, leaving them worse off than they'd ever been, emotionally and financially. Something didn't sit right about her mother dropping everything to be with Samuel.

After her mother hung up on her for the second time, Natalie couldn't stand another minute. She couldn't stand the situation with Derrick. She couldn't stand not knowing what was going on with her mom. And she couldn't stand being alone in that house one more day.

There was a time when her home was her haven. It was the one place where she could relax and release the troubles and situations of the world. But that was before Derrick's divorce became final. He'd made that house his house, and no matter what room she went in, he was there. Memories of their love could be found in every room. The force was so strong that she had to go five hundred miles away from it to keep from going insane.

Natalie came to the entrance of Cameron Oakes, glad that she remembered how to get here. When Margaret had decided to move away, Natalie was shocked that she chose St. Augustine, Florida. She had been contemplating for months making a major move, but Florida? Margaret had spent her entire life in the Northeast. But tiring of the harsh winters and the memories, she opted for sun and relaxation. She'd visited several cities in the Sunshine State, but eventually settled on a place with a strong history and a sense of community. Natalie had yet to experience all that this city had to offer. Over the next four days, she'd hoped that she and her mom could sightsee together.

Coming up to the guard's gate, she gave her name.

Security had been a nonnegotiable amenity for Natalie when she helped her mother search for a place to live. Not knowing anyone, she wanted to make sure her mother was safe and secure. The security guard checked the computer and the gate lifted.

Her mother had added her name as a twenty-four-hour visitor the day she moved in. The active adult development was located just a few blocks from the beach. With its community center and activities coordinator, her mother always had plenty to do and someone to do it with. With at least ten duplexes and four attached homes with side garages, it was large enough to offer many amenities.

As she parked the car in a visitor spot, Natalie's smile widened and she leaned back and rested her head on the seat. After waking up at 5:00 a.m., having a delayed departure, and the fiasco at the rental car counter, she had finally arrived at her destination. The prospect of spending time with her mom suddenly became extremely appealing to her. She hadn't been to visit in almost a year, while her mother had come for a short visit during the holidays. With her busy professional life, she hadn't had a lot of time over the past couple of years to spend quality time with Margaret. Up until this moment, she hadn't realized how much she missed her mother.

Leaving her bags in the car, Natalie walked the short distance to her mother's front door. The temperature was in the high seventies and Natalie was glad she wore a light blue sundress with a thin cardigan over it. It was perfect.

Ringing the doorbell, Natalie shifted from foot to foot. imagining the look on her mother's face when she opened the door. Several minutes passed and no one answered. Unable to tell if her mother's car was in the garage, she peeked in the front window but couldn't see anything.

Ringing the bell again, she anxiously waited for the door to open.

When Natalie finally accepted that no one was coming to the door, she walked about a quarter of a mile to the activities center. If her mother wasn't at home, it was possible that she was enjoying some of the many activities the community offered throughout the day. Walking through the glass double doors, she headed for the information desk.

A large bulletin board was mounted on the wall with a list of all the activities scheduled for today. It was now almost two o'clock, and a movie was playing in the screening room, a book club meeting was going on in the library, there was a salsa class in the exercise room, and the main room was teaching scrapbooking.

Checking in with the front desk, Natalie hoped the young, blond woman sitting behind it could help her locate her mother.

"Can I help you?"

"I'm looking for my mother, Margaret Donovan. I went to her house and she wasn't there. I was hoping that you could tell me which activity she's participating in this afternoon."

The woman looked skeptical and didn't make an effort to look anything up. "We're not supposed to give out any information on our residents."

"I'm sure if you check your records, you'll see that I'm her 'in case of emergency' person." Natalie realized that she was only doing her job, but this day had gone nothing like she had planned.

The woman punched a few keys on her computer. "Do you have identification?"

Pulling out her driver's license, Natalie stood quietly as the woman examined it as if it held some great secret.

Handing it back to her, the woman checked her sign-in sheets. "We don't have her registered for anything today."

Natalie's shoulders dropped. Thanking the woman, she headed back toward her car. Dialing her mother's cell phone, she found her patience slipping quickly when she got voice mail. Still not wanting to give away the surprise that she'd come to visit, she left an urgent message for her mom to call her.

Sitting in her car, she leaned her head forward against the steering wheel. This day was shaping up to be worse than she could ever have imagined. When she got on the plane this morning, she thought surprising her mother and spending some time would give her some answers about Samuel, but also occupy her so that she could put thoughts of Derrick out of her mind. But so far, she'd accomplished neither. Her mother was nowhere to be found and thoughts of Derrick and their crumbling relationship were never too far from her mind. Starting the car, she backed out of her parking spot. The only thing in her stomach was some fruit she had eaten before heading to the airport. Deciding to grab a bite to eat, she hoped by the time she returned her mother would be home.

"Dr. Carrington, you have a call on line one and your next patient is in room four."

Derrick had just walked out of an appointment and was headed to the next. He hadn't heard from Natalie and a part of him wanted to know if that was who was on the phone. Instead of asking the receptionist, he headed to his office to see for himself.

Suzanne watched Derrick move from room to room. His mood was no better today than it was yesterday. Not that she wanted to see him suffering and depressed, but she couldn't help but smile to herself. He must not have patched things up with Natalie.

Suzanne had monitored their relationship and could tell that they had the normal spats of any couple. But this one was different. Derrick and Natalie usually were back on track in a day or two. Not this time. It was going on a week and there were no signs of anything changing. He'd walked around the office giving polite words to his staff and patients, plastering a fake smile on his face, trying to convince everyone that nothing was wrong. It wasn't working. There was something very wrong, and she planned to take complete advantage.

Over the past several days, she had thought about the best approach. With Derrick trying to get over this breakup, she had to play a delicate balance of friendship while positioning herself for more. She'd played it cool for the last couple of days, but now it was time to step it up. Maybe she'd offer drinks or dinner—nothing too fancy, nothing too romantic. Just some place nice where she could start to take his mind off Natalie. Once she got his mind—if just for a little while—she could get to his body and then his heart.

"Suzanne?"

She snapped out of her thoughts to face Sherisse. "Yes, Dr. Copeland."

"I was asking if the latest order of syringes had come in yet. I'd called your name several times."

Looking slightly embarrassed at being caught daydreaming, she started toward her office. "We got an order in this morning. I was just about to check them in."

"Great, let me know when you're done."

"Sure."

Sherisse watched Suzanne enter her office, and then turned the other way to see what had her so captivated. Based on the direction she was facing, it was Derrick's office. Everyone in the office knew Suzanne was interested in Derrick, but to Sherisse's knowledge, she had never made a move. As long as this remained the case, there wouldn't be a problem. But that dreamy, faraway look Suzanne had in her eyes was starting to tell a different story. Sherisse made a mental note to talk to the other doctors about it.

Derrick stood at his desk and picked up the flashing phone line. "Dr. Carrington."

"Derrick?"

He hadn't heard this voice in over a year, but the recognition was immediate. The shock of hearing from the last person in the world that Derrick would want to talk to temporarily stumped him.

"Are you there?"

As he snapped out of his astonishment, his jaw tightened and his eyes narrowed. "You have some nerve, Scott. I should end this call right now."

"Wait, Derrick. Don't," Scott said, rushing through his words. "I know things are pretty messed up between us."

Derrick's sinister laugh relayed the message that what he had just said was a gross understatement. Scott made it sound as if they'd just had a disagreement about something trivial. "Correction, Scott. Things aren't messed up between us because there is no 'us.' There is just you and me and we have absolutely nothing to talk about."

Scott couldn't blame him for not wanting to talk to him.

It had taken him months to get up the courage to make the call. "Your anger is fully understood."

Derrick slammed his door shut and started to yell. "First of all, I'm looking for your understanding. And second of all, you're wrong. I'm not mad—I'm disappointed, hurt, and let down."

Scott tried to speak, but Derrick cut him off. This time his voice was lower and calmer. "You were supposed to be my boy, my friend."

Scott tried to explain. What happened that day had been eating away at him. He wanted to make peace. "Me and Charlene . . . it just happened."

"Oh, spare me," Derrick said. For months after he left Charlene, he had wondered how it happened. Did Scott go after his wife? Did they sneak away for romantic dinners? Did they sit around and laugh about their deception? Did they ever feel guilty? And now that Scott was offering some insight, this was his explanation?

"Come on, Scott. Is that the best you can come up with? Nothing 'just happens.' You didn't magically fall in bed with my wife. You made a conscious choice to betray our friendship."

"Derrick, you don't understand—"

"You're right, Scott," Derrick said, giving him credit for that statement. "I don't understand. I don't understand how one day, you're in my face smiling, hanging out, having a drink, and the next day you're lying in bed with Charlene.

"I don't understand how, even if she stood in front of you completely naked, offering herself, that you would give in. I don't understand how you could stand by my side and watch us take our vows and then become the very person to break those vows."

"I can see you're not ready to talk about this."

"You're damn right I'm not ready to talk about it. And you want to know why? Because there's nothing to talk about. You are dead to me."

Those words cut Scott to the core and he realized how his weak moment had destroyed a friendship that had been special to him. "We're not together anymore—Charlene and I."

The admission didn't surprise Derrick. How could an affair like that last? "I don't care."

"I was just hoping—"

"Hoping what, Scott?" he said, his voice rising to a yell. "That we could start over? Be boys again? Have a few drinks?"

"Derrick—"

"Go to hell . . . and say hello to Charlene when you get there."

Derrick slammed the receiver so hard, it cracked the base. Furious that Scott would even think that a phone call could make right all the wrong that he'd done, Derrick paced his office for several minutes just to calm down. Now that he and Charlene were no longer a couple, did Scott think they could just pick up from where they left off? That man must have been completely out of his mind.

There were some obvious lines that should never be crossed in a friendship. Sleeping with your friend's wife definitely fit into that category. The audacity of Scott to contact Derrick after all this time and expect to explain away this situation appalled him.

"Dr. Carrington, room four."

The intercom jolted Derrick. Walking out the door, he took several deep breaths to calm down. Storming down the hall, he spoke to no one. Picking up the file outside the room, he pushed the door open and stepped inside. Duty called.

Suzanne watched his behavior and thought about that phone call. Who could that have been to get him so worked up? Checking with the receptionist yielded no information. She only knew that it was a man. Whoever had Derrick so upset, she hoped to help ease some of that tension away.

Just past four o'clock, Natalie pulled into that same visitor parking space and cut the engine. Jea had called with a couple of questions, and the president of a women's network group contacted her to confirm her speaking engagement for next month, but no call from her mother, and nothing from Derrick.

Ringing the doorbell, she couldn't wait to see the expression on her mother's face when she opened the door. Natalie rang the bell again and began to think that she'd missed her mom again.

"Natalie, is that you?"

Turning to the left, Natalie saw Margaret's neighbor in her doorway. Having moved in a few weeks after her mom, Emily Docks had become her mother's best friend. They did just about everything together. If anyone knew where to find Margaret Donovan, Emily would. "Yes, Ms. Docks. It's me. I came down to visit with my mom."

"Oh dear," Emily said, concern on her face.

"What do you mean?" Natalie said, alarm bells ringing in her head. Had something happened to her mother?

"She already left."

"Left for where?" Natalie asked, walking across the small patch of grass that separated the two homes.

Stepping out of her door and onto the small porch, Emily leaned against the railing. She was in her late sixties, and her hair had gone completely gray and she wore it in a short Afro. "Did she know you were coming? I can't imagine her leaving if you made plans to visit."

"She didn't know I was coming." This trip was turning into a nightmare. "Where is she, Ms. Docks?"

"On a cruise," Emily said. "She asked me to keep an eye on her house and pick up her mail and newspapers."

Natalie's disappointment immediately turned to agitation. "Are you saying my mother went on a cruise and didn't tell me?"

Emily was a little taken aback by her tone of voice. "Don't get upset with me. I'm just the messenger."

Taking a deep breath, Natalie lowered her voice. She was right. There was no reason to be rude. "I'm sorry, Ms. Docks. It's just that I wanted so much to surprise her, and now it looks like I wasted a trip."

Emily heard the longing in her voice for her mother and accepted her apology. "They left this morning. They'll be back on Monday."

"They?" Natalie asked, narrowing her eyes in suspicion.

"Margaret and Samuel."

Natalie had to stop herself from yelling at the woman who was trying to help her. When did her mother start vacationing with this man? "Are you saying that my mother went on a trip with a man she barely knows?"

"Are you talking about Samuel?" Emily said, appalled at her description. "He's the nicest man. Treats your mother like a queen."

"Ummm," Natalie said, not quite buying into that

description. Deciding it was best to save any additional comments about Samuel for her mother, she let the subject drop. "Thanks, Mrs. Docks, for letting me know. Do you have any other information about this cruise?"

Emily noticed how upset Natalie appeared to be, not just because she missed her mother, but because her mother was with Samuel. Wanting to put her mind at ease, she said, "Your mother is a good judge of character and Samuel's good to her."

"I appreciate you saying that," Natalie said, not the least bit influenced by it.

"Margaret left me a copy of her itinerary. I'll get it for you."

Natalie smiled in appreciation when the woman returned from inside her house with the piece of paper.

Getting back in her rental car, Natalie reviewed the travel information. The boat was sailing at six o'clock. At fifteen minutes past four, she decided to try her mom again on her cell.

"Mom!" Natalie said, thanking God that she answered the phone.

"Natalie? What is it? What's wrong? You sound winded."

"I'm just so glad I got you. Did you get my message?"

"I got it about an hour ago."

Natalie's exuberance slightly deflated. "Why didn't you call me back?"

"I was planning to. I just hadn't had a chance. You know how it is. You rarely have a chance to call me back."

Natalie couldn't argue with that. There was no way to count the number of calls from Margaret that Natalie never returned. "I'm here . . . in Florida."

"What?" Margaret asked.

Not exactly the response that Natalie hoped for, but she

couldn't blame her. She hadn't been the best daughter lately. "I wanted to surprise you, Mommy."

The use of the "mommy" word caught Margaret off guard. "Natalie, is everything OK?"

"Yes," Natalie said. "No . . . I mean . . ."

"Natalie, I'm five minutes away from boarding the ship."

"Mrs. Docks told me."

"Why didn't you tell me you were coming?"

"Like I said, I was trying to surprise you."

There was silence on the phone and Natalie realized she wanted desperately for her mother to cancel her trip and spend the weekend with her. When no offer came, Natalie didn't think she had the right to ask. "You'll be back on Monday?"

"Yes, it's one of those quick trips to the Bahamas."

"I'll be here when you get back."

Margaret hesitated. "Are you sure everything is OK?"

"Yep," Natalie said, letting the lie roll off her tongue. "Have a good time and I'll see you Monday."

"I love you, baby."

"Love you, too, Mommy."

Chapter 13

Derrick rubbed his temples, trying to massage away some of the stress in his life. Between missing Natalie like crazy and Scott's phone call, it was a wonder he was still able to function. Walking out of her house was the hardest thing he'd ever done in his life. He thought she would call out to him . . . stop him. When he opened her front door, he paused, giving her one more chance. He walked through, never hearing a sound.

When the phone call from Scott came today, it sent his blood pressure through the roof. What would possess him to contact him now? After all this time? Now that he and Charlene were no longer together, maybe he realized what a stupid mistake he had made. In Derrick's mind, even if that were true, it was much too little, way too late.

The start of a weekend—he wasn't looking forward to spending the next two days alone. Just after eight o'clock—he should have left the office hours ago, but the truth was that he had nowhere to go. Going home didn't appeal to him, and if he went to his parents', they were sure to ask about Natalie. He could call Damian or Brandon, but it was Friday night, and Derrick was sure they had plans with their wives. He had hoped to work until exhaustion; maybe he could make it through the night without missing Natalie so much.

"Derrick?"

He didn't have to look up to know who stood at his door. "What are you still doing here?"

"I was on my way out and saw your light on," she said. She'd been waiting for him to leave to ask if he'd like to join her for dinner. After saying good night to the other doctors and staff, Suzanne hung around. It was Friday night and he was still at the office, which meant that he and Natalie were still on the outs. "We're the last two people in the building."

"Just trying to finish up a few things."

"I was going to stop and get something to eat. Do you want to join me? There's a spot about two blocks from here."

Thinking of her previous offers, Derrick decided to decline.

Suzanne stepped into the office and pushed the door until it almost closed. "Can I talk to you for a second?"

Derrick noticed the gesture but didn't say anything. "What is it?"

Walking with purposeful strides toward his desk, she shed her white jacket and set it on a chair in front of his desk. This time, the tight, white cotton shirt she wore outlined her braless breasts, the nipples showing through. "Remember I told you I know your moods? That I could tell when something is tearing you up inside? This is one of those times."

Her voice raspy, she barely spoke above a whisper. "You're confused, hurting, and probably feel like you're all alone. If I had to guess, I would bet money that it has to do with Natalie."

She was on point, but Derrick didn't want to discuss it—especially with her. With her standing to the side of his desk, he concentrated on keeping his eyes focused on her face and not the perky mounds demanding his full attention.

Thinking of Will and Natalie, he had to finally admit that they were exactly right when it came to Suzanne and her feelings for him. The attraction she had ran deeper than he ever would have guessed, and it was time to set the record straight. He didn't want to encourage her in any way. While he was all those things that she had just described, that was something he had to deal with alone. "I appreciate your concern, but I'm fine."

Moving around the desk, she kneeled on the floor in front of him, resting her hands on his knees. "There's no need for you to deal with this alone. Nobody should have to deal with their problems completely by themselves."

Derrick stared at her hands before raising his eyes to hers.

Suzanne smiled when he didn't push her away. "I know you've had a rough time lately. There's no need to pretend with me. We've worked together too long."

Gently squeezing the tops of his thighs, she quietly exhaled when he allowed her touch to continue. "You don't have to open up to me and tell me what's going on—unless you want to. Or we can skip all the talking and you can let me take care of you. Just for a little while, you can let me take your mind off whatever it is—or whoever it is. No need to think about tomorrow or the next day—we can just have tonight."

Extending her stroke to the inside of his legs, she inched her way closer and closer to his manhood.

Derrick felt her hands caress his body and he closed his eyes. His personal life was a mess and Natalie didn't seem to want to do anything about it. He'd waited by the phone and checked his e-mail, hoping that she would come to him, and he'd gotten nothing. What did that leave him with?

The offer Suzanne just put on the table was clear. There was no room for misinterpretation. She offered whatever he needed or wanted. She made no secret that she wasn't expecting anything more than this moment. She could ease some of his loneliness, take his mind away from all the thoughts about his personal life.

Opening his eyes, he stared at her. Without removing her hands, he said, "Suzanne, I don't think—"

"Don't think, Derrick." Reaching up, she ran her hands across his chest. "It looks like you've been doing that all day, and it hasn't gotten you anywhere. Maybe it's time to just go with the flow."

"Suzanne—"

"Shh," she said, rising up. "Don't answer me just yet. Take a second and think about it. Think about how good it would feel. How satisfying it would be."

Placing one leg on each side of him, she let her body rub against his growing physical reaction. Entwining her hand with his, she guided him under her shirt until he cupped her breast, her nipples hardening at his touch. Leaning forward, she placed her lips on his.

Derrick froze in the moment as her body rode him. Slipping her tongue inside his mouth, she wrapped her arms tightly around his neck, rocking her most private part against his. A sensuous sigh escaped her lips and that's when Scott's words ran through his mind—*me and Charlene . . . it just happened.*

Breaking contact, he leaned away from her and took his hand from under her shirt. Derrick knew the truth. Nothing *just* happened. There was always a choice. He lifted her off him and stood. The spell that seemed to be over him from the pain of his breakup with Natalie and the phone call from Scott had been broken. "Suzanne."

Adjusting her shirt, she tried to gracefully recover from his rejection. Shaking her head from side to side, she stepped away from him. "Don't say anything."

"You're an attractive woman."

"Especially that," she said. "I don't want to hear what a great person I am from someone who doesn't want me."

"I'm involved with someone else—in love with someone else."

"Natalie? Oh, please," Suzanne said, rolling her eyes to the ceiling. It was bad enough that he was turning her down, now he wanted to throw that woman in her face? "Give me a break. I've heard the rumors. All the times you've proposed. All the times she's turned you down. You've been moping around this office as if your world was falling apart. Now, I don't really know the woman, but I do know that she's a fool if she can't appreciate what she has."

Walking around the desk, she picked up her jacket and headed to the door. Right before walking through, she gave him a final piece of advice. "You can lie with your mouth, but your body always tells the truth. You wanted me. You're a fool if you don't wake up and stop letting that woman treat you any kind of way. Being faithful to someone who doesn't give you what you need is useless."

He heard the distant sound of the office door closing and Derrick sat back down in his chair. *What the hell is wrong with me?* How did he let it get that far? As he rested his head in his hands, Suzanne's words reverberated in his ears. Was he being a fool—holding out for someone who had no intention of coming back? He hadn't spoken to Natalie in a week. Could he still claim that they were involved with each other?

"You made the right decision."

The voice startled Derrick.

"What are you doing here?"

Holding up a small Victoria's Secret bag, Will stepped into the office and took a seat. "A present for my date. I left it on my desk and had to come back. That was a close call."

"Too close," Derrick admitted.

"I told you that woman had a serious thing for you."

"I don't understand how I let it get that far," Derrick confessed, still unable to believe that her tongue was down his throat and his hand was up her shirt.

"Oh, that's easy. She's a beautiful woman and she has her sights set on you," Will said. "That's a challenge for any man to turn down."

"That still doesn't excuse my behavior."

"I didn't say it did."

The two men stared at each other and Derrick nodded in understanding.

"What stopped you?"

Out of all the craziness that had taken place tonight, this was the only part that made sense. "I love Natalie—even if she can't make up her mind about me."

"Good answer."

"It's the truth."

"You told Suzanne you two were still involved."

"Yes, I did."

"But you're not, Derrick," Will reminded him, hoping to push him into taking action with Natalie. "You walked away from her. You let her go."

Derrick didn't want to be reminded of the status of his relationship with Natalie. Will was hoping that this conversation would knock some sense into his friend. "You can't go on like this. You have to do something,"

"What?"

"I really don't care," Will said. "Call her, send her a letter, go see her . . . do something, Derrick, before you drive the rest of us crazy."

An hour later, Derrick opened the door of the small sandwich shop and searched the dining area. As it was only half filled this time of night, it didn't take long for him to spot her. Sitting across from her, he signaled the waitress. "Thanks for meeting me on short notice, especially because of Brianna."

"No problem," Christine said, waving off his concerns. "Damian loves bathing her and putting her down for the evening. He probably won't even miss me."

"Can I get you something to drink or eat?" he asked when the waitress arrived.

"I'll just have a cup of coffee."

"Make that two."

Alone again, Derrick said, "I don't want to put you in the middle of my mess, so I'll understand if you don't want to talk about this. But I was hoping you could give me some insight into Natalie and what's going on in that pretty head of hers. Because, honestly, I have no idea."

"It's about time," Christine said, practically jumping out of her seat with joy. "Out of respect for my friendship with Natalie, I didn't want to butt in where I wasn't wanted, but if you're opening the door to me, I'll be glad to march right in. I can give you exactly what you want."

"Which is?"

"I can tell you why Natalie won't marry you."

Derrick sat back and his face relaxed. He'd been hesitant to contact Christine because he didn't want her to think he was putting her in the middle. After leaving Will, Derrick had sat in his truck, at a loss. Could he and Natalie still be considered together? Could they find a way to work things out? No matter how many questions swirled in his head, one thing was true—Will was right. He needed to do something. That's when he called Christine. Based on what she just told him, it was the best decision he'd made all week.

"I've got that part—she's not ready. The question is, what do I do about it?"

The waitress set their coffee down and Christine added sugar while Derrick drank his black.

"That's where you're wrong. That's not the question you should try to find the answer to."

At his dumbfounded look, Christine continued. "It's not what—it's why."

"Now you've lost me."

Christine thought about all she'd learned about Natalie and her life since they found out about each other. And one thing was clear—Natalie had a very specific reason for not being the marrying kind. "Describe Natalie."

"What?" Derrick said, more confused than he was five seconds ago.

"Describe her," Christine said. "Simply list out her characteristics."

When Derrick didn't start speaking, Christine offered more encouragement. "You've tried everything else to figure this out—you might as well give this a shot."

"You got me there," Derrick said. "Let's see. She's smart, beautiful, independent, self-sufficient, take-charge, a leader."

"Keep going," Christine said.

After hearing all the words that fit Natalie to a tee, Derrick felt his mood slip even lower. "If I do, I'll just keep listing things that show why she's not interested in marriage. She doesn't need anything—or anybody."

"You're half right," Christine said, setting her cup to the side, leaning forward, wanting to make sure her message came across loud and clear. "When I married Damian, I was smart, beautiful, independent, take-charge, and a leader. Like Natalie, I owned my own business."

"You two sound like you have a lot in common. The only difference is that you said yes when Damian proposed."

"That's because Natalie is something that I'm not."

Derrick's pulse started to race and he unconsciously held his breath. This was the information he'd been waiting for. Some piece of data that would shed some real light on Natalie and her ways. "Now you have my undivided attention."

"She's been brainwashed."

Derrick was momentarily speechless. "I would respond, but I have no idea what to say—except what the heck are you talking about?"

Christine took a sip of her coffee before continuing. "Natalie left town today."

"What?" Derrick said, completely caught off guard. "Where is she?"

"Florida."

"Her mom?" Derrick asked, thinking that was the only person she knew well enough to go and visit.

Christine had thought about how much she wanted to share about Natalie with Derrick. She and her sister had built their friendship on trust, and she didn't want to break that bond by sharing too much. But desperate times call for desperate measures.

Natalie had called Christine with the latest information on her visit, including the cruise and having to wait until Monday to see her mom. "How much has she shared with you about her mother?"

Conversations about family had come up periodically between them. Natalie had gotten to know his parents quite well over the past year—first by helping them turn their business around and then by family events in which she was no longer a professional colleague, but the woman he loved. But the reciprocation hadn't been the same. Natalie complained about her mother, ranted and raved about the constant calling, and every now and then shared a little piece of her childhood, but for the most part, he only had basic information. "Her mother had Natalie fairly young and raised her on her own. She told me her father was married to your mother and had an affair with Margaret."

Christine motioned the waitress for a refill. They were going to be here for a while. "Let me tell you a story about Margaret Donovan and how I believe, intentionally or not, she managed to brainwash her daughter."

Over the next half hour, Christine shared with Derrick Margaret's philosophy on men and putting trust in them. When she had first met the Donovans, Margaret was bitter, indignant, and cynical. Having spent most of her adult life hating Henry for what he did to her, she constantly filled Natalie's head with reasons why men, especially married men or soon-to-be divorced men, couldn't and shouldn't be trusted. "Natalie claims that her mother's philosophies are ridiculous, but deep down, I think she believes them, and that's why she can't accept your proposal. She's just been using your divorce as a smokescreen."

"Have you talked to her about this?"

"I've tried," Christine said, recalling the many conversations about getting over her fears and trusting in Derrick and their love. "She won't even entertain the thought."

Everything Christine told him put quite a few things in perspective. Natalie's fears ran much deeper than his divorce or him being ready to commit to another marriage. This was about her and her very real challenges of taking everything her mother had said over the years and tossing it out the window. "I appreciate you sharing this with me, but I'm not sure this information is going to change anything. I've done everything in my power to show her how much I love her, care for her, and want her to be in my life. If she's not ready to accept that, there's nothing I can do."

"That's just it," Christine said, her eyes sparkling with excitement. "I think she may be ready."

"Why?"

"This trip to Florida was a big move for her. She's been trying for weeks to reconcile what her mother filled her head with over the years with her feelings for you," Christine said. Thinking of all the discussions she'd had with her sister over the past few weeks, Christine continued. "She loves you so much, Derrick. She wants to give you everything you want—because she wants those same things. She's just having problems with the arithmetic."

"The arithmetic?"

"You are on one side of the equation and her mother is on the other side. They just don't add up for her anymore. Talking to her mom just may take care of that."

Christine had a strong sense of Natalie and who she was,

and their relationship reflected that. If Christine said that Natalie might be in a better position to talk marriage when she got back from Florida, then he was willing to try again. "I'll call her when she gets back."

Christine reached in her purse and pulled out a piece of paper. "Natalie's going to be there all weekend by herself, waiting for her mother to return from her cruise."

Derrick stared at Christine and started to read her underlying message. "I don't know, Christine, that's taking a big chance."

Pushing the paper across the table, she pointed to the top. "There's a flight that leaves at six-ten in the morning."

"I'm not sure that's the right move," Derrick said hesitantly. What if she didn't want him around? What if they ended up worse off than they were now?

Lowering her finger, she pointed to the hotel information. "You can get a room there—or you can just wait and share Natalie's."

"Don't you think this might be crowding her? If Natalie is trying to work through some issues with her mother, I might not be a welcome distraction."

"Trust me on this, Derrick. When I spoke to Natalie earlier, she was on the edge of losing it. Her mother was gone, you're not around, and she's starting to feel overwhelmed. If she needs anything right now, it's you."

Releasing a slow grin, he couldn't believe that Christine was talking him into this, even though she didn't have to push too hard. He was more than willing to make this trip. He was missing Natalie so much. He might have done it whether she brought it up or not.

Picking up the paper, he folded it and put it in his

pocket. Pulling a few dollars out of his wallet, he set them on the table to settle their bill. "I better get out of here. I have to get up early to catch a plane."

Christine squealed with exhilaration. "You won't regret this, Derrick, I promise."

Chapter 14

Natalie rolled over and peeked at the clock. Just after 9:00 a.m. She wasn't ready to get up and face another day. Sleep had eluded her most of the night, as she tossed and turned, never keeping her eyes closed for more than an hour. At the time she purchased her airline ticket, coming to Florida had appealed to her more than anything. Now that her mother was gone, she was alone—and lonely.

Never would she have imagined her mother heading off for an island trip. She couldn't think of the last time her mother put her off for anything. What if she hadn't shown up? Would her mother have told her that she was going on a cruise? Would she have let Natalie know that she was going away for a long weekend with a male companion? What if there was an emergency? What if Natalie needed to get in touch with her?

Christine thought she was going to Florida for all the wrong reasons. Instead of worrying about Margaret and Samuel, Natalie needed to focus on her own relationships—with her mother and with Derrick. Natalie quickly discounted that advice. Christine didn't understand how vulnerable Margaret could be with this man. What did she know about dating? About relationships? Natalie just wanted to make sure that whatever was going on between her mother and her new friend was on the up and up.

After all that her mother had been through in life at the expense of a man, she should be careful about dealing with men. Finding some sense of peace and happiness after moving to Florida, did she want to risk getting involved with someone? Natalie wasn't about to leave Florida until she got some answers to her questions.

Getting frustrated just thinking about it, Natalie picked up the breakfast menu to order room service. She had planned to be spending time with her mother, but now that that was impossible, she had no idea how she would fill her time.

Scanning the options, she found nothing appealing to her until she came across the cinnamon rolls. The automatic smile couldn't be helped. Her body temperature rose about ten degrees and she longed to feel his touch as she recalled what Derrick had done with that icing. Then the smile left and was replaced by the dull, aching pain that had made its home in her heart since the day he left.

She had stopped crying herself to sleep a couple of days ago, but it didn't stop tears from making unannounced visits at the most inopportune times, like when she stopped at the Chinese place to get takeout or when she checked her luggage at the airport.

Christine hadn't been much help. "Relentless" wouldn't do justice to describe her over the last week, constantly bullying her sister to contact Derrick. But Christine hadn't felt the chill that was in the air when he walked out of her house the last time. There was too much hurt, too much anger, and too much pain. Everything that they had become to each other just wasn't enough to overcome this one issue. She had wanted him to give her time, and he wanted her to trust in him and their love enough to get married. There was no middle ground. And that left her in a hotel room wondering why she felt so alone.

As an only child with a mother who worked all the time, Natalie was often left with a babysitter or by herself. That in no way compared to the experience of aloneness she had today—the loss, the abandonment, the heart that was still breaking.

Losing her appetite, she tossed the menu aside and headed for the shower.

The strong force of the hot water felt good pelting her body, relaxing muscles that had grown stiff from the stress and worry about her mother—and Derrick. Standing completely under the spray, she let the water soak her from head to toe. Closing her eyes, she didn't fight the memory that seeped into her mind.

Derrick and Natalie had just finished their workout in the gym when they stepped into her glass stall. As the water came down on them, Derrick lathered her washcloth and cleansed every spot on her body, gently rubbing her shoulders, her arms, her back, and her legs. After rinsing her off, he retraced with his lips every part he had cleansed. When the heat between them became hotter than the water, he backed her up against the wall and entered her. She had wrapped her legs around his waist, and the rhythm of their bodies meshed with the melodic pounding of the water. With powerful thrusts and screams of ecstasy, they soared to heights high above the clouds.

Natalie opened her eyes and looked around her. With the water continuing to soak her, she had to confirm that she was actually alone. The memory was so strong, so real. She could feel his arms around her, taste the flavor of his skin, hear the sounds of their love.

What was she doing? Why couldn't she give him what she wanted? How could she continue to go on with this pain of loving him and missing him? A couple of days ago, she thought she was all cried out, but as the drops of water mixed with her fresh tears now, the sadness that consumed her indicated that this might be the biggest cry of them all.

Sliding down the wall, she lost all energy to fight. All the control, the independence, the need to be in charge became useless. None of those things mattered without him. They were now replaced with the loneliness of their separation. That emptiness that had been with her since Derrick walked out of her life completely took over. The tears before had been from the anger, from the shock, from the fights and the arguments. These tears were from her heart. A heart that had been snatched out and tossed to the side when he walked out of her life. A heart that, without Derrick, could never be repaired.

When her body had given all it could, Natalie reached up and turned the water off. With what little strength she had left, she dragged herself to the bedroom. Barely drying off, she slipped on her robe and lay across her bed.

What now? With all that was going on with Samuel and her mother, she wanted to be here when her mother returned from her trip. But she finally admitted to herself that she couldn't take being away from Derrick. Reaching for the phone, she dialed. Not sure where the call would lead them, she just needed to let him know that she loved him, needed him, and missed him greatly. When the answering machine picked up, disappointment set in and she disconnected the call. This wasn't a conversation for voice mail.

The knock on the door caught Natalie off guard. No one knew she was here and she hadn't ordered anything. Aware that it was close to ten o'clock, she assumed it was housekeeping. Tightening the belt on her robe, she cautiously peered through the peephole and blinked twice. Without hesitation, she removed the locks and swung the door open.

All thoughts of her mother, Samuel, and the cruise flew from her mind as he stood before her. Her eyes lit up and a smile spread across her face. Whatever had been the barrier between them became irrelevant—his divorce, the proposal, and his ultimatum disappeared from her thoughts. The only thing she could digest was that he had come to her.

Before he could open his mouth, she lunged at him, embracing him with all the power and love she had in her. No regard for consequences, no desire to think beyond this moment—there was only the primal, fundamental need for him. Kissing him with the pent-up passion that had lived in her since the moment he walked out of her house, she slipped her tongue inside his mouth and explored every part as if it were foreign territory. Her hand, around his neck, pulled him closer and closer. As their tongues intertwined, Natalie relished the sweet taste of him. Taking a step back, he kept pace with her as they entered the room, the door making a resounding thud as it shut behind them.

Derrick dropped his traveling bag on the floor and wrapped his arms around her waist. In step with each other, they walked down the short hallway and found their way to the bed. His clothes for the warm weather, sweatpants and a T-shirt, formed a thin barrier to her. When she fell backward, he followed, lining up his body on top of hers.

Sitting on the plane, he had had no idea what he would do or what he would say when they came face-to-face. He'd come to offer support after what Christine told him about her mother and to find a way to salvage their damaged relationship. However, when she opened the door and fell into his arms, all logical thinking went away. With her wet hair, natural face, and short robe, she looked bare—stripped of everything, vulnerable. Her eyes reflected all that to him. Then, in the blink of an eye, all that changed. He saw hunger, raw attraction, and deep desire.

Feeling her body pressed against his caused his need for her to overpower him. The thin robe she wore had almost came undone and her breasts peeked out. Derrick felt his hardness and knew that if he didn't stop now, he wasn't sure he'd be able to.

Sliding beside her, he put some space between them. "Natalie—"

"Uh-uh," Natalie said, closing the distance he created and kissing his face and neck. "No words. No talking." As she moved on top of him, the belt came completely undone and she straddled him, pushing on his growing manhood. Her body was on fire and the swirling questions of why he was here, how he knew where to find her, and what he wanted were set aside. Those things didn't matter to her. What mattered was that he was here, in her room, and in her arms.

Pulling his shirt over his head, she tossed it on the floor. Guiding his hands, she set them on each of her breasts and sighed in gratification as he kneaded and squeezed, causing her nipples to harden.

"Derrick," Natalie said, barely able to contain the fire

that was raging through her. "I've missed you so much. I want you. Right here. Right now."

Sitting up, Derrick placed his lips on hers and switched their positions. As all the love he had for her came pouring out, Derrick's control was rapidly slipping away. There was nothing resolved between them, but he couldn't deny her what she wanted, or what he needed.

After talking to Christine, Derrick had come to understand more about the woman he loved. If Christine was right, then her inability to accept his proposal ran much deeper than her love for him. Armed with that information, he wanted to take things slow, to get them back on track. Obviously, Natalie had other plans.

He had no intention of picking up the physical aspect until he was sure that it was what she wanted. "Are you sure this is what you want?"

Without a word, she slipped her robe off her shoulders and helped him out of his clothes. Taking him fully in her hands, she massaged him, hearing the moans of pleasure that escaped his lips. After protecting himself, he entered her.

With each stroke, all the emotions of their turbulent past seemed to float further and further away. Breathlessly saying his name, Natalie shuddered into complete satisfaction. Derrick, hearing the erotic sounds coming from her mouth, followed with his own release.

Spent, both physically and mentally, neither spoke for several minutes. Finally, Natalie lifted herself up and lay beside him. Immediately feeling the loss of their closeness, Derrick hugged her to him. Slowly tracing his fingers up and down her arm, he kissed her on the lips and stared lovingly into her eyes. "That was some greeting."

"I couldn't help myself."

Smiling at her comment, Derrick said, "I've been miserable without you."

Thinking about her morning episode in the shower, she had to admit the same. "I've missed you so much."

Natalie relished the safety of his arms. "How did you find me?"

"One guess."

"Christine." If she couldn't make Natalie deal with Derrick in D.C., she was going to make her do it in Florida.

Derrick hesitated before he continued. "She also told me about your mother and how concerned you were about Samuel. I didn't want you to be alone."

The room became silent again as both hesitated to speak.

Natalie was the first to break the silence. "Thank you for coming. You have no idea what I was going through before you knocked on that door. I couldn't take being away from you any longer. I called you this morning but got your voice mail."

"I had second, third, and fourth thoughts about coming here," Derrick said. When he had stood in line at airport security, he still thought briefly about changing his mind. "I promised to give you the time you asked for."

Snuggling up closer, Natalie smiled at him. "I'm glad you didn't."

"The risk of your rejection was worth just seeing you again."

"You never have to fear my rejection," Natalie said.

Now, they took their time making love. The urgency and need that tortured him when he had first arrived gave way to a gentleness that allowed them to leisurely please one another.

Two hours later, Derrick and Natalie sat in the hotel

restaurant enjoying a very late breakfast. The receptionist at the activities center at her mother's complex had recommended this hotel to Natalie. Sensing the frustration that Natalie was experiencing, she named this place because of the location and amenities—everything she would need to enjoy and relax over the weekend. Just about twenty minutes away from her mom, the Ponte Verdra Resort served every type of guest with championship golf courses, miles of beaches, a state-of-the-art health club and spa, and several award-winning restaurants.

"Christine said your mom went out of town?"

Natalie's expression soured as she thought about the crazy antics of her mother. "This whole thing with my mother is driving me crazy. First I call and some man answers her phone, and then I come to visit and I find out she's headed off to some island with him."

Derrick watched the peace they had just been experiencing give way to tension. "Have you met the man?"

"That's what's really bothering me about this. I don't know anything about him—where he's from, how old he is, what he does for a living. All I know is that he's turned my mother's world upside down and if she's not careful, she could end up hurt—and by herself again."

She spoke the words with such conviction and Derrick wondered how she could draw such a conclusion. "You just said you don't have any info on this guy, why don't you just assume that he has your mom's best interest at heart? Otherwise, you're going to make yourself crazy over the next couple of days."

"That's easy for you to say," Natalie said. "But my mother has been through the wringer when it comes to men. She gave her whole self to someone, only to have him treat her like she didn't matter. Henry was laughing behind her back and in her face. I refuse to let that happen to her again."

When Derrick didn't respond, she saw his stone-faced expression and realized what she had just said. "I'm . . . I'm sorry, Derrick."

Pushing his plate back, Derrick decided that he'd eaten enough. "I do know what it feels like. You just described my ex-wife. But if I took your attitude, I wouldn't have opened myself up to you, fallen in love with you, and I wouldn't be fighting like hell to make this thing work between us."

The conversation was quickly turning down a road that Derrick didn't have the energy to travel. He came to Florida to be with her, not to dissect their relationship—again. He was here to offer support. Relaxing his shoulders, he curved the corners of his lips and said, "We have today and tomorrow and I've never been here before. How about we see the sights?"

Relief flooded through Natalie at his change of subject. Charlene had truly run a number on him and she didn't discount what he had been through because of it. She hadn't meant to insult him or discount his ability to relate to what had happened to her mother. "We can stop by the tourist's desk on the way out."

Derrick and Natalie scanned the various brochures in the lobby of the resort. After reviewing many of the places to see, they decided to embark on a tour highlighting the African-American experience in St. Augustine. The city was rich with history from all cultures, and they were excited at the chance to learn more about it.

Starting with the Gracia Real de Santa Teresa de Mose, locally known as Fort Mose, Derrick and Natalie were fascinated by the tales the guide was sharing with them.

With the group listening intently, the guide shared the history of the land they were standing on. Over 250 years ago, the area had become a haven for those brave men and women who dared to run away and escape their enslavement in the British colonies of Georgia and South Carolina.

Battling slave catchers and the surrounding swamps, Indians and fearless Africans shuttled the slaves south, instead of north, as the Underground Railroad would, more than a century before the Civil War. In exchange for their freedom, the former slaves gave their service to the Spanish government and converted to the Catholic faith. Fort Mose later became the first legally sanctioned free-black town.

"Can you imagine finding freedom during this time?" Natalie asked, looking at the artifacts that had been retrieved from the town.

"It's an amazing story," Derrick said. His history books in high school hadn't taught him any of what he was learning today.

They ended their afternoon by visiting historic Lincolnville. The African-American community had been founded by slaves who took pride in building a thriving city. With its own businesses and schools, the area not only prospered but became influential in the civil rights movement. The Southern Christian Leadership Conference and Martin Luther King Jr. had claimed this town for part of the movement. Both Derrick and Natalie were impressed and proud of the contributions made by the people who had claimed this land.

Later that evening, they enjoyed a relaxing dinner at an Italian restaurant a few short blocks from the hotel. With the casual atmosphere, Natalie wore a pair of black capri pants with a striped black and white short-sleeved top. Derrick was laid-back in a pair of jeans and a dark blue pullover shirt.

They had both been quiet as they reflected on all they'd learned today about the journey of African-Americans in this state and in this country, and the major contributions they made to this area.

After ordering, Derrick reached across the table and put his hand in hers. "Listening to our tour guide today made me realize how precious life is."

"Derrick, I want you to know that—"

"Let me finish," he said. "I love you so much and I want to be a part of you life. If you're not ready to accept my proposal, that's fine. I just don't want to waste any more time being apart from each other."

"I appreciate that, Derrick," Natalie said.

"But I do have one request."

Natalie wasn't sure she liked the sound of that. "I'm listening."

"I want you tell me about your childhood, your mother, and what it was like growing up."

Natalie didn't understand what he was asking. "You know about my mom and childhood."

"I'm not talking about Henry and his marriage and finding out Christine was your sister," Derrick said. "Those are the facts. I want to know how it affected you, how it shaped you into the person you are today."

Skeptism flashed in her eyes and she stared at Derrick several minutes before saying a word. "Sounds like you've been talking to Christine."

Derrick didn't deny it. "She didn't say much, only that some of your hang-ups with relationships could stem from your mother."

Natalie sat back and slid her hand out of his. "Hang-ups? Who said anything about me having hang-ups?"

Derrick chuckled as the waiter set their dinner salads in front of both of them. "You say you love me and that you want me to be a part of your life, yet you can't commit to me. I call that having at least one hang-up."

"I am committed to you, Derrick," Natalie said, her voice softening. "I don't need a ring or a piece of paper to demonstrate that to the world."

Shrugging, Derrick decided to drop it. Arguing with her wouldn't accomplish anything. He promised himself he would not have this conversation with her again, and he intended to honor it. Picking up his fork, he dug into his salad and he didn't say a word the rest of the night about marriage or commitment.

The next day, Derrick suggested hanging out at the beach and Natalie agreed. Ordering a picnic basket filled with tasty food and drinks, they headed down to the water in the early afternoon. With the temperature close to eighty degrees, the sun was a welcome change from the rainy weather they left behind in D.C. Spreading their blankets, they watched couples and families play and frolic in the water.

As Derrick watched a man teach a little boy how to float, he thought about the family he wanted to have. He and Charlene had talked about starting a family since the day they married, but each time Derrick brought it up, Charlene didn't think it was the right time. "We haven't really talked about this, but I was wondering. Do you want kids?"

"Of course I do," Natalie said without hesitation, opening the bottle of sunscreen she pulled out of her beach bag.

"When?" he asked.

"When I get . . ."

Derrick heard her words trail off, but didn't say anything. *When I get married.* A slight smile escaped his lips as he watched her expression. It was apparent by her sudden quietness that this was the first time she had verbalized the connection between the two. In her mind, children and marriage went together. And she just admitted that she wanted children. That revelation lifted Derrick's spirits.

Removing his shirt, he tossed it on the blanket. "I'm about to hit the water. You game?"

Taking off her sundress, Natalie said, "I'm right behind you."

Derrick's words died in his mouth and he froze as she put her dress in her bag. "What are you wearing?"

Natalie looked down at herself. "A bathing suit."

"I've been to a lot of beaches—some of them with you. That is not a bathing suit. It's more like a sample piece of fabric."

On a whim, she had bought the two-piece as a gift to herself, still wanting to prove she had it. The white strapless top matched the bottom that rode high on the side. Doing a quick turn, she held her hands up. "You like?"

"I'm normally not the jealous type, but I don't want anyone seeing you like this." Looking around, he took note of the several looks of appreciation from some men—and women.

"Ah, don't worry," she said, kissing him squarely on the lips. "What's underneath belongs only to you."

Derrick watched her run to the water. Shaking his head, he wondered how many guys he'd have to punch out before the day was over.

Chapter 15

Monday afternoon, Natalie parked her rental car in the same spot she had parked in three days ago. The only difference was that Derrick was in the passenger's seat. According to the itinerary, her mother's ship should have docked a couple of hours ago, meaning she should be pulling into her driveway in the next few minutes. Anxiously tapping the steering wheel, she periodically peered down the street to see if there were any signs of oncoming cars.

"You're going to give yourself a heart attack if you don't calm down," Derrick said, noticing her watching the street like a hawk. They'd ordered breakfast in, and as the morning wore on, Natalie became more and more on edge.

Putting her hands in her lap, she made a concentrated effort to keep still. It wasn't nervousness that drove her to have the jitters. It was anxiousness and anxiety over confronting her mother about her strange behavior.

A car turned onto the street and Natalie recognized it right away. What she didn't recognize was the person driving the car. *Why is he driving her car? Doesn't he have his own?*

When the car disappeared inside the garage, Natalie got out and started toward the front door.

Derrick got out of the car and walked behind her. Christine had told him that Natalie had gone bananas when she found out about Samuel, but Derrick couldn't have imagined what she meant—until now. Natalie was skeptical and cynical about her mother with this man—ready to pounce. He had no idea how this scene was going to play out.

When Margaret opened the front door, she welcomed her daughter with a big hug. "It's so good to see you."

The hug Natalie gave was halfhearted as her eyes focused on the man bringing in their luggage from the side door.

Margaret released her and followed her line of sight. "Natalie, I'd like you to meet Samuel Delmar."

"It's good to meet you finally," he said, coming toward her with his arms outstretched. "Your mother has talked so much about you. She's got to be the proudest mother I know."

When Natalie didn't move, he lowered his arms slightly and settled for a two-handed shake.

"Samuel," Natalie said, only to be polite. She held his hand for only a brief second.

In the quietness that followed, Natalie took a hard look at the man who had begun to occupy her mother's days and, apparently, her nights. Older than her mother by at least ten years, Samuel seemed to be around sixty. He was shorter than Derrick, and his receding hairline and small-framed glasses gave him a distinguished look. Dressed in shorts and a polo shirt, he appeared at ease.

"Natalie?"

"Huh?" she said, turning her attention back to her mother.

"Are you going to introduce us to your friend?" Margaret asked, breaking the silence.

Derrick stepped forward and offered his hand to her. "Derrick Carrington."

Waving off his handshake, she embraced Derrick like a long-lost friend.

Natalie paused at the gesture and stared at the woman who never wanted to meet her boyfriends, much less embrace them with such enthusiasm. She was normally reserved, slightly mistrusting, and never wanted to let someone know that she truly cared. But looking at her today, Natalie saw some other things that were very different.

First of all, there was the hair. Dark brown, it had started to go gray and Margaret hadn't done a thing about it. Now it was a vibrant shade of auburn and had been cut in layers to softly frame her face. Next, Natalie focused on her clothes. The bright yellow top with a summer skirt would never have been worn by the Margaret Natalie thought she knew. The color was too bright—too alive.

"It's so nice to meet you, Derrick."

Margaret turned her attention to Natalie. "Why didn't you tell me you weren't alone?"

"Derrick came to keep me company while I waited for you to return."

Derrick and Samuel cut their eyes at each other at her curt tone and Margaret said, "Well, here I am. Now what was so urgent that you had to fly down to see me?"

Natalie looked at Samuel before turning her attention back to her mom. "How can you ask that? A man sleeping in your house made this trip urgent."

"Why don't I get us all something to drink?" Samuel said. "Derrick, you want to join me in the kitchen?"

"I'm not thirsty," Natalie said, refusing to look at him.

"I am," Margaret said. "Thanks, honey."

Nodding, Derrick squeezed Natalie's hand before following Samuel down the hall.

When she was sure that they were out of earshot, Natalie glared at her mother. "What is going on with you? Have you lost your mind?"

Margaret took exception to her tone and took a seat on the couch. "Let's get one thing clear. I'm the mother in this relationship and you won't talk to me that way."

Regrouping, Natalie sat beside her mother and apologized. "I call you on the phone and you have a man over. You're taking impromptu trips without telling me. I'm concerned."

"Why?" Margaret asked. "I'm a grown woman perfectly capable of taking care of myself."

"Come on, Mom," Natalie said. "Not when it comes to men. What do you really know about this Samuel guy? You couldn't have been seeing him for more than a month."

"Actually, it's been almost three months and you would know that if you had more time for me."

"What's that supposed to mean?" Natalie asked.

"You know perfectly well what I mean. I call you—you're unavailable. You say you're going to call me back, I don't hear from you. I figured you weren't that interested in what was going on in my life."

"That's ridiculous," Natalie said, feeling a pang of guilt. "I've just been really busy lately."

"And so have I—with Samuel."

"Three months?" Natalie repeated. "What can you possibly know about a guy in three months that you would traipse off on a cruise with him?"

"I know enough," Margaret said, losing her patience

with her only child. "Not that I owe you an explanation, but he's kind, loving, caring, and always has time for me."

"Or maybe he just has time for your money," Natalie countered, far from being convinced that this was a man her mother could trust.

"My money?"

"The inheritance I received set you up quite nicely," Natalie reminded her. "You have the opportunity to enjoy life to the fullest without being concerned about your finances. You don't think he hasn't picked up on that?"

Margaret stood, eyes blazing at her daughter. With her hands on her hips, she worked hard to keep her voice down, but to no avail. "I don't appreciate what you're insinuating."

"Why is it that he's always here? Why is it that he's driving your car? Doesn't he have anything of his own—or is he perfectly fine with mooching off you?"

"Natalie, that's enough."

Both women turned to the male voice.

"Derrick, this doesn't concern you," Natalie said.

"I don't care if it concerns me or not, you have no right to talk to your mother that way."

"But it does concern me," Samuel said. "We could overhear the two of you. As a matter of fact, the *neighbors* may have overheard the two of you."

"Good," Natalie said, stepping to him. "Then maybe you can answer some of these questions."

"He doesn't have to do any such thing," Margaret said, deciding this out-of-line behavior had gone on long enough. "This is my house and Samuel is my guest and I will not have him treated this way."

"Well, I'm your daughter—and have been for longer than three months."

Moving beside Margaret, Samuel held her hand and stroked it gently.

The gesture infuriated Natalie.

"It's OK, Margaret," Samuel said. "If Natalie has questions, I don't mind answering them."

Samuel sat on the couch and Margaret sat beside him. There was no question who her allegiance belonged to.

"You're right, Natalie, I stay at her house. I eat her food. I drive her car. But that's only because I don't live in Florida. I live in Atlanta."

"Why?" she said, surprised. How much more would be revealed to her in this visit with her mother?

"That's where my work is."

"What else is there, Samuel? A wife? Kids? Or just another woman? Why is it that you always have to come here?"

"Natalie," Margaret said, "that was completely unnecessary. You have no right to come in here with your accusations and innuendos."

Samuel rubbed her arm. "Really, Margaret, I don't mind."

Margaret turned to her daughter. "For your information, I've been to Atlanta several times over the last couple of months and none of what you're accusing him of is true."

"What?" Natalie said. Had she really been that out of touch with her mother? "When was this? Why didn't you tell me?"

"I tried, but you were too busy."

"I'm not busy now, so why don't you tell me everything else I don't know about your life?"

"Fine." Leaning into Samuel, Margaret rested her head against his chest. "I'm moving to Atlanta."

"The hell you are."

"That's it," Margaret said, fed up with her daughter's

attitude. "I don't have to sit here and take this from you and neither does Samuel. I want you to leave."

"You can't be serious. You're going to chose a man you've known for three months over me?" Natalie said, her eyes widening in shock.

Margaret stood and walked toward the door. "I'm not choosing anything. Until you calm down and can talk about this like an adult, we have nothing to say."

"I have a better idea," Samuel said, rising to stand between them. "Why don't Derrick and I go get us all something to eat? We should be back in about an hour."

Derrick put his arms around Natalie and whispered in her ear, "Lighten up."

After the men left, both women were quiet.

Margaret sat back down and stared at her daughter, unable to recognize the anger she had. "Natalie, what has gotten into you?"

"How can you set yourself up like this?"

"What are you talking about?"

"How could you forget what Henry did to you? How he treated you? How can you pack up and leave your home for this man?"

Margaret heard the longing in her voice and reached out for her daughter's hand. "Is that where this is coming from?"

"You said it yourself—over and over again—independence, having our own, never giving it all completely to a man. That was the way to avoid being taken advantage of, being used and discarded like well-worn clothes."

The reality of that statement socked Margaret in her gut. Those words had been her mantra for most of her life. She sang them from the rooftops to anyone that would listen. And she had passed that on to her daughter. "Natalie, those were words from a bitter woman who insisted on holding on to the past."

"Those weren't just words, that was your life. You gave yourself to a man who lied, cheated, and manipulated you. Can you honestly say that Samuel won't be the same way?"

Margaret leaned back and exhaled deeply, feeling the brunt of all the emotional damage she had passed on. How could she reverse it?

"Natalie, I have to let go of the past. I've spent twenty-five years of my life pining away for what could have been. I struggled to raise you, barely able to make ends meet at times. I refused help from others and I cut myself off from relationships with men because of one man. When I came to Florida, it was because I needed to make a fresh start. And that's what I did. What with the sunshine, my new friends, and the financial freedom, I transformed into a whole new person—a better person."

Natalie heard the words but found them hard to digest. "I'm happy for you, Mom. I really am."

"But you don't believe what I'm saying?"

Natalie remained silent.

Margaret stood. "Let's go to the kitchen and have a cup of coffee."

Settled at the small table beside the window, she reached for her daughter's hand. "Tell me about Derrick."

The smile on Natalie's face came naturally.

"Aahh, I see he's someone very special to you," Margaret said, giving her hand a squeeze. "I saw the way he looked at you. I think he feels the same way."

"We met over a year ago when his parents needed help from BSI," Natalie started.

"Yet I've never heard of him."

"It wasn't that serious."

"But now it is . . . and I still haven't heard of him."

"I knew you wouldn't approve," Natalie said, barely above a whisper.

"Approve—of what?"

The emotions of having to say that she feared her mother's rejection of her love for Derrick rushed to her head. "Of me falling in love with him."

"Oh, Natalie," she said. "Was I really that bad?"

"You always told me to be able to stand on my own, not depend on a man."

Those words rang true in Margaret's ear. Over the years, she'd filled her daughter with all the frustrations of her failed relationships. She'd done such a good job that her daughter couldn't be happy that she finally found someone she wanted to share her life with. "Seems as if both of us have been living secret lives. How about you tell me about Derrick and I'll tell you all about Samuel?"

Natalie nodded and continued. "Derrick's a doctor who has a thriving practice with three other partners. He's kind, warm, giving, and loves me as much as I love him. He's been married before. His divorce became final a couple of weeks ago."

Margaret held her expression, but couldn't stop herself from asking the question. "Were you two involved while—"

She didn't have to finish the sentence. "No! He was separated and in the midst of his divorce when we met."

The relief was visible as Margaret exhaled a breath she didn't realize she was holding. She'd unknowingly been the other woman and wouldn't wish that pain on her daughter—or Derrick's wife. "I'm glad to hear that."

Natalie hesitated before continuing. "That's why things

have been challenging for us lately. He's ready to commit to me, but I don't think he's over his first marriage."

"You think he's still in love with her?"

"No," Natalie said confidently. There wasn't the remote possibility that he and Charlene would ever be together again. "I think you can't possibly be ready to trust again so soon after a devastating breakup."

"Because?"

"It took you years to get over Henry—surely it would take Derrick a little longer than this to get over Charlene."

Margaret closed her eyes and felt her heart sink at the emotional damage she had done to her only child. She had taken her adult problems and dumped them on a little girl whose only crime was that she listened to her mother. "What does Derrick think?"

"Derrick thinks he's ready."

"What about you—do you want to marry him?"

Just then, they heard the front door, which told them the men were back.

A few seconds later, Derrick and Samuel entered the kitchen cautiously.

Samuel walked over to Margaret and gave her a kiss on the cheek, while Derrick stood beside Natalie, placing his hand on her shoulder.

"Is everything OK?" Samuel asked.

"Yes." Margaret looked to her daughter for confirmation.

"It's getting late, Natalie. If we want to catch our flight, we'll need to leave. If you want to stay, I can call the airline and change our tickets."

Standing, Natalie said, "I really need to get back. Jea's been holding down the fort long enough."

"It was nice meeting you, Natalie."

"You too, Samuel."

The sarcasm that had been prevalent in all her previous words to Samuel had diminished.

Derrick and Samuel walked out to the car while Natalie and her mom hung back.

"Natalie, don't make the same mistakes I've made. Letting my past ruin my future. Derrick's a good man. I know that because I know you. It's OK to love him—completely."

As she gave her mom a hug, a lone tear touched the corner of her eye. She'd come here to remind her mother of the perils of trusting in a man, to put Samuel on notice that he would not get away with treating her mother any kind of way, using her, and ultimately hurting her. But the tables had been completely turned. Her mother had become a vibrant woman, embracing life and all it had to offer. She was moving to Atlanta whether Natalie approved or not.

"You didn't have a chance to tell me about Samuel," Natalie said, needing to begin to make up to her mother over how she had treated her today.

"I'll call you tomorrow and tell you all about him," Margaret said, appreciating Natalie's effort.

"I'd like that."

The ride to the airport was made in complete silence, as Derrick allowed Natalie to digest all that had happened today. After listening to her talk to her mom, he realized Christine and Will were right. She'd had a lifetime to build up the wall of resistance toward what he was asking of her.

Once they settled in their first class seats, Derrick held her hand in his. "Are you OK?"

"Just a little overwhelmed," she said, thinking back to all that had transpired that day. "I thought this was some guy she'd met and was getting to know. Now I find out she's planning to move to Atlanta. It's a lot to take in."

"Natalie, after listening to you talk to your mom, I finally understand. You're not ready for marriage."

"Derrick, I—"

"It's OK," he said with honesty. "Things between us are just fine. There's no need to rush. I'm not going anywhere. When the time is right, you'll know it."

Chapter 16

Tuesday morning was met with a stack of phone messages, a ton of e-mails, and a line of people standing at her door. Natalie rarely took time off from work for this very reason. There was always so much to catch up on when she returned.

Exhausted by the time they pulled into her driveway last night, she had needed all of her remaining energy to change her clothes and crawl into bed. The last four days had been physically and emotionally draining. Grateful to be back, Natalie felt work was the one constant in her life, the one thing that didn't have her feeling up one minute and down the next. This was where she was in complete control.

"Natalie, do you have five minutes to go over the Pickett Contracting file?"

"How about around eleven, John?"

John had been an excellent addition to her staff about six months ago. Snagging him from a public accounting firm had been easy because he had tired of the mandatory fifty-five-hour workweeks and the constant travel. When he saw an opportunity that allowed him to put his skills to work in an environment that made a tangible difference in people's lives, he had jumped at it.

"Can I bring the Henton Industries file as well?"

Natalie saw her lunch break just slip away. "No problem."

"Thanks."

After picking up the phone to begin returning calls, she had dialed three numbers when she was once again interrupted.

"Do you have five minutes to sign these invoices? We have to get these checks out today."

Natalie waved Jea into her office and hung the phone up. She'd have to call later. "Might as well go through them now."

The five minutes Jea asked for turned into twenty, which meant Natalie's next appointment was waiting for her in the conference room.

"So much for being in control," she mumbled as she followed Jea down the hall.

By the end of the day, Natalie was exhausted. She had yet to return all her phone calls and she had only made a small dent in returning e-mails. The grumble of her stomach reminded her that she hadn't put anything in her stomach since that morning.

"Natalie, you have a call on line one and I'm leaving for the day. Did you need anything else?"

"No, Jea. Have a good evening."

The flash of the light blinked for almost a minute before Natalie mustered the energy to lift the receiver.

"You sound exhausted."

Natalie leaned back in her chair and twisted the cord around her fingers. "You have no idea."

Derrick could hear the exhaustion in her voice. "How about you let me cook for you tonight? My place."

"Seven?"

"See you then."

Derrick hung up the phone and thought about the romantic dinner he'd prepare. It wasn't often that he cooked, but he did have a few specialties he thought would work. Things had been tough for Natalie lately, as she tried to figure out what she wanted in her life. Now that they had placed a moratorium on the marriage issue, it took the pressure off both of them.

Gathering his belongings, he made a mental grocery list.

"Looks like the long weekend was good for you."

"Better than good."

Will shut the door and took a seat. "What happened?"

"I hate to admit it," Derrick said, giving credit where credit was due, "but you were right."

"Aren't I always?" Will asked, with a confident grin. "About what?"

"The time I spent in Florida revealed a lot about Natalie. You should have heard the verbal exchanges between Natalie and her mom. Natalie was rude, disrespectful, and refused to listen to reason. Her mother almost kicked her out of the house until Natalie finally calmed down and apologized to her mother for her behavior."

"That sounds like some family reunion."

"But I learned an invaluable lesson. Natalie doesn't just have a problem making a commitment to me, she has a problem with commitment period. She met her mom's new boyfriend and went off. I'd never seen her so passionate about anything. When she crossed the line with her attitude, that's when I realized how deep her fears ran."

"And the ending to this story?"

Derrick knew that everything hadn't been resolved in that

one day, but the tides had definitely shifted for the better. "Everyone called a truce—including me and Natalie."

"Which means?"

"There will be no talk of engagement or marriage until Natalie says so."

Will watched for any sign of frustration. "Are you cool with that?"

"Actually, I am. Regardless of the legal document, Natalie and I belong to one another. I can live with that. If she ever wants more, I'll be ready. If not, I'm OK with that, too."

Will hated to deflate the high Derrick was on, but there was another issue that he had yet to fully deal with. "What about Suzanne?"

The mention of her name reminded Derrick of that night just a few short days ago. What was he thinking? If he ever wished he could relive a few minutes of his life, it would be those. There would be no way he would allow that to happen again. "Nothing. We've only had professional conversations today and I expect it to remain that way."

"You think Suzanne is going to let it remain that way?"

"She doesn't have a choice."

Will wondered if Derrick was discounting the attraction Suzanne had for him. "Are you going to tell Natalie?"

That was the one question Derrick had been avoiding ever since Suzanne walked out of his office, embarrassed and frustrated. Nothing happened; was there really a need to tell Natalie about it with so much going on in her life? "I'm not sure."

Offering some unsolicited advice, Will thought of some of the previous situations he'd gotten himself unintentionally tangled in. "Take if from a brotha who has gotten caught in one too many lies with the ladies, tell her."

"There's no chance of anything ever happening between me and Suzanne," Derrick reasoned. "Do you really think I should risk it by telling Natalie?"

"A word to the wise," Will said, "it's hard to keep a secret hidden when more than one person knows it. If you don't say anything, and I don't say anything, there's still one more person out there who can let the cat out of the bag whether you want to or not."

Derrick didn't like the sound of that. Suzanne made it quite clear that she didn't think Natalie respected or deserved him and that he would be better off with her in his life instead. "You don't think she would?"

Will raised his hand in defeat. "Hey, man, if there's one thing I've learned over the years, it's never to try to figure out what a woman—especially a scorned one—will or will not do."

The knock on the door interrupted them.

Dr. Sherisse Copeland walked in with a file in her hand and a concerned look on her face. At thirty-three she was the youngest doctor in their practice. She'd been planning her own private practice since she started college. "Can one of you come and talk with one of my patients? He's been complaining of pain in his chest, but I can't get him to take an echocardiogram. He wants me to give him something for gas."

"I'll go," Derrick said, rising from his chair. These types of situations were more common than most would think. Patients came in all the time complaining of discomfort, pain, headaches, and that feeling that something "just wasn't right." When the best course of action would require further testing, sometimes in hospitals, some patients became uncomfortable. They feared the unknown and would prefer a Band-Aid type of treatment for the symptom to getting to the real core of the problem. He'd been fairly successful at getting patients to see his point of view; he hoped that would be the case today.

Suzanne watched Derrick walk down the hall in quiet conversation with Sherisse. He'd taken the day off yesterday, but she couldn't get a handle on the details. When he arrived, his mood was better than it had been for weeks—talking and laughing with staff, taking a little more time with patients to find out what was going in their family life. He'd even volunteered to buy lunch for the entire office staff. The first chance she got, she'd find out what had caused this new Derrick to appear.

Hanging his doctor's jacket on the back of his door at the end of the day, he opened it back up to find Suzanne standing on the other side.

"You surprised me."

"Didn't mean to," Suzanne said, attempting to enter his office. When Derrick didn't move, she had no choice but to stand in the door. "I wanted to stop by and see how you enjoyed your time off."

The question sounded innocent, but Derrick didn't like it. It felt as if she was digging for information. The best thing he could do was to be polite and keep his words general. "It was great. I recommend everyone taking a short break every now and then."

"I agree with that," Suzanne said. "It must have done you some good, you seem to be much happier today, in such a better mood. It's such a change from last week, I just wanted to stop by and share in the good news."

The game of cat and mouse had gone on long enough. "I appreciate your concern, Suzanne, but we are coworkers and I would prefer to keep all our conversations related to work."

Holding her smile in place, Suzanne nodded in understanding. "Understood, Dr. Carrington."

He watched her turn on her heel and head back to her office and Derrick unleashed a breath he didn't realize he was holding. He hoped he made himself clear with her. Their relationship was strictly business.

At seven o'clock on the dot, Natalie rang the doorbell to Derrick's town house. The three-story brick home was the end unit in a quiet neighborhood in the northwest section of the city. Running home before coming over, she'd changed into a pair of jeans and a purple peasant shirt. Comfortable, she was ready for a relaxing evening in.

"Right on time," he said, greeting her with a kiss before she entered.

"Something smells great."

Derrick had bought this house a couple of months after he arrived back in D.C. Charlene balked at him spending any money until their settlement had been finalized, but Derrick needed a place to live, so the judge allowed it. The rooms had remained sparsely furnished and decorated for several months until Christine got a hold of it. She couldn't let another day go by without adding some color, some furniture, and a few knickknacks to make the house a home. With Natalie's input, they created a place that was reflective of his style.

The first floor, with a living room, dining room, and large kitchen, was filled with shades of green. The basement had a den with soft, oversized furniture, a plasma television and a custom sound system that played throughout the house. The upstairs consisted of the master bedroom, his home office, and a spare bedroom.

"I hope you're hungry because I made fettuccini with homemade Alfredo sauce, fresh-baked garlic bread, and I have your favorite chardonnay."

"After the day I've had, that sounds like music to my ears."

Soft jazz played throughout the house and, rarely eating in the dining room, Natalie was surprised when he led her to that room. "Oh, Derrick, it's beautiful."

The table was set with china and the dimmed lights and candles cast a soft glow against the walls. Fresh flowers formed the centerpiece and the fragrance wafted through the air. Derrick pulled out a chair for her and Natalie sat.

"Tonight, I serve you. Whatever you want—you name it. It's yours," Derrick said, uncorking the bottle. Filling both of their glasses, he raised his to her, offering a toast. "To the woman who is my life. Thank you for being you. I love you."

Natalie touched her glass to his and felt the power and truth in his words.

Derrick served the food and noticed Natalie was barely eating. "What's on your mind?"

Setting her fork down, Natalie apologized. "I'm just thinking about my mother. I was so rude to her in Florida. I got carried away."

"You said you apologized to her," Derrick said, seeing the guilt still across her face. "I'm sure she understands."

"You don't know what it was like growing up with her," Natalie said, reflecting on her childhood.

"Why don't you tell me?"

That was the same request he had made of her in

Florida—to open up and share it all with him. And Natalie wanted to do that more than anything.

"She was so bitter. All the time. There was no room for joy or happiness growing up. Her life turned out nothing like she planned. Pregnant her second year of college, she lost her educational goals and she lost the man she thought loved her. My entire childhood, I lived with her belief that had she not loved Henry, given him all of her, then her life's dreams wouldn't have been taken away from her."

Derrick didn't interrupt. Christine had shared this with him, but hearing it come from Natalie's mouth, he could feel her pain as she relived those years with her mother.

"When I started dating, it was always the same speech. 'He's not nice enough, Natalie. Be careful, Natalie, you have so much to offer the world. Don't give it all up for him.'"

"Is that what she said about me?" Derrick asked quietly. If that was the kind of talk he'd been fighting against, no wonder she couldn't bring herself to say yes to his proposal.

"I didn't tell her about you," Natalie admitted.

The admission was unexpected. "Why?"

"Because she would say those words and I didn't want to believe that about you."

"Do you?" Derrick asked. "Do you believe that about me, that I would stop you from being who you were created to be? That I would take the precious gift of love that you've given me and treat it with disregard or disrespect? Do you think that I could do to you what Charlene did to me or what Henry did to your mother?

"I know what it feels like to give your everything to a relationship and the other person tosses it away. I've yelled, screamed, and practically beheaded sparring partners at the gym. That kind of pain I wouldn't wish, or inflict, on anyone."

"I know that, Derrick."

"Do you *really* know that, Natalie? Think about it long and hard before you answer. Can you honestly say that I would never abandon you?"

At that moment, it became clear to Natalie why she hadn't accepted his proposal. She had tried to blame it on Charlene, and then on Derrick's emotional state, but she had finally come to see what Christine, and now her mother, had been telling her. It was time to let it go.

When Natalie was growing up, her mother constantly filled her head with opinions and reminders to always maintain control in relationships with men. She could care about them, love them, make them a major part of her life, but never give 100 percent. That was the way she would avoid ending up hurt, disappointed, and wounded.

When she reached adulthood, Natalie prided herself on discounting all those theories Margaret had tried to drill in her head. Just because one man had treated her mother with the utmost disrespect didn't mean that that was all men. She'd admonished her mother on many occasions to set aside that theory and get over some of her anger. But Margaret couldn't do it, wouldn't do it. And up until last week, Natalie thought that Margaret was destined to live out her life alone. But that theory changed when Samuel came into the picture.

She'd seen such a different side to her mother. Margaret had found someone and was giving her all to him, and here Natalie sat, keeping the man she loved at arm's length. That had been her pattern with every man she dated—always coming up with an excuse to end things before they had a chance to truly grow into something more.

With Mark, Natalie thought she was too young. They had dated during their college years and called it quits after graduation. A budding career had been her excuse for not continuing to see Kevin. She'd just started with her CPA firm and she was focused on making her mark. Stanley came along when she was contemplating her future. Did she want to stay in corporate America or was she willing to risk her traditional career to follow her professional dreams?

Each relationship she had shared with her mother, and each time Margaret gave her the same speech. But when Derrick came along, she didn't share anything about him with her mother. She couldn't bear the thought of having her mother lump Derrick into the category that she had put all her boyfriends in. He meant too much to her. The answer to his question suddenly became clear and she felt a weight being lifted off her shoulders.

"Ask me again," she said.

"Do you believe—"

"No, not that question."

Derrick's eyes furrowed in temporary confusion.

Natalie got out of her seat and started around the table toward him. "Ask me again."

Derrick stood when he noticed the serene and peaceful smile on her face and in her eyes. Her body was fully relaxed and the emotional tension that had been present in him gave way to the woman standing in front of him—a woman who seemed to have had an epiphany.

He moved around the table to meet her halfway until they stood a few inches from each other, not touching.

When he had walked out of her house weeks ago, he promised himself that he would never let the words come out of his mouth unless he was 100 percent sure of what she would say. "Do you love me?"

"Yes—but that's the wrong question."

"Do you know that I would never hurt you or abandon you?"

"Answer is still yes—but, again, it's the wrong question."

"Do you know that I'm willing to take our relationship as is, and keep things the way they are?"

"Yes."

"Do you still want me to ask you one more question?"

"Yes."

Derrick held his hand up, indicating for her to wait. Leaving the room, he returned a few minutes later with a small box in his hand. Standing before her, he gazed into her eyes and smiled at the joy he saw in them. Opening the box, he took at the ring. "Will you—"

"Yes!"

Before he could get the words out, she jumped into his arms, putting kisses all over his face. "Yes! Yes!"

Wrapping his arms around her, he swung her around several times. Planting her feet back on the floor, he reached for her left hand and slid the ring on her finger.

Natalie stared at the shining object that gave notice to the world that they were together. The emerald-cut two-carat stone sat high above the diamonds cascading around the sides of the channel setting. Holding her hand out, she giggled like a teenager. "It's beautiful."

"So are you," Derrick said. "Let's seal this deal with a kiss."

"I've got a better way to seal this deal."

With the food left on the table, Derrick led Natalie upstairs to the master bedroom. Removing her shirt, he unbuttoned her pants and helped her step out of them. In seconds he unhooked her bra and buried his face in her chest. "You taste so good," he said.

Natalie had been privy to the expert touch of his hands, but each time the sheer magic of them sent shock waves that traveled from the top to the bottom. A shiver of wanting settled in her stomach.

Rising, he captured her lips, more demanding and more intense than before. The hunger that he ravished her with created a burning desire. His hands explored her body, touching all her pleasure points, until he slid his hand down the front of her black lace panties and caressed her most sensitive spot of all. Moving toward the bed, Derrick gently laid her down.

He couldn't wait another second to be as close to her as two people could become. His hard body lay atop hers and she rose to meet him as he entered her. The force of their union touched the deepest part of his soul and he knew that this woman would be in his life forever.

Chapter 17

Carla's Café was crowded when Derrick and Natalie arrived the next morning. After making love for half the night, they spent the other half planning their future. Now that Natalie had finally said yes, the excitement of planning a wedding had taken over.

"Isn't this a sight for sore eyes?" Carla said, bringing over a fresh pot of coffee and two cups. "It hasn't been the same without the two of you here."

"It's good to know we've been missed," Natalie said, reaching across the table for Derrick's hand.

Carla caught the glare off the ring and shaded her eyes. "Girl, you're shining so bright I'm gonna need to wear my shades." Setting her serving items down, she picked up Natalie's hand and stared at the diamond. "I hope this means you two have finally found a way to stop all that arguing."

"I don't think you have anything to worry about in that category," Derrick said. "We're finally on the same page."

When Carla waved to the other wait staff working that day, they all came over to congratulate the couple, each one of them sharing infamous stories of the legendary arguments that they had witnessed over the past year.

"I can't believe some of the things I've made you put up with this past year," Natalie said as the crowd started to disperse.

Carla smiled at the happy couple, but added with playful sarcasm, "We'll see how much things have changed when the bill comes."

Derrick had started to laugh at the joke when someone caught his eye. Suzanne stood outside the window watching the festivities. With Natalie's back to the door, she didn't notice. Looking as if she was about to come in, Suzanne changed her mind and just stood there. The sadness in her expression told him that she had seen the ring and understood that he and Natalie were not only together, but getting married. He had informed her that any communication between them would be at the professional level, and while he didn't think he owed her anything, at some point today he would tell her, officially, that he and Natalie were engaged.

Flashes of that night entered his mind and he remembered Will's statement about secrets. Would Suzanne be brazen enough to tell Natalie about that night, or would she be mature enough to realize that that scene would never, ever be repeated? Giving him an unreadable smirk, she turned and headed down the street.

"Derrick?"

Looking back at Natalie, he said, "Sorry, I zoned out for a minute."

"I was asking if you wanted to meet me for dinner tonight at Lenny's."

Putting Suzanne out of his mind, he winked. "You bet."

Arriving at the office an hour later, Derrick had just a few minutes before their management meeting started. Every other week, the four doctors scheduled time to review financial and medical information, and any other business items related to their practice.

When Derrick walked into the small conference room, Sherisse and Jeff were already there. Will, as usual, was running late. "Good morning, everyone."

Neither said a word and Derrick paused before taking a seat. Their faces were grim and it was easy to tell that something wasn't right. "Somebody want to tell me what's going on?"

The two doctors glanced at each other, but neither spoke.

Derrick didn't like the vibe that was coming from both of them and said so.

"We'll wait for Will before we go into anything," Jeff said, getting silent approval from Sherisse.

"I don't think so," Derrick said. "There's something going on and I refuse to be the only one in the room that doesn't know. If this has anything to do with our medical practice, tell me now."

"Fine," Sherisse said, opening her folder with handwritten notes. "I hate to be the one to tell you this, Derrick."

Derrick's heart pounded in his chest. Her expression told him that whatever bombshell she was about to drop would have a tremendous impact on his life. "What is it?"

Taking a deep breath, Sherisse looked at Jeff, who encouraged her to continue. "You've been accused of sexual harassment."

"What!" Derrick exclaimed, jumping out of his chair at the outrageousness of it. "I have been nothing but professional with all of my patients. My record shows that—"

"This isn't a patient, Derrick."

Jeff's words caught him off guard. If it wasn't a patient, that meant a staff person was making the claim. The first name that came to mind was Suzanne, but even she wouldn't stoop to lying.

"Is this some kind of sick joke—a late April fool's gag?"

"I wish it were," Jeff said. "Before you got here, one of our employees asked to speak to Sherisse."

"Who?" Derrick said, even though, deep down, he already knew the answer.

Sherisse looked down at her notes. "Suzanne came to see me first thing this morning. She said she hated to do it but didn't think she could let this kind of thing happen again."

"I have to tell you, man," Jeff said, "when Sherisse brought this to my attention, I didn't believe one word of it, but it's our obligation to investigate."

"Investigate what? I haven't done anything wrong."

"Her story is pretty damning," Sherisse said.

Sherisse looked down at the paper in front of her. "He asked me to take off my jacket and to come around his desk. As a single parent, I couldn't afford to lose my job, so I did what he asked. He asked me sit on his lap and he placed his hand under my shirt, cupping my breast. Then he kissed me. At this point, I could not value my job over my dignity and I quickly got up, gathered my belongings, and left."

"That is the most ridiculous thing I've ever heard."

"But is it true?"

"No, Jeff, it is not true," Derrick said, boiling over with anger that he had to sit with his colleagues to justify himself.

"So you're saying you didn't touch her breast or kiss her?"

Derrick paused at the question. Technically speaking, he had, but it was not in the context that Suzanne was presenting. If anyone had a right to claim harassment it was him—not her.

"Derrick?" Sherisse said, a sinking feeling in the pit of her stomach. "Did you?"

"Yes, he did." All three turned to the voice as Will stepped into the conference room. "Sorry I'm late, but I got tied up with an unexpected delay."

Everyone in the room knew that was code for spending the night with his latest girlfriend and oversleeping.

"What do you know about this situation?" Jeff asked.

"I know that Derrick kissed Suzanne. I know that Derrick had his hand up her shirt. And I know that Suzanne instigated the entire scene."

"How?" Jeff asked.

"I was there." Will went on to explain about the forgotten gift and what he overheard.

Both Jeff and Sherisse breathed sighs of relief. A lawsuit would not only be bad publicity, it could cost them a fortune to defend and an even greater amount if they lost.

"Wait a minute," Derrick said, as Sherisse and Jeff relaxed. "You guys actually thought I was capable of this? That I would use my position for sexual favors?"

"Calm down, Derrick," Sherisse said.

"The hell I will. I spent my entire life building my career. You think I would throw it all away for a quick hit? With her? With any woman in this office?"

"It's not a matter of whether we believed her, it was that she had the potential to do some serious damage to our practice," Jeff said. "You can't blame us for asking the tough questions. We had to know what we were up against."

Derrick sat down in frustration. Everything they said was true. If the tables had been turned and one of them had been accused, he would do the same thing.

"Everyone in this office knows that Suzanne has a crush on you," Sherisse said, thinking of the day she had caught Suzanne gazing at Derrick's office. "This could really have blown up in our faces."

"It still can," Will reminded them. "She can still file a claim, get a lawyer, and go through the process. It's going to be our word against hers."

"I'm going to talk to her," Derrick said, heading for the door.

"No, you won't," Will said, grabbing him by the arm. "You shouldn't be alone with her again."

"Will's right," Sherisse said. "Talking with her may only make matters worse."

"So what do you suggest?"

"I suggest you take a couple of days off," Jeff said, "until we can sort this all out."

Derrick started to protest, but decided against it. It was what was best for the practice.

"I also suggest we all talk to her," Jeff said, "allowing her to have an attorney there. I don't want it to be construed that we're trying to force her to change her mind."

"How soon can we get that arranged?" Derrick asked, anxious to get this over with.

"Since she came to me, I'll go back and talk to her. I'll arrange a date as quickly as I can."

As hard as it was, the group moved on to other business, and in another hour the meeting was adjourned.

Will followed Derrick and entered his office right behind him.

"What?" Derrick said after his door was shut.

"Stay away from her."

"Meaning?"

"Meaning I know you," he said, able to read his mind. "The first chance you get, you're going to corner Suzanne and give her the third degree on why she's doing this—and that will make things worse."

"I can't believe she would do this. Does she know what she's putting in jeopardy? My career, her career, this practice, the patients that we serve?"

"You already know the answer to your questions anyway. You know why she's doing this. You not only rejected her, but now you're back with Natalie."

Derrick remembered seeing her this morning outside the café. Was that when she decided to do this? "She saw us this morning at the café. She saw Natalie showing off the ring."

Will let out a slow whistle. "Did you say ring?"

In all the chaos this morning, Derrick had yet to tell Will about his engagement. "That's right. She said yes—willingly and without fear."

Giving his friend a bear hug, he patted him on the back. "Congratulations, man."

"Thanks."

Not wanting to put a damper on the celebration, Will said, "There's one more thing you should be thinking about."

"What?"

"Two more people know your secret now," Will said. "And two attorneys will soon know of your secret. The list is growing. Are you comfortable with your odds in Natalie not finding out?"

Derrick thought about his words and the truth in them. If Natalie found out from anyone but him, it could break their bond of trust forever.

* * *

The buzz of excitement ran high at the offices of BSI. Not since they had received a huge grant last year to extend their services did any other event warrant such a celebration. Everyone at the company gathered inside Natalie's office to congratulate her and view the ring that had all the women in the office oohing and aahing.

"That man has taste," Jea said, holding her hand up and turning it from side to side. "Whenever I get engaged, I'll be sure to have my fiancé take a lesson from yours."

"Does this mean that things are getting serious with you and David?"

"Oh, please," Jea said, completely discounting her statement. "That man was last week's news. This week it's Corey."

"And next week?" Natalie asked.

"Who knows?" Jea said, as if she already knew next week Corey would be old news, too. "I did meet this guy named Drew at happy hour a couple of weeks ago. He called last night. We might do dinner next week."

"I don't think I'll ever be able to keep up with your dates."

"Hey, I'm young, single, and free," Jea said, prancing around the room like a model. "You're not supposed to be able to keep up with them."

"I believe you've had more dates this year than I've had my entire life," Natalie said.

"And I'm just getting started," Jea said.

Once the office had cleared, Natalie picked up the phone and dialed. "Mom?"

"Hey, Natalie."

"Is this a good time?" Natalie had learned to respect her mother's time and not assume that she should always be at the mercy of Natalie's schedule.

"Of course."

As she shared the news of her engagement, she could feel the relief and happiness from her mother through the phone lines. Even with everything that had happened between them, there was still a small portion of her that feared her mother's rejection. Hearing the sincere words of happiness from her mother made her feel complete.

"You've made the right decision, Natalie. I'm happy that my messed-up past didn't ruin your ability to love—and have a full life with this man."

"Me too." Natalie hesitated before continuing. "How is Samuel?"

Margaret smiled when she didn't hear a hint of accusation in Natalie's voice. "He's fine. I'm going to visit him in Atlanta this weekend."

"Tell me about him."

"He's been a widower for almost five years. He owns two car dealerships and he loves to travel and spend time with me."

Natalie spent the next twenty minutes listening to Margaret talk about Samuel. Her words of endearment about him reminded Natalie of when she talked about Derrick. Maybe this Samuel guy wasn't so bad after all.

After hanging up with her mom, Natalie was unable to concentrate for most of the morning. Shutting her door, she went online and began doing something that up until yesterday she never thought she would do—search for wedding dresses.

"Natalie, Christine is here to see you."

Clicking off, Natalie closed her browser. "Send her in."

"OK, I came over as soon as I could. Your message said it was urgent." Christine had been on edge ever since Derrick left for Florida. She hadn't heard anything from either one of them and she had been too afraid to call. She was dying to find out what happened.

Warning her staff not to say anything about the engagement to Christine, Natalie put her hands in her lap, hiding them from view. Getting rid of all traces of a smile, she motioned for Christine to take a seat.

"What is it?" Christine asked, realizing this was not good news.

"It's Derrick," Natalie said, with sad eyes and a somber expression. "How could you send him to Florida knowing how tense things were between me and my mom?"

Christine stared at her sister and her heart almost stopped. Her only goal had been to get Derrick and Natalie talking—to hopefully find a way to repair their broken relationship. Judging from Natalie's response, her plan backfired. "Natalie, I was just trying to help. I wanted the two of you to work things out."

Panic crossed Christine's face and the gravity of her mistake formed a small tear in her eye. Natalie couldn't let her game go on any longer. Removing her hand from under the desk, she held it out to her sister.

It took a few seconds for Christine to realize what Natalie had done, and as soon as it hit her, Christine stood and smacked her hand. "You little sneak. You had me believing I'd really messed up."

"Serves you right," Natalie said. "Butting into other people's business. You can start apologizing by taking me to lunch."

"Based on the results this trip got you, *you* should be buying *me* lunch."

Natalie grabbed her purse, and the two women giggled and laughed their way out of the office.

* * *

Derrick took a seat opposite Natalie's chair and opened his menu. Natalie talked nonstop about her day, informing him of all the good wishes she'd received from family and friends.

By the time they'd ordered their meals, Natalie realized she had been having a one-way discussion, barely letting Derrick get a word in. "I'm sorry. I've been monopolizing the conversation."

"No problem," Derrick said. "I'd rather have no other conversation than this one—about our engagement and about our life together."

Natalie heard the words, but nonetheless, wondered if he had something else on his mind. She watched him carefully, especially his eyes. He was concerned . . . worried. This look was not new to her. It was the same expression he wore the first time he had come to her office and at Damian's birthday party. "Is everything OK?"

Derrick had debated all day about how and when to tell Natalie about Suzanne. It was no longer a question of "if." He chickened out on the way over and didn't think he could wait until the end of the evening. So in tune with his moods, she'd already guessed that something was going on.

The waiter arrived with their salads and Derrick took advantage of the momentary reprieve.

"I spoke to my mom today."

Derrick paused at her words. He knew they were making progress and he hoped that this latest conversation kept them on the right path.

"I told her about the engagement. I never thought I would say this, but she was supportive of my decision."

"I'm glad to hear that."

The words were there, but his mind wasn't. "Derrick, what's going on?"

Setting his fork down, he reached across the table for her hands. "There is something I need to tell you."

Natalie's pulse quickened and her stomach dropped. "I've never seen you this serious. Are you OK? Are your parents OK?"

"I'm fine," he said. "I spoke to my parents this morning and told them the great news about us."

"Then what is it?"

"I want to tell you something, but I want you to promise that you'll hear me out."

Natalie's defenses immediately went up. "Fine."

He could already hear the short tone of her voice. There was no easy way to do this, so he might as well just spit it out. "It's about Suzanne."

The name was the last word she expected to come out of his mouth.

"Suzanne and me."

Natalie pulled her hands away and set them in her lap. "You slept with her."

"No," Derrick said, disappointed that that was her first assumption.

"Then what happened between you two?" she asked, the accusation already there.

All of a sudden, spitting it out became very difficult and Derrick searched his extensive vocabulary for the right words. "You and I had been arguing. I thought our relationship was over. I was hurt, alone."

"And . . ."

Derrick told her the details of what had happened in his office—from the moment Suzanne walked in until she sat on his lap, all the way up to the kiss. When he finished, she began to gather her belongings. "Where are you going?"

"You asked me to hear you out and I did. Unless there was something else you left out?"

"Please sit down, Natalie."

"I've heard enough. I'm going home."

"Just like that?"

"Oh, I'm sorry," Natalie said with fake enthusiasm. "What am I supposed to do, order dessert? Have an after-dinner drink?"

"You're supposed to talk to me—not walk away."

"Don't tell me how I'm supposed to react to something like this. You have no right."

Derrick had to agree with her. He was the one who messed up.

"Don't you think I've heard enough? She's got her legs wrapped around your body, your hand up her shirt, and her tongue down your throat. What other fun details of that night do I need to hear?" Natalie's voice rose several decibels and her hands started to shake.

"You need to hear that I pushed her away, told her that I was in love with you, and never to approach me like this again."

"Oh, how nice of you to do that, Derrick," Natalie said, unable to calm down. "Now, was this little speech of yours while she was bumping and grinding against you, or after?"

"Natalie, listen—"

"No, you listen," she said, refusing to hear one more word out of his mouth. "You knew this when we were in Florida. You knew this last night when you proposed. Why are you telling me now?"

As she stood, her voice was rising and several other customers were looking their way. "Can you please sit down so we can talk about this?"

Refusing to move, Natalie said, "Answer my question. Why now?"

Derrick hated to have to even say the words. "She's claiming sexual harassment. This could ruin my career."

Natalie's jaw dropped and she found herself teetering between emotions. One part of her wanted to scratch his eyes out for allowing this to happen and the other side wanted to go to him and comfort him. But the first part won out. "Is she right?"

"What! How can you ask me that? I told you what happened."

"Are you sure you didn't encourage her? You two looked mighty cozy when I interrupted your lunch. Maybe it was she who pulled the plug on your little late-night tryst—and not you."

Derrick couldn't fault her for the anger, but he couldn't believe that she would think he was capable of doing what Suzanne had accused him of.

"Do you honestly believe that, Natalie?"

The question cut Natalie to the core. The memories of them making love over the past couple of weeks came to her mind—their time in Florida, the proposal last night. "No, Derrick. But that doesn't change that you allowed her to come at you like that and that you have a suit hanging over your head."

Relief flooded through Derrick that she believed he was innocent. "There was a witness."

"Who?"

"Will returned to the offices to pick up a package he left. He overheard the entire thing. He can confirm that she came on to me and I turned her down."

Seeing her rigid stance soften just a little, he said, "Can you please sit back down so we can talk about this?"

"I don't think so, Derrick," Natalie said, turning to leave. "I need some time."

"I understand. I'll take you home."

"That's OK. I'll take a cab."

The waiter returned with their entrées and set them on a tray stand beside the table. Noticing the tension, he didn't make a move to put the food on the table.

"We've changed our minds," Natalie said, heading from the door.

The waiter's confused face turned to Derrick. "Sir?"

Hastily handing him his credit card, Derrick rushed to the door. He looked up and down the street, but she was nowhere to be found.

"Can I help you?"

Derrick turned to the valet. "Did you see a woman, about this tall? She had on a tan coat, black bag. She just came out of the restaurant a few seconds ago. She was in a big hurry."

"Yes, sir. She got a cab just a few seconds before you came out the door."

"Damn," Derrick said, going back inside the restaurant. What should he do now?

Chapter 18

Natalie opened the box of Oreo Double Stuff cookies and stuck one in her mouth. Before she finished chewing, she said, "Did I tell you he had his hand up her shirt?"

"Three times," Christine said.

"No, I think it was four," Danielle said, grabbing a handful of cookies.

"Give her a break, guys. Can't you see she's upset?" Tanya said, setting a tray full of drinks on the table.

Instead of going home, Natalie had called Christine, who told her to come right over. By the time she got there, Tanya and Danielle had already arrived. All comfortably dressed, they shed their shoes as soon as they arrived and lounged around Christine's family room.

"You're damn right I'm upset. I agree to marry that man and he tells me that a week ago he was all over some woman?"

"I think what he said was that a woman was all over him," Danielle clarified.

"Is there really a difference?" Natalie said, eating another cookie. "The result is the same."

"Which is?" Tanya asked.

"Which means that he's just like a man. No matter how hard you want to believe that they won't do you wrong or treat you with disrespect, they manage to find a way to do it."

"I used to feel the same way," Tanya said. "Brandon considered himself such a playa when I first met him. He probably dated more women than he could ever keep track of."

"How did you learn to trust him?" Natalie asked.

"He built his track record with me. He proved to me over and over again that he was a changed man."

"That's one man in what . . . millions? Derrick is doing just the opposite—he's showing me that he's just like all the rest."

"I'm not excusing his behavior, but—" Danielle started.

"Whatever you say next has to be an excuse for his behavior."

"All I was going to say was that you need to decide if you're going to let this come between you and Derrick."

"Too late for that," she said, popping another cookie in her mouth. "It's between."

"How long are you going to let it stay that way? Forever?" Tanya asked.

"Are you suggesting that I forgive and forget?"

"No, but I am suggesting you think about whether you want to stay with Derrick and work it out. Brandon and I wasted so much time because of pride or anger. I'm just suggesting you take a look at what you want and if it's Derrick, do what you can now to work it out."

"*He* messed up," Natalie reminded all of them. "I'm not doing anything to get back on track. If anyone has to make that effort, it's Derrick."

"I agree with Natalie. Why should she be the one trying

to figure out how to fix this situation? He created this mess. Let's sit back and see how he fixes it."

Raising her glass of wine, Natalie held it out to Danielle. "I like the way you think. That's exactly what I'm going to do. Let Dr. Derrick Carrington figure out how to get me back."

Danielle raised her glass in support of Natalie's position. Glancing at the other women, Christine raised hers. All three women looked at Tanya. Finally she joined her glass with the toast.

Saturday night, Natalie sat in front of the television surfing channels. Her girlfriends had called to see if she wanted to do dinner, but she wasn't in the mood to go out. It had been three days since Derrick's confession and he was working hard to get her back. When she arrived at work on Thursday, there were three different flower arrangements for her. Everyone in the office thought he sent them in recognition of their engagement, but the note begged for her forgiveness and he asked to see her.

Friday, she'd arrived home to a delivery of a box of her favorite chocolates. Declaring his love and telling her how much he missed her, the card asked her to call him. She'd eaten the last of the chocolates this afternoon but hadn't contacted him.

The doorbell rang and Natalie didn't need to wonder who it was. Still not ready to face him, she couldn't go on ignoring him forever. At some point, she had to decide what she wanted to do—walk away or stay.

Sliding her feet in her slippers, she clicked the television off and headed down the hallway to the front door.

Her breath caught as she saw the face on the other side. "Mom?"

"Yep," she said, opening the screen door and stepping inside.

"What are you doing here? When did you get here? Why didn't you call me? How did you get to my house?"

"Derrick picked me up from the airport."

Looking past her mother, she saw Derrick's truck pull out of the driveway. Focusing her attention back on her mom, she took her overnight bag out of her hand and set it by the stairs.

"Show me where I can freshen up and then you and I are going out for a good old-fashioned mother-daughter dinner."

"We're not going anywhere until you tell me what's going on."

"Still stubborn, I see."

Natalie just glared at her mother.

"Derrick called and told me about this Suzanne thing. He just wanted to make sure you had someone to talk to if you needed to. It was my idea to come see you and he offered to pick me up."

"But—"

"Why don't we continue this over dinner? I'm starving."

Natalie changed into a pair of jeans and a cropped top and her mother chose a casual wrap dress with short sleeves. Natalie still couldn't get over her mother's change in style. She looked as though she kept up with the latest fashions.

Once they were seated in the Thai restaurant, Margaret didn't waste any time getting to the point of this unexpected visit. "Are you going to let that little harlot take your man away from you?"

Natalie laughed at her biblical vocabulary. "Harlot?"

"Whatever it is you young people call it these days—are you going to let her take away the man you love?"

"Mom, it's not that simple," Natalie said. Suzanne might have instigated, but Derrick participated.

"Why not?"

"Because he wasn't going to tell me if it hadn't been for the sexual harassment claim," Natalie said. "That's the same as lying."

"Who gave you the sole rights to emotional roller coasters?"

"What are you talking about?"

Margaret was hoping that she could get her daughter to see things from a different perspective. "Why are you the only one who can be on an emotional roller coaster, not knowing what you want or want to do next from day to day?"

"Personally, things have been tough for me, lately."

"And they haven't been for Derrick?" Margaret said, challenging Natalie to look at it from his point of view. "In a matter of weeks, you turn down his proposals several times, the two of you break if off, you didn't want to talk to him, you didn't want to see him. You don't think all those things were tough on him? You don't think he was confused, frustrated, angry, and wondering if there was ever going to be a time when the two of you would work out your problems?"

"He let her kiss him . . ." Natalie reminded her.

"I know what happened and I'm not defending his actions, I'm here to talk about what you want to do about it."

"I shouldn't have to do anything about it."

Margaret felt so sorry for her daughter. And she blamed herself. She'd given her tunnel vision when it came to men, and now that she had the chance to break out of that tunnel, it was a tremendous struggle. "When Henry told me he was married and that he had no intention of leaving his wife, I was devastated. Over the years, there were men who were interested in me. There were times when I got asked out, but I was so destroyed by what Henry did to me that I let him come between me and any potential man who could have loved me. I've wasted a lot of years living but not being alive. Are you going to let Suzanne do that to you? Let her take away your chance for love?"

"You're asking me to forgive Derrick."

"I'm asking you to follow your heart and do what you believe is right. Because you deserve to have what you truly want."

Monday morning, Derrick sat in a conference at a downtown law firm waiting for the meeting to start. He still couldn't believe that Suzanne was going through with this. She knew that there were no grounds for her accusations, yet she insisted on having some action taken against him.

"How are you holding up?"

"As well as can be expected, Will."

"Sherisse just called. She and Jeff just arrived. They should coming through those doors in a few minutes."

"Is Suzanne here?"

"Yep. She and her attorney are waiting down the hall. We'll get started in a few minutes." Will watched Derrick pace up and down the room, his fists clenched and his body straight and tight. "Remember what the lawyer said. You don't say a word. No matter what she says, you let our attorney handle it. After today, Suzanne will no longer be a problem for you."

"That only takes care of one of my problems," Derrick said, thinking of Natalie. He'd dropped her mother off and hadn't heard a word from her. He could tell Margaret was sympathetic to his situation, but that didn't mean she had any influence over what Natalie ultimately decided to do. Whatever Natalie wanted, he was going to find out today. As soon as this meeting was over, he was going to her.

"I know it's been rough on you two, but you've come too far for it not to work out," Will said, pulling for this relationship to work. "Give her time, man, she'll come around."

Sherisse and Jeff entered the conference room, followed by Winston Floundry, their attorney. Winston had been briefed on the scenario and didn't think this case was going very far. Once everyone was seated on one side of the conference table, Winston reminded them of what would happen.

"We'll hear her story, and then I'll ask some questions. But under no circumstances are any of you to speak." Eyeing Derrick, he said, "Especially you."

He buzzed his secretary to bring in Suzanne and her attorney.

Derrick sat up straighter and clenched his fists under the table when she walked in. It took everything in him to keep his mouth shut, but Winston had already warned him that any outbursts from him would not help the situation.

Once everyone took a seat, Marshall Jones started things off.

"I'm representing Ms. Spencer in this matter. We are prepared to file charges against Dr. Derrick Carrington and the medical practice of Proctor, Cain, Copeland, and Carrington for sexual harassment and a hostile work environment. However, if this meeting can produce an agreeable resolution to this issue, we will forgo formal proceedings."

Derrick opened his mouth to speak, but Winston cut him off. "We called this meeting because we want to get a better understanding of Ms. Spencer's claims. It is my understanding that she told her story to Dr. Copeland, but I, as well as Dr. Carrington, would like to hear it."

Opening his file, Marshall removed some papers and started reading from his notes.

"If you don't mind," Winston said, turning his eyes toward Suzanne, "I'd like to hear it directly from her."

Derrick stared at Suzanne with eyes filled with hate. Could she really sit in this room and tell this lie? Could she look him in his face and say that he harassed her?

Suzanne cleared her throat several times before starting to speak but didn't buckle under his stare. "Dr. Carrington called me into his office under the guise of discussing the work schedule of the staff. Once I entered his office, he complained about the temperature and told me I'd be more comfortable if I took off my jacket."

A vein popped out of Derrick's neck and Will nudged him on the leg. Holding his tongue, he let her continue.

"When I came around his desk, he hugged me at the waist and pulled me toward him. Losing my balance, I fell in his lap. That's when he reached under my shirt and touched my breast. When I started to protest, he kissed me."

"And what happened next?" Winston asked.

"I told him I couldn't, scrambled off his lap, picked up my belongings, and left." Suzanne's voice wavered and she cast her eyes downward, ashamed. Her attorney handed her a tissue and she discreetly wiped her eyes.

Derrick watched the entire scene and almost stood up to start clapping. This performance was worthy of an Academy Award. When was she going to stop the dramatics and tell the truth?

"Thank you, Ms. Spencer."

"As you can see by her story," Marshall said, "Dr. Carrington is in a position of authority and has direct influence over my client's career. She's no longer sure she can perform her duties. Her career advancement has been greatly compromised by the actions of Dr. Carrington.

"In light of this, she'll have to begin searching for a job, which could take months to secure. And as you can tell, she has suffered great emotional distress. Now, a lawsuit can be a long drawn-out process, taking years to work its way through the system. Not to mention the cost to your medical practice in terms of attorneys' fees, bad publicity, and the possibility of lost patients."

"Cut to the chase, Marshall," Winston said, cutting off his monologue. "What do you want?"

"One hundred fifty thousand dollars."

"What?" Derrick said, no longer able to keep his mouth shut. It was like dealing with Charlene all over again. Her wanting something for nothing.

"Please excuse his outburst," Winston said, eyeing him to calm down. "As you can guess, this would be upsetting to anyone accused of these charges."

"As it would be to the woman who suffered at the hand of his inappropriateness," Marshall reminded him.

"Before we discuss any possible resolution, may I just ask Ms. Spencer a couple of questions?"

"I'm not sure I'll allow her to answer them, but go ahead."

Winston opened his file and started firing off his questions. "Ms. Spencer, can you tell me what time this event took place?"

Getting an OK from her attorney, she said, "Around eight p.m."

"Who was in the office at this time?"

"No one."

"So it's your word against his?"

"Yes," she said confidently.

"Was the door shut?"

"Not really. It was cracked."

"Ms. Spencer, are you aware of the security system your office has?"

Suzanne eyed her attorney at the strange question. When he nodded his approval, she said, "Yes."

"How does it work?"

"What do you mean?" she asked, unsure about this line of questioning.

"How would someone get into your office after hours?"

"They would slide their security card across the panel and the door would unlock."

"Is there a point to this?" Marshall asked impatiently.

"I have the records from your security company that have Dr. Will Proctor entering the building at seven fifty-seven on the night we are talking about."

For the first time, Suzanne's confidence faltered and she shifted in her seat.

"Where is his office in relation to Dr. Carrington's?"

Suzanne didn't answer right away and Marshall eyed his client. "Down the hall and to the left."

"Would he have to pass Dr. Carrington's office to get to his?"

Suzanne didn't answer and she looked to her attorney for help, of which he could provide none.

Realizing the light was becoming clearer on his line of questioning, Winston closed his files and set them aside. Folding his hands in front of him, he stared directly into her eyes. "We've heard your offer, and we are declining.

You go ahead and file your charges, and when it gets to court, the jury will hear from Dr. Will Proctor and his version of what he overheard that night, standing right outside the door."

"Which is?" Marshall said, completely confused as to what was going on.

"Which is that Suzanne had a crush—a thing—for Dr. Carrington. Everyone at the office knew it, his girlfriend knew it, and even the women at a café they frequent knew it. Suzanne knew my client was at a vulnerable point in his life and decided to make her move. *She* removed her jacket, *she* placed his hand under her shirt, and *she* kissed *him.*

"Now there is one thing that we do agree on. She's probably no longer able to work for these doctors. So I give you a choice, you can either drop this ridiculous claim today and I won't go after you for my attorney's fees or we'll see you in court and I'll parade every last one of these people in there to testify against her."

Marshall looked at his client in complete shock. "Suzanne?"

Suzanne focused her eyes on Derrick and, this time the tears were real. The reality of what she'd done began to sink in. Rising out of her chair, she picked up her purse and walked out.

Closing his files, Marshall stood and shook hands with Winston. "There'll be no lawsuit."

Derrick left the conference only feeling half elated. Suzanne had been taken care of, but that left Natalie. Declining lunch with his colleagues, he got in his truck and turned on his cell phone. The message light blinked and he checked his messages.

"Derrick, it's Natalie. I'd like you to come by tonight. I should be home around six."

That evening, Natalie paced in her living room. She'd dropped her mom off at the airport that morning promising to visit her next month. Checking her watch, she found it was almost six o'clock. When the doorbell rang, her heart skipped a beat.

"Thanks for coming," she said, leading him into the living room.

"I got your message." Derrick sat down on the sofa and waited. He had no idea what would come next. Was she going to give him back his ring, ending it once and for all, or was there a chance that she wanted to stay together? For the time being, at least she was still wearing the ring.

Natalie remained standing. "My mom told me that your meeting with the lawyers was scheduled for today. How did it go?"

"As expected," Derrick said, "Suzanne was caught in her lie and she won't be filing any lawsuits."

"What happens now?"

"Now I try to put his episode behind me. She's no longer with our office." Derrick paused before he continued. "I want to apologize again for what happened with Suzanne and for not telling you. I was wrong. It sounds trite—but something like that will never happen again."

Natalie took a seat beside him. "Derrick, when you told me about Suzanne, all the stories my mother ever filled my head with about men came to the front of my mind. I couldn't get past her past to my present."

Derrick braced himself for whatever would come next.

"But I don't want to focus on the past anymore. I want to focus on my future." She reached out for his hand. "My future with you."

Staring down at their entwined fingers, Derrick didn't want to misinterpret what she was saying. "Does this mean that you'll be my wife?"

"Yes," Natalie said.

Closing the distance between them in an instant, he hugged her tightly. "I don't want a long engagement."

"Neither do I."

"I say we seal this deal with a kiss."

"I've got a better idea," she said, leading him up the stairs.

Epilogue

Natalie slipped on the sheath dress and turned to look in the mirror. With her hair piled high on her head with the crown on top, she looked, and felt, like a princess. It was hard to believe that in the next few minutes she would be walking down the aisle. After everything she had gone through with Derrick and her mom this year, this day had been but a fantasy to her.

"Come in," she said at the knock on the door.

Margaret entered the dressing room at the church and took a long look at her only child. "You are absolutely stunning."

Natalie beamed at her compliment but had to let her know that she paled in comparison to her mom.

"Did you ever think this day would come?" Margaret said, fussing with Natalie's dress.

"Not in a million years," Natalie admitted. "Who would have thought that the past was keeping such happiness at bay?"

"I'm proud of you, Natalie."

"I know, Mom," Natalie said. She'd heard her say this

a hundred times. "I have my own business. I'm independent. I'm able to take care of myself."

"All those things are true," Margaret said, "but that's not what I'm most proud of."

"Really?" Natalie said, feeling like a little girl. "What is it?"

"I'm most proud of you today. For going through what you went through and still being able to stand tall on this day—with me."

Natalie gave her mom a hug and pulled back when she felt the tears. "We spent too much time with that makeup artist to ruin it just a few minutes before the wedding."

Pushing back the tears, Margaret nodded in agreement.

Another knock at the door interrupted.

Christine came in looking beautiful in a tea-length dress with matching scarf. "Wow. Both of you look radiant."

Margaret turned to Christine and saw the same features she'd always seen—Henry's eyes and his complexion. But this time, there was nothing—no hurt, no bitterness. "Christine, it's so good to see you."

Christine glanced at Margaret to be sure she'd heard correctly. The few times that their paths had crossed, Margaret hadn't had one kind word for Christine.

"As you can see, Christine," Natalie said, "my mother really has changed."

Twenty minutes later, everyone took their places and the music started. Natalie took her time marching down the aisle. She wanted to savor every moment of this day. Glancing around the church, she smiled at all the people who had come out to share this special day. Just a month after her engagement to Derrick—it was amazing what could be put together in such a short period of time. The flowers, the dresses, the candles, everything was perfect.

Taking her place at the altar, she turned to face the

audience. Just then, the wedding march began. The double doors in the back of the church opened and her mother stood there in a beautiful cream satin gown with a lace bodice and a short train. Natalie had never seen such a wonderful sight in all her life. Cutting her eyes away from her mother, she looked at Derrick, who sat on a pew in the front row. Their day would come soon enough.

Just as her mother approached the minister, Samuel reached out for her hand and guided her the rest of the way. They began to take their vows before their friends, family, and God.

The wedding reception was in full swing when Natalie finally had a moment to find Derrick. "Doesn't my mother look happy?"

"Almost as happy as you. I can't believe I agreed to wait another three months before our wedding."

"Don't worry, it will be here before you know it."

"I can't wait."

"Neither can I."

Dear Readers,

Many of you have asked for Natalie and Derrick's story and I hope that you found it worth the wait. They had their share of challenges, but love prevailed. Please feel free to drop me a note at *doreenrainey@prodigy.net.*

Until next time . . .

Doreen

ABOUT THE AUTHOR

Doreen Rainey graduated from Spelman College in Atlanta, Georgia, and currently resides in the Washington, D.C. area with her husband of twelve years, Reginald.

The award-winning *Love Series* includes *Foundation for Love, Can't Deny Love,* and *Pursuit of Love.* Her other works include *Just for You, One True Thing,* and *The Perfect Date* in the anthology *A Thousand Kisses.*

Please visit Doreen at *www.doreenrainey.com* or e-mail her at *doreenrainey@prodigy.net.*